The Counterfeit Brit

RACHEL EISENWOLF

The Counterfeit Brit
Eisenwolf – 1st ed

Published in the United States of America

ISBN – 13: 978-0-6157-2007-4
Library of Congress Control Number: 2012952403

Thanks to Zane Kesey for permission to use Further
as this cover's backdrop.

www.TheCounterfeitBrit.com

Break Maiden Books

FIRST EDITION

To the illegal alien in all of us

ᔏA NOTE TO READERS᛭

Although my own experience at the "Purple Parakeet" spanned over a year, for the sake of continuity, the events in this story have been compressed to take place over a three month period.

Also, in order to maintain anonymity in some instances I may have changed identifying characteristics and details such as physical properties, businesses, occupations and places of residence.

All other physical descriptions and conversations have been recreated from my combined memories. In order to further protect the privacy of individuals, I have blurred and composited personalities, and changed all names.

Any resemblance to actual persons, living or dead, is purely coincidental.

THE
COUNTERFEIT
BRIT

Accidental Accent

It wasn't a deliberate plan or anything. I mean, I didn't just wake up this morning and decide to become English. That would've been weird. But, then, to call my accent accidental isn't really accurate either. Because I'm not turning myself into somebody else by mistake, exactly, am I? I guess you could say I'm doing it accidentally on purpose. It's like this.

My name is Rebecca Lamb. I'm thirty, a perpetual student, and out of a job. My boyfriend has ditched me. And here I am in Berkeley, California, with an expired lease and exactly three hundred dollars to my name.

This is how I first find out about it. The Purple Parakeet youth hostel, that is. According to the website, it's a cozy retreat that services a variety of tourists traveling through San Francisco. The rates are cheap: Twenty dollars per night. They have a rec room, a sauna, and a free breakfast. Needless to say, I give them a call.

"Purple Parakeet," answers a sing-song-y male voice.

"Hi, do you have a girl's dorm bed available for tonight by any chance?" I ask, hopefully.

"Yes we *do*. Where ya calling from?"

"Berkeley," I tell him. I notice there's a hint of local pride in my voice, like I'm still pleased I've managed to make the big move from New York.

"Oh, too bad, we don't take people from the Bay Area. We're a hostel for travelers. *Travelers,*" he emphasizes.

I want to explain to him that I've only been in California for a year, that I'm originally from Connecticut, that I'm going home for August and just need a place to stay for two nights in order to interview with the only school that replied to my teaching application. I consider how I can phrase a sentence that will cover everything.

"Well, the thing is…" I start, glancing out at my alley view.

"We *don't* take Bay Area residents," he repeats. His voice is flat, final.

Sensing too much explanation will make me sound more complicated than compelling, I continue tentatively. "But… I've only been in California… for…"

"Goodbye," he cuts in abruptly.

Slouching down on my mattress, I listen to the dial tone echoing in the empty room. The insult of being hung up on registers but is too secondary to resonate. I have bigger problems. My lease is up. The other hostels are all booked. I can't afford a hotel. And now the Purple Parakeet won't let me stay.

I hover nervously over the phone for another moment, as if waiting for it to reconsider, before slipping on my flip-flops and traipsing over the shaggy puke-orange rug toward the only room in my apartment in which I can't hear my neighbor burping intermittently through the hollow walls.

As I wait for my tea water to come to a boil a wave of dread washes over me. It's not only my usual anxiety about how suddenly, after ten years of hiding out in college, living like an heiress on student loans, I'm here at thirty, with $120,000 of debt, being thrust into the economic system, together only with a third-rate degree and my exaggerated fear of work. My fear today is of the more visceral variety. It's the primal fear of not knowing where I'm going to sleep tonight. And this, I suppose, is how the whole mess begins.

****

By the time I get back to my bedroom the fear spiral that's taken root in the kitchen has snowballed into a sort of crisis. I know that may sound a little overblown, but I'm serious. It has. It's hard to describe exactly why everything feels *so* charged but somehow I've worked myself up into a genuine panic over this and I can't seem to work myself back down. Perspective is lost. And with the new tenant moving in tomorrow, there's no time to spare.

I think hard and fast, racking my brain for a solution. Nothing comes. Taking a few preoccupied sips of my milky tea, I then reach for my phone, press redial, and connect, once again, to the Purple Parakeet. If a foreigner is what they want, a foreigner is what they'll get.

"Purple Parakeet," answers the same man as before.

"Hel-lo," I chirp, shamelessly. "Would you hap-pen to have a bed available for tonight?" in my best English accent.

"Yes, we do," he says.

This time he is friendly. It's like walking through the sensor gate at the airport. I've made it through to the other side. Now, I feel decent. I feel like I belong.

"Oh, fan-tas-tic," I answer. And that is that.

I'm definitely relieved. But not surprised. See, I've always been pretty good with accents. In sixth grade I was Eliza Doolittle's understudy in the school play. And then there was that sophomore year abroad in Arundel, England.

In any case, although my little triumph fills me with some uneasiness, when I get back to packing I notice it's with more vigor than before; my one way outbound ticket has been stamped, at least, and if nothing else, this leg of the trip is officially over.

Shoving everything into my pack, I pause only in order to admire the gray zip-front sweater Gotthard (the boyfriend who ditched me) gave me just before he went back to Holland and I moved out here. A fresh wave of self-pity washes over me as I imagine, with the benefit of hindsight, that the gift might have been some kind of guilt-ridden kiss-off. Still, I roll the sweater up carefully and place it neatly down the side of my already overstuffed pack.

Then I take one last grateful glance around this empty room that no longer represents my life. Halfheartedly I even attempt to affix a symbolic beginning, middle and end to the last twelve months. But this doesn't quite take. See, although the relationship is over, officially, Gotthard and I are still in regular contact. And I still feel like I'm trapped in this game of Crazy Eights with him, wherein every time I adjust to how he says he wants me to be, he puts down a different card.

In my best attempt to ward off these weightier thoughts, I then shimmy under my pack, hoist myself up off the dusty floor and concentrate, instead, on fiddling with all the straps until I'm so wedged in that I can barely distinguish the extra thirty or forty pounds.

And this is when, out of nowhere, something shifts. Suddenly, just like that, I decide I'm not going to survive the rest of the summer at my mother's in Connecticut, while waiting to return to subbing in the fall. No. It's time to do what I've been telling myself all year would be irresponsible to do at this stage of my life. It's time to run away.

On the Road Again

The Bay Area Rapid Transit carries me all the way into downtown San Francisco. Once above ground again I station myself on the curb of Market Street and wait in anticipation for my next link, an old wooden F trolley, which arrives within a few minutes. I step aboard.

"Sor-ry," I say to the driver, as I cross the threshold. "Do you take notes?"

It takes him a moment to register that by notes I mean dollar bills. When he does he seems pleased with himself, and in turn pleased with me. I put a dollar in the fare machine and spin around awkwardly under the weight of my backpack to look for a seat. A woman up front squeezes herself and her shopping bags to her right in order to make room for me.

Dropping the pack off my shoulders, I take a seat beside her on the narrow plastic bench. "Oh, thank you ve-ry much."

"England or Australia?" she asks, expectantly.

"Oh, yes," I start. I pretend to be caught a little off guard. "England."

"We were there two summers ago. We loved it," she offers.

"Really?" I reply, affecting a sort of gracious curiosity I can imagine an English girl might. "Whereabouts were you?"

"Oh, we were in London, and then in Bristol. My husband has relatives from there. We went back to see his great aunt."

Smiling much more deeply than usual, I say, "Oh, how nice! You had a good time, then?"

"We loved it. You have such a beautiful country! I'd love to go back."

With as much humility as I can muster, I reply, "Oh, thank you. That's ve-ry kind."

I can't help feeling a little proud of being from such a beautiful place.

She notices the crumpled city map in my hand. "Where are you trying to get?"

"Oh, thank you ve-ry much," I express preemptively, as I point to the marked dot on my map.

"You want to get off at the Ferry Building. It's the stop just after I get off."

I bow my head demurely. "Oh, thank you ve-ry much, in-deed."

She gestures to my backpack. "It looks like you're on a big trip there."

"Oh, yes, I'm heading to Mex-i-co. To teach English for the summer," I say, trying on my new idea.

I notice my usual apologetic, little-girl, I'm-thirty-and-without-a-plan-and-still-floating-but-if-I'm-saccharine-sweet-I-hope-you-won't-treat-me-like-a-loser voice seems to have vanished while uttering these words.

"Oh, how great! Wish I were going to Mexico! Are you headed there today?"

Feeling further buoyed up by the hint of envy, I explain, "In a few days. I've still got to map out my route."

"You're not going by yourself, are you?"

"Yes," I announce. "I'm on my own."

"You brave, brave girl."

I soak this up too.

"Have you done this trip before?" she asks, as she pulls the stop-requested cord and begins gathering her bags.

"I haven't."

"But, you're used to travelling on your own?"

"Sort of," I say, trying to remember the last time I took a trip by myself.

"Well, do be careful," she then adds, more seriously.

"Thank you," I say, with a pause intending to convey thoughtful consideration. "I will."

She is gazing at me, almost a little sentimentally now. "It's been lovely talking with you."

I angle for a balance of formality and warmth. "Likewise."

"Have a wonderful time," she says.

I can see the exchange has been a real treat for her. For me, too, though for different reasons. After a year of brooding and social isolation (an unwelcome effect of my slow-dissolving relationship) it's exciting to be in a conversation at all.

On her way out the door she hesitates on the steps, waves once more, and calls, "Cheers!"

"Cheers!" I call back.

A pimply-faced teenage boy immersed in a copy of *Nineteen Eighty-Four* and a bag of popcorn glances up at me.

The trolley starts moving again and I sit back in my seat and pull my pack closer to me, as if out of concern for overflowing too much into the aisle.

I feel pleasantly conspicuous as we hurtle down Market Street. The backpack is my new identity. It's like magically returning to student status again – a break from explanations and expectations. I'm traveling. It's enough.

Then the trolley comes to another screeching halt.

"This is the Ferry Building, folks. Pier One," the driver calls out. "The beginning of the line."

****

Once I get off the trolley it takes me a few moments to gather my bearings. Then, locating the barely visible street signs, I make my way across the ample intersection, and begin my ascent up Broadway, in search of the Purple Parakeet. I pass mostly only blighted warehouses and strip clubs. I search on. The Purple Parakeet is supposed to be situated in a neighborhood called North Beach, which the hostel's website refers to as being a lively district, in the heart of San Francisco.

Meanwhile, the sun is getting hotter and my backpack straps are beginning to rub against my jacket and to dig into my shoulders. Stopping for a minute to give the tightness building around my throat a chance to relax, I rest my hands on my knees and my pack flat across my back.

In a way, I don't mind the discomfort. It keeps my focus on tangible goals, like finding water and making my way up the steady incline ahead, which, in turn, keeps me from thinking too much about what's going to happen when I actually get to the hostel.

Finally I spot a deli. I duck inside. Placing a big bottle of water and a pack of gum on the counter, I decide to shift into high gear with my new accent.

"Do you know if the Pur-ple Par-a-keet is ne-ar here?" I ask the man behind the counter, wondering if my face is matching my tones.

"You're three blocks away," he says. "Go right out of here, and it'll be about three blocks down on your right. You can't miss it. That's $2.02."

"For the di-rec-tions?" I joke, handing him three crumpled bills.

He flashes a toothy smile. "Yeah, right."

Then he glances down at his empty free-penny dish. "You got two cents?"

"Oh, sure."

I dig back into my pocket and pull out handful of change and some sweaty lint.

"They're the copper ones," he assists.

****

Back out on the street, a stubby doorman with mirrored sunglasses is standing before one of the strip clubs that line Broadway.

He whispers to me as I pass. "Naked ladies inside. Ladies welcome."

I can't think of anything to say back so I just carry on walking, determined not to let his presence make me change my posture.

Before long I spot the same three-story purple Victorian that was on the website. It looks grimier than it did in the picture, as if covered by fumes from the constant flow of traffic. Nevertheless, I approach the still-elegant gold door and peer through an oval, beveled glass window.

With this one action the seedy air of the neighborhood fades into the backdrop, and my nervousness about checking in upgrades to the very forefront.

Suddenly I'm filled with reservations. What if I don't even make it through check-in? I consider just backing out of the whole thing, the way I used to climb down from the high dive as a kid. I still could back down. I still could, I suppose, just get on another bus and go stay at Luke's.

I stayed with Luke when I first moved out here. Aside from still being the only friend I have in San Francisco, Luke, like Gotthard, is someone I met back in New York. We were all living in the same building, International House, which was a student housing community and a hotbed for foreign students on a mission.

To say the least, Luke's mission had gone a little bit wayward since then, though. Calling to mind his San Francisco apartment, still doubling as his headquarters, I remember why going back to Luke's place is out of the question. There is, really, only one thing to do. I take a deep breath and ring the Purple Parakeet's bell.

Getting through Customs

Just as I am being buzzed in, a man with a shaved head and a broken arm is coming out. He pauses to hold the door open for me with his shoulder as I waddle through under my pack.

I make out the words "Glasgow Belongs to Me" written in orange marker on his cast.

"Thanks," I say, gratefully.

He nods. "At's orite."

Extracting what confidence I can from his brief friendliness I head up the uneven turquoise steps to the lobby.

"Hel-lo, I have a res-er-vat-ion," I practice saying to myself, while pressing the words closer to the front of my mouth, in between my lips and teeth. "Rebecca. Re-bec-ca. Rebec-ca."

My heart thumps at the thought of being distinguished by any one of the real Brits who might be on the premises. Fifty rooms. One hundred and fifty beds. Inevitable.

I continue to prepare: "Can't. Rather. Bother. Promise. Water. Com-mon."

At last I mount the top of the stairs. The unexpected décor of the lobby calms me down, or at least distracts me some.

With velvet drapes dripping from fourteen-foot ceilings, burgundy wallpaper, and an ornately carved mahogany front desk, it seems more like a stage set.

Overhead teeters a crookedly hanging chandelier, missing some of its more prominent teardrop crystals. I step further in.

The guy sitting behind the desk is wearing a puffy North Face coat and a wool hat, even though it's August. He is perched on a high stool, legs bent, with his bare toes clinging to the edge of the front desk. He looks around twenty-five.

Something tells me he's not the same guy I talked to on the phone, but I still approach the desk cautiously and decide not to speak until spoken to. I am uncharacteristically patient as I stand for what seems like ages while he finishes the conversation he is having with another guy dressed in similar attire.

"You should've been at the Boom Boom Room last night, man," he says.

"Yeah?"

"No lie."

"Too bad, the gig I was at was pretty average."

"Yeah."

"Yeah, seen a lot better."

"Yeah. Hey, bro, you wanna try to get to Vegas next weekend?"

"Yeah, I'd be down for that."

"Cool."

Finally there is a pause; their conversation seems to be over. He waits another few seconds, though, as if groping for something more to say, before finally looking at me.

"Checking in?" he asks.

"Yes, thanks," I say.

"Reservation?"

"Yes."

"Name?"

"Lamb."

He taps at his keyboard. "Rebecca?"

"Uh, yes," I agree.

"ID?"

"Sure."

Rummaging through my bag, I pull out the kid leather wallet Gotthard's mother gave me, which is, for the first time, suitably, too short to hold American currency. I fumble a little for my ID, trying to draw some attention to this favorable inconvenience.

Then, wearing my best poker face, I remove my driver's license and hand it to him.

He begins typing something, then pauses. "What are *you* doing with a California driver's license?" he asks.

"My dad's American," I offer. There's just the slightest tinge of self-satisfaction in my voice, as if, being English, I perceive this to be an exotic distinction.

More importantly, though, my confidence rises slightly due to being able to give an honest answer.

"Oh. Anyway, that's sixty dollars. Twenty for the key deposit, forty for the bed. Two nights. You'll get the key deposit back."

I hand him three twenties. Not good. I haven't even left San Francisco and I'm already down to $240.00.

He passes me a key attached to a plastic parakeet key chain.

"So, here's your key. You're in room fourteen, on the second floor. You're bed four-D. And be sure to be in your own bed or else our manager will pull you out of it in the middle of the night. Got it?"

"Got it," I reply, permitting the final T to explode.

He has a slightly preoccupied look on his face while he raps two pencils on the desk like he's playing the drums.

"Umm, there's no smoking, eating or drinking in the rooms. You can do all of that in the rec room," he says, pointing behind me to the double doors with one of the pencils.

"Okay, well," I return, in a more tentative and polite manner than I'm accustomed, "thanks ve-ry much."

He leans back in his chair and stretches his long legs back out.

"Yup."

I pick my pack up and try to sling it carelessly over my shoulder, surprised to find myself feeling dated, suddenly, in my once-hip early nineties Patagonia parka. This and all other thoughts are fleeting, however, in contrast to the almost mad whirl of pleasure I am feeling from having made it past check-in.

Still, I am careful to keep my delirium in check. Making my way through the rambling old building to my room, I stare steadily downward at the tears in the turquoise carpeting and trudge lethargically up the stairs, like a journey-worn traveler.

Phew. I already feel relieved. Completely relieved. Which is, of course, a little on the shortsighted side, considering this is only the very beginning of my journey. Except at this point, naturally, I still have no way of knowing it's just the beginning. Or just how *far* from my former life I'm actually headed.

A Night on the Piss

After a few minutes of puttering around the dimly lit second floor hallway I arrive outside room fourteen. Propping the door open with my hip, I drag my stuff inside. Right away I am greeted by a fragrant alchemy that suggests Satya Sai Baba Nag Champa incense amalgamating with a mildewing bathing suit salvaged from the bottom of a backpack.

A girl is already in there. She's lazily sprawled out across one of the upper bunks wearing a Chang Beer T-shirt and a pair of skimpy orange underwear. She doesn't move a muscle.

I take an unhurried look around my home for the next three days. The cramped space includes two wooden bunk beds, a stack of folded linens, a toothpaste-speckled mirror hanging above a tiny corner sink, a list of items (such as cigarettes) not allowed inside the dorm room, and a window (its ledge doubling as an ashtray) overlooking a parking lot.

Locating bed four-D, I throw my pack down with a little sigh, trying to appear more exhausted than I really am. I figure this is the most probable frame of mind to be in, while on the road and everything.

Moments later, the girl is hanging idly over the edge of her bunk, gazing down at me. Her face is an endearing assemblage of apple cheeks, blonde eyelashes and frosted lipstick.

"Tired?" she asks, in a voice that's scratchy and in an accent that's

…English.

"Oh, hi. Yeah, absolutely knackered," I reply, still careful to keep my tongue as low as possible in my mouth, since I don't know who knows who around here.

She dog-ears the page of the copy of *Hello* magazine she's holding and tosses it over her shoulder. "So, where ya coming from?"

Figuring it might sound suspicious to be exhausted as a result of traveling from the East Bay, I go with, "New York."

"No, I mean what part of England? You're English, right?"

"Oh, right. Arundel," I say, choosing the name of the town in which I studied during my sophomore year abroad.

She has a vague look on her face. "Where's *that?*"

I fiddle casually with the lock on my backpack for a moment, as I gather momentum.

"West Sussex, near Brighton."

"Right."

She unwraps a twisted towel from around her head without seeming to find anything unusual about this.

Still, I lower my eyes in an attempt to ward off any more questioning. Then I follow up as quickly as cadence will allow.

"How about you?"

She wears a quietly pleased countenance. "London."

"Right, how long have you been in San Francisco?" I continue.

"We've been here for three nights. May stay on for a while."

"From London?"

"No! God, no! I'm on an around-the-world," she informs, a little indignantly. "Been going since March."

I attempt to assuage any offense with added interest. "Oh, wow! On your own?"

"Originally, but I've linked up with a few people in Thailand. So there are three of us now," she explains.

I keep the questions rolling while she begins picking the dirt out from under her toenails with a tweezers.

"So, how do you like San Francisco?"

"To be honest, I don't even know," she replies. "After Las Vegas and L.A. we're just so knackered. We've hardly left the hostel. Recharging our batteries, really."

As I strain to keep up the accent I observe that my voice sounds much more narrow and constricted than usual. Still, what I lose horizontally, I seem to gain vertically. Like the horses on a merry-go-round, my tones are now free to glide up and down almost indiscriminately.

"To-tally, I can well im-ag-ine!" I reply.

"It's a pretty good hostel, though," she offers. "You can smoke here, which is great – for America."

She glances down affectionately at some sort of Asian character tattooed on her ankle.

"I know, that's annoying here, isn't it?" I reply.

"God, yes, it's *mad*. And how about the *ice* in everything!?" she continues.

"To-tally," I concur. "And then there's all the bloody air conditioning."

She hits her hands on the bed emphatically. "Exactly! I keep saying to Duncan, one of the blokes I'm traveling with, that I've been freezing the whole time we've been here and it's doing my head in. He says I'm driving him crazy with my whinging."

I concentrate on my choice of phrasing. "Are you not get-ting on, then?"

"Well, no, he's joking," she says. She has an obvious look on her face, with which she unwittingly warns me not to over-focus on form at the expense of context. "But actually, to be honest, ever since Laos, it has been going a bit pear-shaped. I think he fancies me, is the thing."

I take advantage of the distraction she provides. "And you're not keen?"

"Well, I was. We got on great in Thailand. But, I've started to go off him a bit. To be honest, I think I fancy his mate."

"Hmm," I say, as I open the heavy, built-in wooden trunk beneath my bed and shove my backpack in. "Sounds like a bit of a... pic-kle there."

"It's a bloody nightmare!" she replies. "Especially since I think Ian, his mate, feels the same. By the way, I'm Sharon."

I stand up. "Rebec-ca."

"What are you up to tonight, then?" she asks.

"I don't know. Nothing much."

She looks at me sideways. *"Nothing?"*

"I mean, I haven't made plans, yet," I add, justifying myself.

Her eyes light up. "Fancy a night on the piss?"

Looking at her blankly, I sift through my memory bank to distinguish the expression from *taking the piss*.

She registers the apparently visible shift in my expression.

"A night on the piss?" she repeats, mockingly.

"Right."

"Blimey, Rebecca, how long have you been away from home? Anyway, we'll probably just end up drinking here anyway. We're all pretty skint."

****

"So, for how long were you in New York, then?" Sharon gets around to asking me an hour later, on our way downstairs.

I take a quick breath.

"About ten years."

"Really?" she asks. She sounds confused. "How could you stay for so long?"

"Oh, my dad's actually American," I say, cautiously. I'm aware that it could be the beginning of more origin-related questions.

"Well, that's pretty handy, isn't it?" she returns. She rummages through her wallet for her passport. "What do you drink?"

"Oh, I don't know. Spirits, wine. Anything but lager, really."

I wonder if there's a difference between lager and beer and what it could be.

"Great, same. Do you want to each put in five quid and share a bottle of rum?" she asks. "I've still got some Coke in the fridge from last night."

"Sure," I say. "I have no idea what the conversion rate is like at the moment, though. What's five quid? Around seven dollars?"

"Oh, yeah, sorry, no, I meant like five dollars. I'm still thinking in pounds."

"What kind of rum should we get?" I ask, attempting to exchange the currency conversation for something less specific.

She looks at me with a little leer. "I don't suppose they have Pusser's here?"

I sense not knowing won't signify. "Oh, I'm not too sure, real-ly. I haven't been drinking in ages. What about Captain Morgan's?"

Sharon covers her eye with one hand, like a patch, and pushes open the double doors to the recreation room with the other.

"Aye, aye, Cap'n," she says. "A good idea."

The recreation room itself is huge – a converted sort of ballroom, with giant arched windows, and a high, lavishly molded ceiling covered with the chipping remains of painted murals depicting Greek gods and goddesses.

To the right, there's a pool table. One of its legs is propped up by two phone books, to compensate for the uneven floor. And just beyond that there's a big industrial kitchen, complete with a metal island at its center and scores of well-scratched-up Teflon pans hanging from a ceiling rack.

Sharon and I are waved over by two guys sitting in one of four red plastic booths lined up along the far wall. She leads the way across the sticky floor. I follow closely behind, weaving my way through cigarette smoke and past the extended feet of travelers who aren't about to move them.

"Hiya lads," she calls, as we approach the booth.

A guy wearing a pair of mirrored Oakleys, still moving his head to the music, speaks first. "Oright, old girl?"

"Oright," Sharon returns.

He nods at the marijuana-covered table. "We're just settling in, we are."

"So I see," she replies. "Well done!"

She gives them each a little hit on the shoulder, and I guess that they are Duncan and Ian, the guys she said she's been travelling with. Then she motions to me. "This is Rebecca."

The two guys nod at me nonchalantly.

"This is Duncan," she continues, pointing to the one with the sunglasses. "And that's Ian."

I nod back, trying to mirror their level of enthusiasm. "Hey."

Then, I remain, hovering awkwardly. I'm caught between wondering whether it's unusual that I'm still standing and wondering whether sitting down without being asked would seem too presumptuous.

Meanwhile, Sharon is already seated at the table, intently picking seeds out of a little pile of marijuana.

I decide I am welcome to sit down. An invite isn't forthcoming, but neither is it necessary.

Glancing down at the ripped up booth with wires sticking out from every which way, I begin, "Oh wow! Looks like it's been a while since these have been here."

Nobody answers. I am stating the obvious, wasting energy, talking too much.

I grab a badly stained nearby pillow and throw it as indifferently as possible over the wires, despite a definite sense that sitting directly on the exposed wires without noticing would really be the most appropriate.

Ian remains buried in his magazine.

"Great track," Duncan mumbles to himself, as he fiddles with his mini-disc player. "Nice one!"

Although I can tell it's not from unfriendliness, the lack of conversation unsettles me. Picking up a blue lighter off the table, I begin flicking it absentmindedly.

"Don't waste my fluid, please," Ian comments, without looking up.

I return the lighter to the table. "Sor-ry."

My feeble attempt to appear engaged barred, I resort to bobbing my head to the unfamiliar music. This has the reverse effect, however, and makes me feel even more noticeably uncomfortable.

I try glancing in the direction of a gangly youth in a Guatemalan poncho seated at the next table over. Although he appears to be pretty engrossed with his Ramen noodles, which by the way he's eating straight from the pot, something approachable in his manner tells me this is my best bet. I allow my gaze to linger on him for longer than normal. About five seconds. Finally, he senses my stare and looks up. His convivial expression is encouraging. It occurs to me that he probably feels every bit as alienated as I do. I smile openly.

"Hey," I offer.

"Ganesha's name be praised," he replies, evenly. Then he returns to his noodles.

Shrinking back, I resume the head-bobs, while I wait for someone to break the indeterminate silence. I wait. And wait.

"Is it always this crowded in here?" I finally blurt out, compulsively.

Ian slowly looks up from his copy of *Rolling Stone*. He gives me a pointed stare. Then he goes back to his reading, having effectively communicated that no rescue remarks will be offered.

I sink lower in the booth. I am not doing well here. But, I don't quite grasp why, or understand how to stop myself from going under. I try to focus on my breaths. They're short and shallow. Ragged, even. *What is wrong with me?*

Just then, by some miracle, Ian puts his *Rolling Stone* aside.

"So, where are you coming from, lass?" he asks me.

I am delighted, and determined to give short answers from here on in. "New York."

"And before New York?" he continues. He assumes I'm a traveler.

I decide to stick to my own plot for as long as possible.

"Well I was there for ten years," I say.

"Ten years! How'd you manage that?"

"Oh, my dad's American," I say, relaxing a touch as I flag the half truth.

"Oh, okay. But, then," he looks confused, "how *old* are you?"

"Thirty."

"No way!" he hisses. He is shocked by the confession.

Feeling forced into playing the role of the flattered aging woman, I say, "Well thanks, but I really am, actually."

"Never!" he continues.

I pull my right leg up into the booth and rest my chin on my knee.

"Well," I explain, matter-of-factly, "my theory is that everyone usually lies about their age. So when someone actually is their age you think they look younger because it's usually forty-year-olds saying they're thirty."

"Good man, good man," Ian calls, falling out of our conversation in order to address the arrival of a blotchy-skinned youth sporting a spiky mohawk and a T-shirt with a contemptuous slogan written across his sunken-in chest. "What took you so long?"

The kid approaches our booth and casts a brown bag down on the table. "*What* a bleedin' effort!" he huffs.

"What happened, then?" Duncan asks. His tone is chipper.

"Fucking Americans is what happened. The bloke down the road wouldn't let me get it without ID that says I'm twenty-one like! I said, 'C'mon mate, you must be joking.' But, the geezer won't budge and I have to leave all the gear there, come back here, wait five minutes for the bleedin' Mr. Bean at the front desk to buzz me in, back up stairs for me passport, *back* out to the offy, and now I've forgot the fags."

"Easy, Seamus, old boy. You sit here and have a beer. I'll go back out," consoles Duncan.

Seamus looks immediately more relaxed. "Oright, then. Fair enough," he replies.

"Hi," I try, as he falls into the booth.

Seamus glares at me. "Oh, for *fuck's* sake!" He is grabbing his butt with one hand and reaching for a pillow to stick under it with the other.

"What *now?*" queries a Scottish brogue from the next booth over.

Seamus ignores the question, shakes his head in frustration, and swings a mud-covered combat boot up onto the table.

"Fucking Amerrrricans, eh?" sympathizes the brogue, its possessor slowly rising over the top of the booth to get a look at who he's addressing.

Sharon points timidly toward me. "Careful, she's half Yank."

"Oh, sorry, old girl. No offense like," returns the Scotsman. He reaches his arm over his head backwards to shake my hand, in an easy, at-home kind of way. "Anyway, should've known – nice teeth and all that."

I take his outstretched hand. "Thanks, I'm Rebecca."

"Angus. I used to weigh almost fourteen stone, you know. They called me Fatty Paddy. Can you believe it?"

I observe his elfin build, delicate features, spiky baby-fine blonde coiffure. Only Saint-Exupéry's *Little Prince* comes to mind.

"Fatty Paddy?" I ask.

"I'm a quarter Irish," he explains. "But, can you believe I was that *fat?*"

"I can't," I say.

"I can't either," adds Sharon, with an arched eyebrow.

Angus takes a long drag of his cigarette and stares at her.

Ian glares at Angus. "Have you got an exta fag, then, Angus?"

Angus breaks out of his trance. "Sorry, mate, got it off him," he says, pointing across the room. "Drag?"

"Drag?" Ian asks. "What's the *point* of a single drag?"

Angus looks back at him blankly. "You need more drink, like, don't you?"

"Don't think it's the drink I need more of, mate. Maybe something else I need less of, isn't it?"

Angus gestures to Ian's bottle of vodka in the middle of the table. "Mind if I pour myself a wee bit of voddy?" he asks.

Ian shakes his head incredulously. "You're a tightfisted git, aren't you?"

"Oh, go on, why don't you tell me how you really feel?"

"Why don't you buy your own bloody booze for a change?"

"I'll take that as a *yes?*" Angus asks, jauntily reaching for the bottle and filling his pint glass halfway up with Ian's booze.

This transgression is followed by several more minutes of bickering until Angus, finally giving in, begrudgingly hands Ian a *fiver* in order to cover his costs. Next, perhaps in an effort to draw a clear distinction between principles and stinginess, Ian then starts offering the rest of us gratis beers from the brown paper bag he has safeguarded under the table.

"A Becks for Becks?" he asks, when he gets around to me.

Although I don't like beer, I feel obliged, maybe because of the way he has the paper bag so guarded, to show some appreciation for the gesture by accepting.

"Oh, thanks very much. That's ve-ry kind."

"Did I hear you say you were *thirty?*" Angus asks me.

With the majority of hostellers being under twenty-five, I'm well aware that my extra five years are like a lifetime here and also are probably placing me squarely in the confirmed-loser demographic. Still, I figure if I act mildly self-conscious about being thirty and in a youth hostel, it might keep him from considering for himself whether I'm too old to be here.

"Yes, I'm afraid so," I say, owning up to the derogatory status.

"Amazing!" Angus says, as his eyes pop. "I wouldn't have said a day under thirty-five!"

I take a prim sip of my beer and smile. "Oh, cheers for that."

"The Americans are pretty naff, though, you must admit," he adds.

Before I have a chance to answer, he interrupts himself. "Oh my God," he shouts, "I'm going to slit my wrists over here! Can someone please change the CD!"

"You don't like "Scarborough Fair," then?" I ask.

It's the first song of the night that I do like or, for that matter, recognize.

"Not on a Saturday night, pet," he admonishes.

"How long have you been here?" I ask. I'm in awe of how at home he seems to be.

"A month. I'm trying to find work, you know? But nobody wants to employ me," he says, looking at me mischievously. "They just want to fuck me!" He tosses his head back and cackles. "I'm doing laundry here for the moment. Just to pay the rent, like. What part of England are you coming from?"

I pause internally, not liking to be lying directly for the second time already. "Arundel."

"Arundel," he repeats, mocking my accent. "My God, you're so *yah* Rebecca, aren't you?"

Having no idea what this means, I protest. "No, I'm not."

"Yes you are. Isn't she *yah* Sharon?"

"She is a bit posh," Sharon confirms, looking up from her project. "But she's lovely."

The reassuring smile on her face that's telling me it doesn't matter manages to make me feel two times the imposter.

"Anyway," I start. I want to shift the focus. But I can't risk asking him where in Scotland he's from without being sure where Scotland even is. "So, how old are you?" I ask.

"Yah," he says, still teasing. "No, funny you should ask. I'm twenty-one tomorrow!"

"Real-ly?"

"Uh huh, Twenty-one in San FranDisco. Not bad, eh?"

"San Frantastic, really. Are you going to have a... a... par-ty?" I ask, choking on *party*. I realize I can't pronounce it, with its super long, broad A, without sounding, I suspect, even more *yah* than before.

"Defo. Are you going to be here?" he asks.

"Yeah, til Monday," I say.

"Great. You know, you look like Jennifer Capriati, a little."

Limited in conversation, again, I hesitate. I don't dare to ask who this is, lest it be a UK household name. "Really?"

"Defo. Identical wavy brown hair, olive skin, blue eyes. Total doppelganger. Don't you find?"

"I'm not sure, I suppose I've never really heard that before," I answer, without answering.

Frogs, Poms and Aussies

"So, who'd you find the *nicest* downstairs, then?" Sharon asks me, later that night, once we are both snuggly settled into our sleeping bags.

"Angus. Definitely."

"Are you taking the piss?" she asks.

"No, I'm not taking the piss," I insist. "I really did think he was the nicest."

"Well, yes, Angus is *fit* but he's a bit Darren Day, isn't he? I was talking about between Duncan and Ian."

Unable to dispute anything without knowing what *fit* or *Darren Day* means, I just say, "Oh, right."

"So?"

"I'd say Ian, then. He seems maybe a lit-tle more dynamic than Duncan. Though maybe it's not fair to say because we don't know what Duncan is like since he was off in his own world listening to his mini-disc player most of the night, wasn't he?" I return.

I am amazed by how much more face, mouth, and lip movement being English requires.

"There, he is a bit boring, isn't he? Now you can see what I've been lumbered with since Laos. I mean, bless, but..."

"No, quite right," I reply, supportively.

"Do you think I can get away with..."

Just then the door swings open. The light from the hallway, along with two girls, resembling giant tortoises under their enormous backpacks, spill into our room.

"Zey are sleeping?" whispers one of the girls in a heavy French accent.

"Hi," I say in the direction of their shadow. "We're awake."

"Allo!" they return in unison.

"The light's behind you," Sharon offers.

The taller one flips on the overhead light. "Sank you. We are not waking you?"

"No, we're just chatting," replies Sharon. "Welcome to room fourteen."

"Sank you, it's a pleazure, we have just moved from ze ozer hostel, do you know it?"

We both shake our heads that we don't.

"Ze ozer girls were so rude zere. When we came in in ze night zey were getting so crazy. And *everyone* comes in late sometimes, no?"

"Too right. If you want to be alone, you have to get a private," says Sharon, authoritatively.

"Exactly," the girl continues. "And, moreover, it was so sterile zere. We were not even allowed one beer zere. I mean, I take a wine every night since I am twelve years, we are not childrens here!"

"Well, rest assured, you won't have that problem here," offers Sharon.

"Good!" the girl exclaims. "Anyways," she continues, as she catches her breath, "never mind only zis. So, you are coming from Englands?"

Unwittingly sparing me a lie, Sharon answers for us, "We are, indeed. And you?"

"Yes, yes, we're coming from France. We're here for ten days, zen we will travel around California, and zen we will go to Canada. We will try to find work zis fall and winter as ski instructors."

"Fun," says Sharon.

"Oui, we hope so. And you? You are traveling togezer?"

"No, actually, we just met today," I say.

"Oh, you looks like, eh, old friends."

"Nope," I reply.

"Maybe you are from near together in Englands?"

"Not too far," Sharon says, looking up at me. "Becky, how far is Arundel by train from London?"

"About forty-five minutes," I say, automatically, based on a ten-year-old memory of fewer than ten train trips to London.

"Rubbish! It's much farther than that," she counters.

"No, perhaps you're right," I say, catching myself. "It's been an age since I lived there. Maybe more like an hour and fifteen minutes."

"At least!" she insists.

While Sharon explains the best calling cards with which to call Europe and gives them directions to the shop that sells them, I pretend to study a map of Mexico.

What am I doing? This is crazy. These phrases, questions and references. It's only a matter of time. I'm going to get busted. I'll never make it til Monday.

"Becky is your name?" the taller tortoise asks me.

I am drawn away from my psychic drama and back into the warmth of the moment.

"I am Vanessa and zis is Celia," she continues. "I am just reading Vanity Fair with the heroine's also Becky. It is really enjoy, but sorry, I must be reading it in French."

"Oh, real-ly? I've never read it. I love actually French writers," I say, finding myself now slipping into a broken-English British accent. "I love Moliere but, also, sorry, only in English. His grave I saw at Père Lachaise. I was surprised, real-ly, by how short he was."

"Oh, oui, Père Lachaise. You have spent much time in Paris?" she asks.

"During my…" I am nearly saying, "During my sophomore year abroad in England, I went there for two weeks," but then I remember that I *am* English.

"Not really, I've only been once for two weeks," I say instead, as I realize, reluctantly, that to make room for the new version of myself, some of my own experiences will have to become obsolete.

"Is pity, no? We live so close. But, it is always ze way. I have only been once to Englands also."

****

As I listen to the sound of Vanessa and Celia brushing their teeth and washing their faces, peppered with soft whispers about their plans to rent bikes and cycle over the Golden Gate Bridge the next day, I am struck by how simple and complicated everything is at once. On the one hand, I can't remember an environment so easy since summer camp. On the other, I can't ever remember an atmosphere so fraught.

Despite all anxiety, though, what strikes me most is how cozy I feel. The sound of Sharon's breath as she sleeps makes me feel cozier, still. And as I drift off, I find myself hanging on to her breaths.

After just a few hours of sleep the sound of a blaring car alarm coming from the parking lot beneath our window wakes me up. I climb down the wooden ladder attached to my bed and manage a crash landing on the radiator.

"Bloody hell," I call out in a stage whisper. The cut on my toe is exacerbated by the burden of having to don an accent in the middle of the night.

"Are you okay," Sharon asks, groggily.

"Yes, thanks. Just stubbed my toe on the heater."

"Do you need a plaster?"

A *plaster? A plaster?*

"No, that's okay," I decline, deducing she's offering me a Band-Aid, but finding continuing a conversation in this moment to be a more painful prospect than walking down the hall with an uncovered split toenail.

****

Wide awake from the pain of my toe and a blinding light from the hall, I limp to the bathroom. My bladder is about to burst from a year's allowance of beer and rum. A barefoot guy in a pair of pink swim trunks is already there, leaning his pro-surfer body up against the wall outside bathroom number three. I take my place behind him.

"Queueing for the loo at two in the morning. It's all a bit hectic, isn't it?" he says to me, as if we already know each other.

"Yes, it's shocking," I reply.

I get the feeling he's been traveling for a while.

"Is, isn't it? And the worst bit is they're probably in there having a shag. Slags."

"Completely," I concur. He stares at me as if he's waiting for me to finish my sentence.

"And you don't even have your flip-flops on," I add. Then I cringe at the coarseness of my own implication.

"Flip-flops? Dolls, I know you're a Pom and you can't help it, but they're thongs, okay?"

I gather from this that he must be Australian and that Pom must be slang for Brit.

"Okay, then."

"Too many Brits in this hostel," he says. "I mean, where is everyone else? No offense to you personally, dolls."

"Oh, none taken, I ass-ure you," I reply.

He slams a fist on the bathroom door. "Hey! Move it in there!" he shouts.

"I'm taking a *shit* for Christ's sake!" calls back an angry German accent.

The Australian grins mischievously from behind long wisps of limp, sun-bleached hair. "Well do it *faster!*" he orders.

There's a stunned silence followed by an outraged, "No!"

"Yes!" counters the Australian.

Just then another door swings open and a girl wrapped in an orange sarong with an afro and a barbell-shaped earring lodged in her eyebrow is standing in the doorway.

"I'm sleeping. We're all sleeping," she says, in a Brooklyn accent. "You two need to shut the *fuck* up, okay?"

"I'm so sor-ry," I say, sheepishly. I half expect her to be able to hear through my accent and identify me as a fellow East Coast American.

She studies me a moment and rolls her eyes. "Yet another sorry-ass Pom," she says, before she closes the door.

"Charming girl," I say.

"That's Tamika, the breakfast bitch from hell," he tells me.

"And don't you forget it, you dried up old crocodile!" Tamika's muffled voice calls back through the door.

"Cow!" he shouts in return.

Then, touching my arm, he says, "C'mon. The loos upstairs are better anyway."

I follow him down the hall.

"So, matey. Why're ya limping? Too much grog?"

"Stubbed my toe," I explain, through a squelched yawn.

"When'd that happen?"

"About five minutes ago."

"Okay, okay, hop on," he offers.

"Sor-ry?"

"I mean, you look fairly solid," he says, with a smirk. "But I like a challenge. Hop on, I'll give you a lift up the stairs."

"Well, that's very tempting. And flattering. But I think I'll pull through," I say.

He has a look of sincere intent in his right eye and sarcasm in the other.

"Oh, go on," he insists. "At least take my arm then."

Against my better judgment, I throw an arm around him and let the weight off my foot, too affection-starved and buzzed to care.

"There ya go, matey," he says, his left eye looking more neutral suddenly.

We hobble up the stairs together. His sun-freckled shoulder, smooth and warm, is like an anchor.

"You're doing great, soldier," he coaches.

I laugh, too brightly. "Right, thank you."

It occurs to me it's the first physical contact I've had with anybody in a year. I search for something more to say before my silence gives this thought away.

"Okay, here. You take the Feng Shui loo," he says, once we arrive outside decrepit bathroom number seven.

I fumble for something to say back. Anything.

"Wow, it really stinks in this hall, doesn't it?" I ask.

"I don't smell anything. You must have a nose like a fox."

"Well, actually, I…"

"You *are* a fox?" he asks.

"I've always just had this super keen nose, I guess."

He searches my face with an amused smile.

"Too keen, at times, real-ly," I add.

"Yeah, I think you're a fox," he says, as he waves a mosquito away from his arm, nods goodnight, and then disappears before I can come up with anything more to say.

First Day of School

I wake up the next morning to what sounds like the dumping of endless garbage cans of glass into the back of a truck.

"Blimey," Sharon mutters, to nobody in particular. "That's a nice way to start the day."

I breathe heavily, toss frantically and pretend to still be asleep. It's grueling enough to have to talk first thing in the morning, let alone in a flourishing accent.

Another thirty minutes and both the French girls and Sharon are dressed and out of the room. I lie in bed for another half hour, relishing the ease of not having to pretend anything.

Following a long, hot shower, I then rearrange my mouth and lips and head down for breakfast.

"Sor-ry," I say to the third newly arriving traveler I nearly crash into on my way downstairs.

I am shot another half-bewildered look and hastily switch lanes, concluding they're all English and therefore walking up the left side of the staircase and down the right, according to custom.

Still, despite all the kinks, I realize I'm also excited about resuming my role. While my thoughts are still uneasy, my body registers only a steady buzz.

Downstairs, sleepy travelers, some barefoot, crowd the chilly kitchen. I take my place in the procession, which winds chaotically around the kitchen's giant metal island, and survey the bounty: a giant bowl of bagels, plastic tubs of government-grade butter, cream cheese, and peanut butter, three kinds of jam, a heaping pile of sliced bananas and oranges, and a little, token, presumably left-behind, jar of Marmite.

Despite the total abundance, the atmosphere has a sort of Last Supper feel to it. Like some kind of Darwinian game show, there's plenty of reaching and grabbing as the contestants lunge across one other in order to set plates of food aside, or to toss already-man-handled bagels back into the bowl, as they upgrade from plain to sesame or poppy.

Tamika, the so-called breakfast-bitch from the hallway last night, is leaning up against the counter chopping unpeeled bananas into fours. I stand quietly by, hoping she won't recognize me. Just then she looks up and points the end of her large white knife in my direction.

"Don't touch that dial!" she shouts. She's addressing the kid standing behind me, though, the kid whose hand is now backing away from a knob on the kitchen radio.

"Take it easy, I was just…"

"…about to lose your key deposit?" she threatens, finishing his sentence.

"You can't take away my key deposit for adjusting the flippin' volume!" he starts.

"You wanna bet?"

"Crikey," the kid mutters, indignantly. He has no choice but to recognize the chain of command.

Stretching for a scoop of cream cheese, I offer him a look of commiseration. But he doesn't seem to notice. He's too busy arranging his vertically cut pumpernickel bagel on the conveyer belt of the giant toaster. I almost tell him bagels are actually designed to be cut and toasted horizontally. But, out of an interest in avoiding associations with all things American, I hold back.

As I make my way out of the kitchen into the rec room, Angus flails his arms at me from across the room. This, of course, is a big relief. The last thing I wanted was to be seen anxiously looking around for him or Sharon. Or, worst of all, sitting alone.

"Oi, Becky! Party's over here!" he hollers.

I wade through the usual sea of people and approach his table.

"Hiya. Hap-py Birthday!" I say.

"Oh my God," Angus coos, appreciatively. "You remembered!"

"Was just telling Anna about you," he says, gesturing to the young woman sitting beside him. "Becky's the one who has been away from Britain for ten years and still has the most British accent of anyone," he tells her.

Pulling myself up to the table on a gray, rolling office chair, I shake my head vociferously. "Nooo!"

"Anyway, this is Anna. She's working here too," continues Angus.

She greets me with an easy smile and dark, intelligent-looking eyes.

"Nice to meet you," I say. "What are you doing here?"

Once again, my vowels are drawn out; my consonants are clipped. I have to keep my mind on each and every word, each syllable. It is almost like speaking a foreign language; like asking where the post office is in newly learned Italian. The process is exhausting. And it's only nine o'clock.

"I clean the toilets," she returns, with an accent I can't quite place.

"Real-ly?"

I try to hide my surprise that she's cleaning toilets, let alone admitting to it, behind a bite of bagel.

"Yeah, I love working here," she says, oblivious to my embarrassment. "I really want to stay but my visa will run out. And my flight's already Wednesday."

"Right, what a pain," I say. Something in her beam doesn't let me feel sorry for her.

"I'd just love to stay on and not go back."

"Where are you from?"

"Brussels."

"Oh, how lovely. What do you do back home, then?" I continue. I am probing to discover what could be worse than cleaning toilets.

"I study. Engineering."

"Wait!" Angus interrupts, grabbing my knee. "Rebecca, you have to see. See *him?*" he asks, pointing across the room to the guy I met last night outside the bathroom. "He's my favorite."

"Oh yeah?" I say, only just now realizing *Darren Day,* as Sharon called Angus last night, must be Cockney rhyming slang for gay. "I think I met him by the bathroom last night. Is he Australian?"

I can't stop noticing the subtle sound shifts taking place, separate even from the words requiring obvious pronunciation changes, as I alter the shape and movements of my mouth.

"Yeah, he's called Stacy. He's been here just over a fortnight. Halfpipe champion, you know? Doesn't he have the hottest little body in town?" Angus asks, in a camped-up tone.

"Dish," I reply, agreeably.

"You fancy him, too, Rebecca, don't you?

"No, he's all yours," I say.

"No, you fancy him."

"No, real-ly I don't," I insist.

Angus looks at me shrewdly. "Rrrroooole out the polygraph!" he shouts, at the top of his lungs. "Rebecca's going to get a snog tonight!"

I knock him gently on the arm. "Shut up! Are you mad?"

"I know, I'm such a tart," he smiles. "All of my friends are slags. But, mark my words, I'm going to get a shag tonight. By hook or by crook!"

"By hook or by crook?"

"Yes, by hook or by crook!" Angus confirms.

"Well, can't say I've ever heard that expression applied to a shag before," I note. "But I'm sure you will."

"Cheers for the vote of confidence. What are you up to right now? Want to go for a wander?"

"You don't have to do any laundry?" I ask.

"On my birthday? I hope not. It'd be pretty Triple O if I did, wouldn't it?"

"Yeah," I say, not daring to ask what…

"Out of order, that is," he supplies.

Getting to Know You

Outside, Angus and I meander down Broadway, past the strip clubs and the pungent stench of urine, chatting about *home,* and allowing familiarity to catch up with and affirm a premature sense of kinship.

It's peculiar. The affinity feels real. As long as I don't allow myself to think too much about what I'm doing, that is. Cunningly, I steer our conversation toward more immediate topics, areas unrelated and on the surface – to the subjects that don't require more lying from me.

"So what do you want for your twenty-first?" I ask, as we turn onto Columbus.

"A pair of Diesel trainers. That's about it. And a butt-plug."

"A butt-plug? That's disgusting!"

"I tried to get Sharon to do a whip-around and get me a butt-plug with it," he continues. "They're pretty dear, you know. Around fifty quid. You think she'll do it?"

I look at him hopefully. "No, you're taking the piss, surely."

"No way. I want one!" he laughs.

"Anyway," I add, "if so, that's real-ly disgusting."

"Get over yourself," he returns, dismissively, though without much actual edge.

"What's that supposed to mean, then?" I ask.

"It means you've led a sheltered little life in wee Arundel."

"Ha! You have no idea."

"Of what?" he asks.

"Of my experience."

"As if! You may have lived in New York for ten years, but you still act very wee-Arundel, you know," he asserts.

"Right, well, if you must know," I begin, in an effort to avoid withholding more information about myself than absolutely necessary, "when I first moved out here I lived with a virtual por-nog-rapher."

"You? No way."

"Yes way. I'm afraid so," I say. "It's a long story. He was a friend from New York."

Angus nudges me in the rib with his arched eyebrow. "Do I smell a porky-pie?"

Recalling *porky-pie* to be Cockney rhyming slang for lie, I continue, "No, seriously, it's true."

"Bollocks."

"No, honestly. Luke's from Eng-land, too," I continue. "I mean, he's a lovely bloke. Not your typical por-nog-rapher."

Angus gives me a cockeyed look.

"Real-ly, he isn't. I mean, he's got a mouse-pad with his dog's picture on it. His dad's even a *vicar*. If you can picture that?"

"How'd you meet then? Were you a stripper?" Angus laughs.

"Well, he wasn't doing it when I met him, was he?"

"Oh."

"He was on this PhD course. Economics."

"So were you getting a PhD, then?"

"No, we were just living in the same student housing building. Once Luke started shooting porn in his dorm room he just chucked the course, though. Then he moved out here."

"Mental!"

"No, I know."

42

I contemplate the peculiar cachet relating Luke's story always seems to carry, as well as why I always seem to enjoy telling people about it.

"Then what?"

"Well, then he moved out here and began producing. When I arrived here I was skint. He let me crash at his house rent-free for like three months."

"So, why aren't you staying with him now?"

"It wasn't worth it."

"Free rent? Not worth it?"

"I was lit-erally living around dildos being sterilized in pots on the kitchen stove or drying on the dish rack. And so-called *bonking machines*," I lament. "So, it's not that I've never been exposed to all of this stuff. But I just choose not…"

Angus interrupts, dreamily, "Sounds like heaven."

"Well, not exactly. Unless heaven involves boiling eggs in ket-tles on the sly."

"Huh?"

"If I didn't Luke would get all wound up. Seriously, he thought *I* was mental for not having the faith in his dishwasher to sterilize the pots properly."

Angus laughs. "The pots that sterilized the dildos?"

"Correct."

"Wicked! You loved it."

"Not at all. Quite the opposite," I snap. "I mean, for one thing it's just not romantic. It's like this street. I mean, even if I were a bloke, I could never get turned on inside one of these strip clubs. The women aren't being themselves. And the only thing that turns me on is… earn-est-ness, sin-cer-ity."

"Is he fit? Does he still live here?" he asks.

"He is, actually. And, yes, as far as I know."

"I want to meet him! Invite him to my party tonight?"

"Yes, okay," I start, slowly.

As I peruse the spit, gum, and vomit-stained sidewalk, I frame a new picture of just how much vigilance this fake identity thing is going to require. I mean, while I'm tempted to be able to convince Angus of Luke's existence, inviting Luke would also mean confessing my scheme to Luke and risking Luke's getting drunk and telling everyone everything. These are precisely the kinds of details I have to be aware of, if I'm going to remain safely one step ahead.

"What is it?" Angus presses.

"Well, it just might be a little weird for me actually, since we've faded out of con-tact, you know?" I say, commencing with the earliest of an endless succession of backpedaling scenarios to come.

"Whateva," Angus says. "He sounds like good fun."

"He is. He was. But living there wasn't," I continue, thinking out loud. "I mean, he's a lovely guy."

"You already said that."

"Well, he is. I mean, he's a real friend. Totally sound. But, I was in this long distance relationship with this bloke – this bloke I really love. And being at Luke's just made it all the more depressing. The atmosphere of porn is so soulless, especially in contrast to being in love."

"I can imagine that, actually," Angus says.

I realize it's the first time I've felt relaxed enough with anybody to talk about Gotthard. Or, maybe, that anyone's felt relaxed enough with me to listen.

"You can?"

"Yeah, I've just been blown out last week myself. I mean we were only going out for two weeks but it's still really gutted me."

"I'm sorry," I say.

"You should be. It's your fault," he jokes, banning the canned condolence. "I don't know," he continues, "I just feel really let down by myself. I was going to say by Jonathon, but it's myself. I

44

always put myself out there and make myself vulnerable. I just feel worthless sometimes. You know what I mean?" he asks.

"Yeah."

Struck by his candor, I hold back the impulse to put an arm around him. Instead, I rescue him along more culturally appropriate lines. I change the subject.

"Do you play Scrabble?" I ask.

"*Love* Scrabble."

"Does the hostel have a board?"

"Defo, two. We can play later. When we get back."

"Okay."

"Let's go halvers on a packet of bickies and go to the park for the avo, though," he adds.

"Pardon?"

"Split a pack of bickies and hit the park? Let's splash out on a packet of Chips Ahoy, then. A dollar forty each. They're gorgeous. Have you *never* tried them?"

"Oh, yeah, sure," I agree.

I make a mental note of *halvers*.

Angus and I then pass the rest of the afternoon lying around in Washington Square Park, making idle chitchat about how *naff* the people playing volleyball look, and discussing other likes and dislikes that connote perhaps more to personality and sensibility than to nationality.

When the sun starts to go down, we spend another hour inching ourselves clockwise around the park in an effort to stay under it before we finally give in and head back along Columbus toward the hostel.

Walking home, the warm evening air dances around us and smells like summer friendship. Except for everything, I don't feel as if I have anything to hide from him.

Finally, we make it back to the hostel. After hauling ourselves up the steps of what feels like one of San Francisco's steepest streets, we arrive outside the rec room's back entrance. Angus fiddles with the combination lock.

"The code is four-five-six, by the way," he says.

"Cheers."

"How glamorous-like, eh?" he observes. "Late for my own birthday party."

Then, attempting a dramatic entrance, he kicks open the wooden double doors with the sole of his worn sneaker.

We are met by blaring ragtime piano music, the distinct aroma of marijuana, and a room full of people milling around with red plastic pint glasses.

A man wearing an upside-down garbage bag is pointing a long metal spoon toward a bearded hippie seated at a light green piano across the room. "So, let's hear it for Banjo Bob!" he shouts.

Some of the crowd cheer in unison at this. Others are too absorbed in conversation and consumption to notice.

Angus glances over at a few people climbing up on chairs to dance to a remix of "If You're Going to San Francisco."

"We should have left the park sooner, Becky. It's kicking off a bit earlier than usual in here tonight. But, never you mind."

Grabbing me by the arm, he then pulls me through the crowd of people toward the pool table, which is now covered by a giant piece of plywood, a red sheet, and four, large, metal pans filled with creamy-looking casserole. A sign beside it all reads, "Vegetarian Shepherd's Pie."

"Rebecca," he instructs, "get us two *big* plates and meet back at booth two. I'm going to dash out for a bottle. We'll wolf it down, lay our foundation, like, then we'll get going with the whiskey."

"Over and out," I say to his back as he drifts away.

I pause before I take my place in the food line. "Thanks for the din-ner! It looks amazing!" I call to the man in the kitchen wearing the garbage bag apron.

"Save room for the cake!" he replies.

"A cake too?"

He then signals that it's okay for me to bypass the big "Kitchen Closed" sign and come see what he's doing.

I inch my way around the blackboard barricade, covered with what looks, perhaps, like hardened pumpkin pie thrown at it on a previous occasion, and enter the kitchen.

Up close he looks different. Around fifty. An aging hippie. A cross between Robert De Niro and Fred Flintstone, though with black, threatening eyes set even closer together than either of theirs. He gestures proudly to his cake in progress.

"Wow!" I say, following the prompt. "Do you do this every Wednesday?"

"Nope." He is concentrating on squeezing icing through a cone shaped out of waxed paper. "Parties every Wednesday and Friday night. But cakes only on birthdays."

"Cool."

"Yup, that's why we're the *best!*" he exclaims.

"Well, your cake cer-tain-ly looks impressive," I say, Englishly.

"Don't touch this one," he jumps, as if I were going to. "Here," he says, handing me a stack of pictures. "Have a look at these other cakes we've had. The one on the top is the one I made for Dylan's birthday."

"Oh, right."

"I was older then, I'm much younger than that now!" he croons, conveying what's inscribed in icing on the cake in the picture. "We played my Dylan bootlegs until four in the morning. *That* was a fun night!"

I am suddenly aware that *this* is the man who I spoke to on the phone from Berkeley. I don't know how I know. I just do.

"Well, it's really kind of you to give all of this lovely food away," I offer, more meekly. "Is it your hostel, then?"

"Nope, see that guy over there?" he says. He points to a great, jolly-looking man with two, long, whitish-gray braids. "That's Harrison, the owner. I'm Alan, the manager. Be sure to tell him you think I throw a great party."

Smiling serenely, I reply, "I will, with pleasure."

Then I get a peculiar feeling in the pit of my stomach. The fake naturalness I'm peddling has a funny aftertaste. It fools my ear, but not my belly. And I wonder if he can taste it too.

"Don't forget," he reinforces.

"Of course, I won't."

"Good."

"This party is *amazing!*" I then add. I am over fawning now, like a waiter behind a peppermill. I'm hoping, I guess, that an abundance of appreciation, in some unknown way, can atone for my trickery.

****

Breaking away from Alan, I finally make my way out of the kitchen and back into the crowded rec room. Angus, already back from the liquor store, is reclining in one of the booths.

"You rinsed the forks, right?" he confirms, as I place our silverware and plates of shepherd's pie on the table before him.

"No, they were clean," I say.

"I know, but you have to rinse anyway. Some people just wipe them off with a towel and put them back in. Seriously."

"You're joking?"

"No, seriously. You can't be naive."

"Oh, okay," I say. "I'll just go and wash these off, then."

"No, it'll take too long with that dishwashing queue in there. Leave it. Let's have a drink," he says.

I take a seat and adjust to the idea of eating off a dirty fork.

"Right."

Angus winks in the direction of his whiskey and pushes an empty glass in front of me.

"And I know you're not going to let me get pissed alone on my birthday," he warns.

I affect the attitude of a seasoned drinker. "Wouldn't dream of it."

"Good." He then dumps the Scrabble letters on the table and begins turning them over. "That was quite the Coca-Cola moment we had back there this morning, wasn't it?" he asks, carelessly.

"Was, rather," I agree, pouring myself my first ever shot of whiskey. "It can be so..."

Angus grabs me urgently by the forearm and manages to spill my shot of whiskey on the board. "Dish alert!" he exclaims.

"C'mon, Angus!" I reprimand, familiarly.

But he just ignores the spill and ticks his head anxiously in the direction of the door. "Dish of the day, eh? *Eh?*"

A good-looking new arrival, wearing a beat-up jean jacket and a patina of self-assurance is entering the scene.

"Party's over here!" Angus shouts instinctively, motioning him over. "Dish of the day, eh, Becky, eh?"

I'm torn between wanting to indulge Angus and wanting to avoid playing the bawdy slob myself.

"Not too shab-by," I finally return.

"Too right he's not."

"I do rate that look," I observe.

"Nice ruddy complexion," Angus adds.

"Yes, nice rustic man-ner in general," I say.

"That too. Like the shoulder-width. Like that a lot."

"Yeah, I agree," I manage to squeeze in, just before said dish is literally positioned over us.

"What's the crack?" he asks, brushing a slow hand through the uneven edges of his shiny brown hair.

"Pull up a seat," Angus instructs. "We need another player."

He flashes us a temperate smile. "Nah, no thanks," he says. "Girlfriend's just gone out for a bottle. I think we're going to… "

At the mention of the words *girlfriend* and *we*, Angus, personally betrayed, abruptly dumps the conversation on its ear.

"Oh my God!" he shouts. "We can't be playing Scrabble anyway! It's eight! I'm Tweeeennnnty-Onnneee!"

"Are ya then?" the guy replies.

But Angus only pushes himself upward until he's standing in the booth towering over the rest of the room and broadcasts to the crowd, "Hello everyone!"

He is waving one hand in the air for silence and pressing the other against his chest, as if overcome by emotion.

"Tonight I'm twenty-one! I'm from *Scotland!* And I just want to say… *My heart feels warm!* …and you, YOU," he shouts, pointing to a random, puzzled-looking spectator, "know *exactly* what I'm talking about!"

Hoovers, Bin Liners, and Loo Roll

I open my eyes the next morning to see a stocky young woman with a navy handkerchief in her hair standing over my dorm bed nodding her head in agreement with herself.

"Shall I just skip the hoovering, then?"

"What?"

"Yeah, go back to bed, it's only five past ten anyway. I'll give it a miss in here today," she confirms.

"Oh, cheers," I say. My head throbs.

I look around the empty room. My eyes rest on the hem of my gray flannel skirt. I've slept through my alarm. I've missed my sole teaching interview, too. It was the whole reason for staying here these last days. And now I've missed it.

Rolling over on my side, I stare at my stern skirt and the confining lifestyle it suggests. I entertain the idea that the skirt together with a pair of nylons has actually always left me feeling more uncomfortable, more separated from myself, and more like a phony, than this accent has yet to do.

Running my fingers along the cracks in the lavender wainscoting alongside my bed, I can't help feeling secretly relieved. The last thing I wanted to do was squeeze myself into that skirt in the first place. But I couldn't have justified skipping the appointment. With the same spirit of surrender, I conclude I can't possibly make it to Mexico and back on $220.00.

I know I should leave. If I had more money, I know I would leave. But, I can't. I don't. I temper my own reservations by reminding myself I won't be staying long. A week or two at the most. I'll figure out something else to do. It's not a crime.

****

Back downstairs I loiter at the border of the empty kitchen. Tamika, the bitchy server, is in there mopping the floor. I notice some sweat beads gathering on her forehead and that the left side of her lip appears to be raising involuntarily, a little, but I don't connect any of this to my presence.

"Any chance I can still get one bagel?" I ask, after another moment.

At this, however, Tamika slams her mop down, shakes her head in an overdone, disgusted sort of way, and then begins explaining, in an artificially slow, patronizing, and *loud* voice, "There is no 'just one bagel.' There *is* no breakfast after ten. *Over.* Don't you *get* it?"

Some others, still lingering in the rec room over their breakfasts, observe the spectacle.

"Don't think she gets it, Tamika!" calls a voice from the crowd.

This garners a few chuckles.

"Right, thanks anyway, that's cool," I assure her.

I'm irritated by the too-obliging tone my new accent seems to lend to almost everything I say, causing that line between humility and humiliation to become an even finer one than it normally is.

Shuffling away from the kitchen, I then make my way across the crowded room and over to the first available table. Collapsing down as carelessly as possible, I reach for an abandoned pamphlet on the history of the Golden Gate Bridge. Then I pretend to be deeply absorbed by it, as if I'm not thinking about being the out-of-the-loop new arrival who just got yelled out of the kitchen.

After a long drawn out couple of minutes, I'm rescued by Angus's voice.

"Back from Mexico so soon?" He is looming over me with an articulate smirk. "How was it, then?"

"Ah, yes, I didn't make it, I'm afraid."

"So ya didn't, so ya didn't. Becky, you rascal, you."

He pats me on the head condescendingly and produces a poppy seed bagel.

"Oh, thanks! How'd you get *that?*" I ask.

"I've got the stroke around here, darling."

"Guess so."

"No, actually," he confesses, "I just nicked a few while Tamika was in the sprinkler room. Eat it surreptitiously, though. It's ridiculous anyway. Who's getting out of bed before ten after last night?"

"Surreptitiously is a big word," I observe.

"Frankly," he replies, ignoring me and looking disdainfully at the pamphlet on the table, "I *never* want to see the Golden Gate Bridge!"

"No, nor do I. By the way, did you hear all of those car alarms going off last night?"

Angus takes a seat. "Who didn't?" he replies. "Pissed as I was, I didn't sleep any – at all."

"Same here."

"Lucky for me, I'm young, though, so I just jacked-off all night," he adds.

"That's nice."

"My roommates didn't think so."

Touching my hand distractedly he then jumps up and rushes over to the sound system.

"Hey, what *is* this shite!?" he demands, as he opens the carousel and removes the CD.

Someone too slouched down in a booth to see shouts back, "We're listening to it!"

"Sorry, pal, it's shite," Angus explains. His tone isn't unfriendly, just declaratory.

"Well, you better not be putting on any more of that sitar crap, man," the voice threatens back, acquiescing.

"No, no, I promise," replies Angus, agreeably. "It's *Travis*, mate."

I watch my new friend walking back from the stereo.

I can't stand this deceit. How can I go on pretending to be friends with this person who thinks I'm somebody else? This isn't normal. It's crazy.

I consider just telling him everything and ponder possible phrasing: "Angus, you'll never believe it, but…" "Angus, can I tell you something?"

Just then Alan, the aging hippy manager, enters the scene.

"Angus!" he bellows. "Have you seen Seamus?"

"It's not *my* day to watch him, is it?" Angus replies.

A storm clouds over Alan's face. "Angus, yes or no? Please. I'm not in the mood!"

"No, I haven't. Why?"

"He's supposed to be vacuuming today. I have to go somewhere. I don't know where he is and I can't do the vacuuming. I don't *like* this!"

"Sorry, Alan, I don't know," Angus returns, more deferentially.

"*Damn* him!" Alan shouts, attempting to slam the swinging door behind himself as he exits.

Angus looks over at me and carelessly lights a cigarette. "See how mad he gets when he's late for his rage management class?"

"Yeah, funny. He's got a pret-ty fierce temper, hasn't he?" I observe.

"Positively *cantankerous.*"

Motioning for a single drag of tobacco, I privately determine not to risk telling *anyone* about me for now.

I head back up to my dorm room and spend the next hour alone in my bed, alone in my head. To say the least, I feel conflicted. It wasn't supposed to go this way. The hostel was only supposed to provide a few nights shelter. But, somehow, nobody is catching on to the accent. It's going swimmingly. I am amazed by how adept I am at carrying out the charade. I'm making the first friends I've had in over a year. And I like everything about this place, from the sense of community and camaraderie to its faintly decadent culture and the nourishing food. The fact is, after catching a glimpse of what feels like some kind of an enchanted commune, the thought of contorting myself to return to the outside world just does not appeal. How am I supposed to leave when this is exactly where I've always wanted to be?

On the other hand, this can't go on indefinitely. None of it's real and all of it's dangerous. I'm deceiving them. Any minute I'll be busted. Then ostracized. It's inevitable. I have to leave before that happens. But, to go where?

Without an answer in sight, I return to the kitchen, where I find the omnipresent Angus now rifling though the sticky cubbyholes lining the kitchen wall.

"What are you looking for?"

He looks up.

"A decent tea bag. Like looking for the Holy Grail. Or for a light off a Californian. Which is basically the same thing."

"Too right," I say.

And just like that I feel restored. It doesn't make any sense, but being back in my character is where I feel safe; albeit within a fiction, it's the only place where I seem to be back amidst some semblance of reality.

"What are you up to tonight, then?" he asks.

"I don't know. I'm shattered. I thought I'd try to get some sleep tonight," I say. "Why? Scrabble?"

"*Don't* think so, dear. I want to go clubbing. In the Castro." He swings his arms in a series of dance moves. "Ya wanna come?"

I whine, apologetically. "Clubbing? Really? I don't think I can."

"Sure you can. Nobody else here can dance anyway. Haven't you ever seen the Americans? They just sort of pose from side to side.".

"No, I can dance, thanks. I meant go out," I explain.

"Oh, don't be daft, you're not *that* old," he teases.

"Come again, wee laddie?"

"Well, why not then?"

"Too skint," I confess. I hope he won't press it.

"Too skint to go for a dance? Now that's pretty pathetic. Anyway, you can tap a tenner off me," he offers.

"No, I mean I'm really skint," I insist.

"You can't be that skint. How much do you have left?"

"Bugger all, really."

"Rubbish. You must have something."

"Two hundred and twenty dollars."

"At all? Or in cash?"

"At all."

"Wow, Becky, you're even worse off than I am, if it makes you feel any better. I've got seven hundred quid and a credit card. And I'm only twenty-one."

"Yeah, that's a nice thought," I say, happy to keep my $120,000 student loan debt to myself.

"Seriously, Rebecca, that is pretty pointless to be that broke and have no job and to think you were going to go to Mexico with it."

"Yeah, no, I know. My plan was to work for room and board but all the vol-unte-er programs I found on-line you actual-ly have to pay for."

"Triple O!" returns Angus. "Well, anyway, you're pretty relaxed for having $220.00 left. What are you going to do?"

"I'm not sure, exactly. But I'm trying not to panic."

I figure if I don't panic, it won't turn into a crisis. And I'm eased by the knowledge that, for now, at twenty dollars a night, I still have eleven days left to figure something out.

"Then come out clubbing and spending with me tonight."

"No, I can't," I insist.

"Or, why don't you just start working here?" he asks.

"No, I can't," I say, knowing for sure I couldn't allow myself to kick the deceit up another notch by staying here longer, and actually working. No matter what.

"Why not?"

"I have to set up a flat and stuff, don't I?"

"With $220.00, nutter?" he asks.

Feeling cornered, I reply, "No, I know. I have to think it over today."

"I mean, seriously, Rebecca, what else are you going to do?"

"I don't know," I nearly snap. It's a lose-lose: To have scruples is to prevent myself from taking a job I need; to abandon them is to create a new set of problems.

Angus presses on. "It would just be to cover the rent, like."

Finally, putting aside what he doesn't know, I allow myself, for an instant, to be seduced by his voice of reason.

"Well, what would I do anyway?"

"Hey Al!" he calls across the room.

Alan snarls. "What now, Angus?"

"Is there any work going at the moment?"

Yanking a mop out from behind a stack of flattened cardboard boxes, he asks, "Who wants to know?"

Angus points to me. "Have you met Becky?"

"Didn't I meet you the other night?" he asks me, squinting his eyes.

"Hi, yeah, but no, that's okay," I say. I'm still convinced that accepting a job would be too brazen a move.

"She could clean Bagby. Louisa leaves in a few days. You could train with her today. You want to clean Bagby?" he asks, fixedly.

In spite of everything, I reply, "What's Bagby?"

"It's another building down the street. But it's a part of the Parakeet."

"Can I con-sid-er it?"

"Sure, you can con-sid-er it," he says, mocking me. "But it'll be gone in fifteen minutes."

"Okay, I guess I'll take it, then," I say.

"Hooray!" hollers Angus.

I experience an immediate sense of comfort accompanying the settling of my practical concerns. Yet, of course, this is mingled with a strange and sudden sense of escalating fear. I've just committed to staying on longer in disguise.

"And how easy was that?" asks Angus.

"Hey Angus, I've got to tell you something," I blurt out, in a sudden attack of guilt.

His blonde eyebrows arch in curiosity. "What's that, darling?"

"Just that I'm… well, no, just thanks for arranging that," I say, instead.

He looks at me as if he's taken aback by my humility.

"Pleasure, treasure! And every three hours of work equals a free night. So, now you won't have to fret, pet."

****

After quelling my cash concerns Angus disappears to his laundry duty. Alone, once more, I settle into my favorite booth and slip back into private bewilderment.

In an attempt to gain some clarity, I pull out my notebook. Across the first page I scrawl the words:

Ruse or Ruthlessness? Caper or Crime?

"Becky?"

I look up from my journal entry with a cautious nod.

"I'm Louisa. You're supposed to train over at Bagby with me today?"

Casually, I move my arm in order to cover my entry.

"Yes, yes, thanks, Alan just told me about you," I say.

"Well, I'm heading over there at half eleven, so if you want to just be ready around then?"

I try to remember whether half eleven means a half an hour before eleven or a half an hour past it.

"Right. I'll get my skates on, then."

"Why? It's only half ten," she returns.

"Oh, right, cheers, I thought it was later. Half eleven it is, then. Should we meet here?" I ask.

"Yeah, that'll be grand. Just wear your worst clothes. It can be a bit of a Bagby over there, if you know what I mean?"

****

At half past eleven Louisa returns and leads me over to some bottle green lockers at the far end of the rec room. She fills a black bag with rolls of toilet paper from one of them, hands me a stack of folded sheets, and kicks the locker shut with her foot.

"The bagels are delivered by the same people who deliver the loo-roll," she informs.

"Real-ly?"

"Yup."

We head over to Bagby, passing several little whitewashed townhouses and a tattoo shop along the way. Louisa, in keeping with what seems to be a social standard around here, makes no effort to converse. I follow suit.

After a while, we pass by a facially pierced teenager sprawled out on the sidewalk, leaning up against a parking meter.

"Spare some change for a cup of coffee?" he asks, holding out a paper cup.

"Funny, was just about to ask you the same thing," replies Louisa.

This exchange seems to break the trance altogether because after this she suddenly starts talking.

"Alan, the manager, he's a complete fucking knob, by the way."

"Is he?"

I figure from her tone that a *knob* is a bad thing.

"Defo. I hate to leave this place," she adds. "It's a great place to save up some dosh if you don't have papers but, seriously, he's too much. Everyone hates him."

"Where are you going after here?" I ask, trying to change the subject.

"I'll probably just head down the coast to Mexico for a while. Then back home. I'm just gagging to get away, you know, before heading back home to Uni."

"Yeah, I hear you. That should be cool," I say, trying to relate, as we approach the graffiti-covered back door to the Parakeet's satellite.

Inside, I follow Louisa throughout the little building (a cozy saltbox that's been converted into extra private rooms for couples), as she pulls blue paisley sheets, which smell like the aerosol deodorants and floral lotions young people buy, off the beds, and shows me where the loo-rolls, Hoover and bin-liners, as she refers to them, are kept.

"Do your own laundry while you're down here, for free," she offers. "You're not allowed to, but I always do."

"Oh, smashing!" I exclaim. Privately, I shrink at the idea of breaking any more rules.

****

By the time Louisa and I get back to the main hostel, the other staff is already congregated around a big rectangular table in the middle of the rec room. I'm super excited about becoming a certified part of the scene. But I keep my cool.

Instead, I casually take the bag of empty beer cans we retrieved from Bagby over to the recycling bin. Reaching way up, I dump them all in, extra unenthusiastically. Although my black sweater (tied around my waist to cover my butt in these tight pants) falls off in the process, I find I don't really care that much anymore. The general lack of sleep, perhaps, fosters a state wherein there isn't enough surplus energy left to worry a lot about things like how wide these too-tight cords make my butt look or about whether people want me to sit down or not.

Then, claiming the seat in between Angus and Sharon, I join my sort of peer group, with minimal uneasiness.

Angus, meanwhile, doesn't notice me. He's too busy leaning over the shoulder of Louisa, who in turn is entirely engrossed with putting the homemade-filter finishing-touch on her latest joint.

"Louisa," he's saying, in a pesky whisper. "Those other people from the other night are coming over. There's no getting rid of them. Just pack it heavy in the front, light in the middle, and heavy at the back."

"Okay, okay, I already have. Keep your *voice* down!" she snaps back.

"Sorry pal," Angus replies, softly. "Pass it over here, though, darling. Over here first. Okay?"

Finally Louisa appraises and then lights her completed handicraft. Following a lengthy hit, she then passes the joint, as instructed, counterclockwise to Angus. In contrast, he takes a series of shorter hits, pausing, leisurely, in between each and every one.

The impatience of the rest of the group soon becomes palpable. And I watch in amazement at how impervious Angus is to their fixed stares, to their psychic pressuring. At how skilled he is at keeping the focus on himself.

An intrepid American, settled in at the other end of the table, is the first and only one to take a stab at the situation.

"Hey, bro," he finally calls to Angus, "I'd hit that. Mind if I get a drag off that bad-boy?"

The attempt doesn't fly, however. Although the American's phrasing is cool enough, his tone, sounding just a hair too invested in the outcome, undercuts his case. And Angus just smiles elusively. Although he knows he's obliged to share the communal drug, he is only prepared to *share* once all actual marijuana from the front third of it has already been smoked.

"I feel awake, Louise!" he then whispers, turning lazily in my direction.

"It's good stuff, eh?" I respond. "But she's actually Louisa, pal."

"No, get it? Get it? I feel *awake* Louise!" he repeats, in a funny accent.

"Oh, okay, I get it. From *Thelma and Louise*, right? Ve-ry funny. I love that movie."

He presses his face up to mine. "I feel *awake* Louise," he repeats.

"That's great, Thelma."

"Why don't you have a drag, Louise?" he asks me.

"Oh, no thanks."

"Why not?"

"Because I don't usually smoke."

"Oh, go on," he insists.

"No, real-ly, I won't have a good time. I'll just get all depressed and intro-ver-ted, you know, Thelma?" It strikes me as odd to hear myself saying something so honest about myself in so dishonest a voice.

At this, Angus starts laughing uncontrollably, and proceeds to drop the lit joint into his pint of beer.

"Oh my God, *Louise,* I am *so* sorry!" he cries, immediately, to the real Louisa, before she has a chance to react.

Louisa observes the calamity.

"That's fine," she replies, coolly. "But you owe me ten dollars."

A shadow of horror flits across Angus's face at the mention of being charged but then, just as quickly, he recovers the hilarity.

"Well, what a buzz-kill!" he exclaims. "I *don't* feel awake, Louisa."

"And you're not getting any of this one," Louisa adds, more curtly, as she embarks on a second roll.

"Okay, okay," Angus snaps back, indignantly. "You don't have to get all crazy-lady-crazy-lady! It's not like we can't dry it out in the oven. Right?"

"Sorry, Angus, but you can't just be dropping all of our joints in pints, can you? I'm sick of it."

"Fair enough, Louisa," concedes Angus. "But it *was* an accident. Wasn't it?"

"Yes, I know that," she replies, softening. "Just, this music is doing my head in. That's all."

Angus concurs, with a disgusted look on his face. "I know, what *is* this?"

Louisa looks over at me. "Rebecca, since you're not smoking, can you change the CD, then, please?"

"Oh, real-ly? I ask, hesitantly. "But, what if someone's listening to this?"

"No. Go Becky, it's your go," Angus overrides. "This music is not going to be possible, and it's your go."

I waver a moment before I succumb both to pressure and to feeling flattered they think I'm even up to the job.

"Okay, then," I say.

Contemplating my strategy en route to the stereo, I resolve to imitate Angus's performance from the day before. With my head held high, I then step up to the stereo and open the CD carousel.

Immediately some guy rushes over, shouting at me in an Irish accent, "Hey! We're listening to that!"

"Sor-ry, but it's shite, pal," I explain, as neutrally as possible.

He hesitates awkwardly. I can hardly believe I'm pulling it off — he has no choice but to defer to my calm clarity.

"Who do you think *you* are?" he challenges.

As hard as I'm trying to copy Angus's diplomatic nonchalance from the day before, I'm thrown by the roughness in his tone.

"Easy. Just nobody likes it," I try. There's a little less confidence in my voice now.

"You're an *English* bitch!"

"*What* did you call me?" I ask, indignantly.

I'm unable to help feeling pleased by so official an initiation and have to be careful not to seem too delighted.

"You heard me. I called you an *English* bitch!"

I force a frown. "Don't *think* so," I say, gravely.

Radiating an almost visible rage, he snatches his CD out of my hand. "Well I *do!* I know so!"

"Doesn't change the fact that it's shite!" I shout back.

"*You're* shite," he retorts, conclusively.

He then glares at me for what seems like ages until at last he turns away and storms back over to his posse.

With my legs shaking like crazy, I do my best to storm back over to my own.

"That went well," Sharon observes, as I reclaim my seat.

"Yeah, right."

"Bloody *Irish*," she then adds, in a disdainful whisper, meant for my ears alone.

"I know," I assure her, in solidarity. *"Typical!"*

Into the Fold

After a few more days I start to feel as legitimate as the other hostellers, or at least as much a bona fide member of the gang as I do a complete and utter fraud.

I'm still consumed with the question: "Am I real or am I a phony?" But the answer is becoming less and less relevant in any practical sense. My contentment here is definitely real, which I figure has to count for something.

Today, in particular, I feel especially at ease. It's been raining outside all day long and the stormy weather has somehow managed to turn the rec room into even more of a safe haven than it usually is. Inside, the wind is howling wildly past the huge stained-glass windows that line the rec room walls, and all of us hostellers are home, together, with nowhere to go and nothing to do.

In any case, by sheer chance, it's on this day that Harrison, the owner of the place, sidles across the room and motions to the empty seat across from me.

"Anybody sitting there?" he asks.

"No. Please!" Being joined by the Purple Parakeet's very own founder is an unexpected thrill.

He places his plate and pint glass of water down on the table and falls heavily into the empty seat.

"There's just no getting rid of this stuff, is there?" he asks. He's referring to our plates of leftover shepherd's pie.

I smile submissively and take a few self-conscious mouthfuls.

"So, I hear this is your hos-tel," I then start.

He nods his head softly, with a simultaneous reserve and warmth.

"Yeah, yup."

"Well, can I just say, thank you for the delicious food and that this is an *amazing* place! I've lit-rally never seen anything like it. You must be ve-ry proud to have started it."

His eyes chuckle, as if mocking me mocking him. "Okay. Who put you up to this? Alan or Isaac?"

"No! No, really, I may be gushing, but it's true. I'm just traveling and I'm amazed to have sort of stumbled across this in-cre-dible environment!"

He looks at me in disbelief. "Is that so?"

"Yes, real-ly! I can't imagine you don't hear it the whole time," I marvel. "Oh, yeah, and your manager, Alan, he throws a fan-tas-tic par-ty," I add, keeping my promise to Alan.

"Well, thank you. That's very nice."

"Sure," I reply, softly.

Although I'm satisfied that he's accepted my appreciation as genuine, I can't help being needled by the thought that if he ever finds out the accent were a farce, he'd take the compliment to have been one too.

"Doesn't Becky remind you of Jennifer Capriati, Harrison?" chimes in Angus.

"The girl who repainted room seven?" asks Harrison, turning to look at me. "Yes, maybe some."

"No, Jennifer *Capriati!* Tennis. Hello? My God, Harrison, you're just totally out of it, aren't you?"

"Must be," he says.

Then he soaks a bit of sauce off his plate with a crust of bread, and looks at me. "You're English, right?"

I freeze. My whole being is suddenly invested in his eyes, as I strain to detect what he is about to ask me.

"Yes," I reply, reluctantly.

"What do *you* think of these shepherd's pies?" he asks.

I'm so relieved I practically cry out, "Delicious!"

"Yeah, I think they're pretty good, too, but I was just wondering because there are a few pans left over and I heard some kids say they just don't taste anything like shepherd's pie. I don't know. Maybe we should go back to pizzas."

"Frankly, Harrison," cuts in Angus, "your only problem is with the beer. I don't want to be too cheeky, but clearly two kegs is never going to be enough. We need to have three kegs from now on. Don't you think?"

"Well, Angus, I don't know. I think what you could mean is that you just didn't get laid the other night," interprets Harrison.

"My God, cheek of the week!" Angus replies. "And so crude, like. Becky, can you believe him?"

"Ve-ry cheeky," I agree.

"Is, isn't it?" he asks again.

"Very cheeky, indeed," I confirm, loyally.

Then I lean back in my chair and bask in the bosom of all the warmth and familiarity. I know it is complete folly, but I can't help savoring the sensation, I guess, of really belonging somewhere.

****

Later that night, as I lie in bed, with Sharon quietly reading one of her British tabloid magazines a few feet away from me, I think about the people here. About how easy-going they are. They all seem to just sort of accept me without really even knowing me. And I think about how much I prefer this to the other way around, as it was with Gotthard.

Then I listen, carefully, until I can hear, clearly, a sample of the lost relationship's myriad conversations playing back to me in my head.

"You've had too many guys. I can't feel comfortable with a girl who has *had* so many guys," he'd lamented for the first two years.

"But, I love *you*. I only love you," I'd insist.

"Yes," he'd say, once I'd finally managed to convince him that I'd meant it. "But, you'll never hold a job. The *problem* is you avoid responsibility."

This became his new mantra as well as the force behind my decision to drop out of my second MA program and start a new life, as a substitute teacher.

"So," he'd ask, ambiguously, "you're still *subbing?*"

Picking up on the undertones, I'd proceed with caution. "Yes, I thought you just wanted me to…"

"What?" he'd counter.

"You said the problem…" I'd begin, but then I'd always abort the delivery, acquainted as I was with his no-win negotiations.

He'd bait more forcefully. "What?"

"Never mind. Yes, I am," I'd surrender, instead.

"Rebecca," would then resume the inescapable indictment. "To some extent you're an exception, but if I'm totally honest I still can't really respect a girl whose slept with over six or seven guys."

"Rebecca?" But now it's Sharon's gentle voice speaking my name.

"Yuh?"

"Mind if I turn out the light?"

"No, Shazzer, I'm cream and crackered myself," I say, with one last homage to my new identity before hanging my accent up and placing it back in the closet for the next eight hours.

She leans down from her bunk to reach the light switch.

"Completely. Same here. Night, Becks."

"Hmm. Night."

"Nice to have the room to ourselves for a change," she mumbles, sleepily.

"Um, it's brill, isn't it?"

I wait a few minutes to make sure she's not going to add anything more before entering back into my own thoughts.

Lying there in the darkness, I feel like an undeclared transvestite. I am finally one of them, finally at home, so long, I suppose, as it all remains a secret.

Stripes, Spots and Friendly Games

The next morning I remain in bed while I listen to someone in the next room over hitting their snooze button every five minutes for about an hour. By the time it stops and I get up, it's already after ten. Once again, I've managed to miss the cut-off hour for the free bagel breakfast.

It's fine though. Now that I'm going to be cleaning Bagby, the adjunct hostel, three days a week I won't be quite as dependent on the free bagels as I was before.

See, things are already on the upturn. And before long I should have enough money to do the right thing. That is, to move on. That's what I'm still telling myself at this point anyway.

After a quick shower, I rifle through the built-in trunk beneath my bed for something to wear. Slipping myself into some worn-out cords, a T-shirt, a wool hat, and my flip-flops I manage to achieve, I think, just the right balance of I'm-too-relaxed-to-worry-about-being-cold along with I'm-comfortable-enough-in-my-own-skin-not-to-care-about-looking-like-I'm-trying-to-stay-warm.

Then it's downstairs.

Once in the kitchen, I hunt among the identical-looking, brown paper grocery bags that line the fridge's floor until I find the one, way in the back (absorbing somebody else's leaky yogurt and spilled tomato sauce), with my name written on it. Then, hauling it up out of the trenches, I transport my disintegrating bag onto the big metal island in the middle of the kitchen and begin stitching together my first homemade meal.

Just as I am applying my finishing touch (and my latest prop) to my coastal cheddar cheese sandwich, a well-tanned woman with David Bowie's cheekbones and a distinguishing set of crow's feet sails into the kitchen.

"Branny's pickle!?" she exclaims.

"Is, indeed," I return, with knowing enthusiasm.

Licking the side of my finger, I am transported back in time to my year abroad by the condiment's sweet and savory flavor.

"Where'd ya find *that?*" she asks, in what I've begun to discern as an Australian accent.

"Brit import shop downtown, actually."

She sticks her neck out and smiles, indicating the desire for a taste. I hand my sandwich over to her, hostel etiquette somehow requiring me to relinquish my first bite to this perfect stranger, and doubly so since I've seen her around with Harrison, the hostel's owner.

She peers at me through her big, half-moon eyes as she sinks her large, off-white chompers into my sandwich.

"Ta," she says, as soon as she's chewed enough to be able to speak again.

I smile, placidly, not so much because I like the idea of her eating my cheese, but because it means I'm acclimating to hostel culture, too.

"Yum," she returns. "You'll have to give me the address of the shop later. I'll put it up on the main info board."

"Defo."

"So, not going around town today?" she asks, changing the subject.

"Nah, not today. Recharging my bat-teries, really."

"I hear ya. Traveling can be exhausting."

"To-tally," I concur.

She walks out of the kitchen and pulls a giant ladder from the wall.

"Do me a favor, then?" she calls.

"Sure!" I exclaim, eager to be the good egg wherever I can be.

She takes off her worn cowboy hat and ties her honey-brown Botticelli-like mane up into a loose knot.

"Hold this ladder for me a few minutes while I change the bulb?"

I lunge forward to brace it and watch as she moves higher and higher up the rungs.

"Be careful," I suggest, pointlessly.

"Yeah, Harrison got two of 'em from the boat yard for seventy-five dollars. Been great for fixing the roof," she calls down.

I size up the building. "Here?"

"No, at home," she returns, confirming herself to be Harrison's girlfriend or wife.

"You fix the roof yourself?"

"Yup."

"I love a competent woman," I say.

She glances down, sardonically, while unscrewing the giant bulb from the ceiling.

"I mean, I can change a tire," I elaborate.

She makes her way back down the ladder. "Cheers, mate."

"No worries," I reply, opting for the quintessential Australian colloquialism.

She walks across the room and flicks the light switch.

"Looks great!" I suck up.

"Yeah, the yellow bulb's a lot better, eh?"

"Yeah. Gives it more atmosphere."

"I'm Zoella, by the way," she offers.

"Re-*bec*-ca."

She looks at me curiously. I freeze up. *I used too much emphasis on my second syllable?*

"You interested in working here?" she asks.

"Oh, yes, actually."

"Great!"

"No, I mean, I already am. I'm going to be doing Bagby."

"Cleaning Bagby?" she asks, banning the use of euphemism.

"Yes, cleaning," I affirm.

"Oh! Great! Good on Alan for spotting you. We could use a crew with a bit of enthusiasm."

"Well, this is a great place," I say.

Just then Angus peeks his head into the rec room. "Zoella?" he asks, languidly. "Could you come out here please?"

"What do ya need?" she calls.

"We've got a couple of *undesirables* trying to check in," he says, in a stage whisper. "They want to speak to a manager and Alan's at lunch."

"If it's not one thing," she starts, shaking her head.

"Yeah, it must get pret-ty tedious," I say. "But, I can imagine they all probably just want to be able to experience this amazing..."

"No, you can't be so soft," she admonishes. "The people in this town just don't seem to realize this place isn't for locals. It's for travelers, and for *foreigners*. For chumps like *you!*"

****

I fix myself a second sandwich and settle into a booth to do a little escape-eating. Zoella scares me. Her features are too pointy. And conversation with her felt edgy. Along with Alan, the manager, she's the other one I'll aim to avoid.

I mean what a thing to say: "The people in this town just don't seem to realize this place is for travelers, and for *foreigners*. For chumps like *you!*" It's like, c'mon, how guilty does that make me feel? Don't get me wrong, it's not like *I'm* begrudging *her* for believing me now or anything crazy like that. I know I started this whole thing. But, I guess, like having a good dance partner, where it can become hard to tell sometimes who is leading and who's following, it must be said, some of them *are* doing some pretty precise mirroring.

I really only ever wanted to pass, to get by. Being given any kind of partiality just makes me feel like… well, like some kind of villain. As if I really *am* such a scoundrel after all.

I grab my sandwich and make my way over to my favorite booth, where I take an enormous bite, intended, at once, to both comfort and to absorb the profusion of nervous energy suddenly swirling around in the pit of my stomach.

Yet, just as I begin to head down this road and lose myself in the flavor of my food, someone from across the rec room hollers to me.

"Hey, gray T-shirt! Wanna finish his game?"

"Me?" I gesture.

He glances around the empty room with his shoulders up and his hands out. "Who else? Fin has to split. You wanna finish his game?"

"Oh, I would, but I can't play," I call back, croakily, as I choke down the rest of my mouthful.

"You're all right."

"No, real-ly, I don't play. I mean, I've hardly ever played," I explain.

"Go on, who cares. Give it a go."

"Oh, no, but I real-ly can't," I insist.

I'm annoyed by how fussy I sound. I wish I did know how to play pool or at least had the courage to step up to the challenge and be comfortable being uncomfortable.

"Don't be such a bore. Now, get over yourself and c'mon over here and give me a game, lass. Here," he says, holding out the pool stick for me to take.

"Well, okay, then. Thanks."

Following him over to the pool table, I cling only to my cheese sandwich and to a dismal memory of the other time I tried to play at college once in New Hampshire.

He offers me an outstretched hand. "Will."

"Rebecca," I return, shaking it heartily.

"English or American rules?" he asks.

"Whichever you like."

"Okay, I say we play English rules, even though we're in America, since we're both English. Or what about a hybrid? No calling shots and no two shots on a foul. Friendly game. You wanna break?" he asks.

"No, that's okay, you break."

"No, you break, you need the practice," he says.

I get a strange sensation. As if there's suddenly really nothing at stake.

Taking the stick from his hand, I attempt to break the triangular arrangement of balls. I graze them but none of them move. I fight off the impulse to apologize.

"You weren't kidding. You really can't play," he teases, chalking up his stick indifferently.

"Okay, try this," he says. He hugs the dark green felt with his two front fingers and hangs his weight on them. "And then," he says, demonstrating, "nice and easy, all right?"

I am drawn to watching what he's doing and listening to what he's saying – all while trying to remain concentrated on my own language, speech and bearing. I sense something is going to have to give.

"Now, go on, try again."

"Right, thanks, I appreciate it," I say, managing to avoid feeling pathetic, while realizing, to my amazement, that what seems to be giving is my capacity to remain focused, too, on the neurotic nature of my more usual concerns.

My shot actually breaks the triangle of balls and sinks a purple.

"Well done," he says.

"Thanks."

"Where are you from anyway?" he asks.

I survey my shot options.

"Hang on, can't multi-task," I say, as I miss my next shot by about a foot.

"Sorry, I put you off."

"No, that's okay. Arundel. How about you?"

He leans in low for a shot along the bank and looks up at me with a little smile as his ball drops staccato-like into the far left pocket.

"Bournemouth. Keep it under your hat, though."

I smile back, tentatively, without knowing where Bournemouth is or understanding the nuance of what he's telling me.

"How long have you been here?"

"About a fortnight. We've been trying to crack into some moving work but there's not a lot of work going at the moment. How about you? You're working here, right?" he asks.

I am struck by the idea that somebody could have been aware of me at all.

"Yeah," I say. "Well, I start officially tomorrow."

"What'll you do?"

"Clean Bagby. It's part of the Parakeet, down the street."

And on we go, shooting pool and small talk for well over an hour until suddenly Alan bellows into the room, "Rebecca! You've got a phone call!"

"I do?"

He walks away, unwilling to repeat himself.

Handing Will the pool cue, I nod at him in a way that signifies my intended return.

"Wait, I'm coming," I then call behind Alan, wondering who in the world could be calling me here.

Dueling with the Opposition

I close the phone booth's accordion glass door around myself.

"Hello?" I ask, apprehensively.

"It's me."

I freeze.

Me is Gotthard. The relationship has been over for a year, officially, but not really. We still haven't fallen out of regular phone calling or e-mailing, and his voice still holds the power to chill me.

"Oh, God. Gott, hi," I stumble. I marvel at how he's managed to track me down.

"Hoi, hoi," he says, impervious to my surprise.

"How did you find out I was staying here?" I whisper.

He ignores my question. "What's up?" he asks.

"Nothing. How are you?" I return, disliking both the way he always obtains more than I offer as well as the way I defer to his strength of purpose.

"I'm fine. How about you?"

"I'm okay," I say. My tone is a little wounded sounding. "I haven't heard back from you in over a week."

"Uh huh."

I water my accent down as much as possible. "Didn't you get my e-mails?" I press.

"Yeah, I did."

Suddenly I am torn between self-pity and rage.

"Well, then why are *you* calling me?" I jump.

"Whatever."

"No, not whatever," I scold, under my breath. "I told you to e-mail me a time *I* could call you. Why do you think I didn't mention the name of the hos-tel in my e-mail? It's too risky."

"Yeah, right," he says, dismissing my reprimand. "Why don't you knock off that annoying accent?"

"Oh, I know, I'm sorry," I concede, equally irritated by it. "I was just about to say… why don't I get a calling card and call you back in a minute, from the street?"

"No, I don't think so."

I experience automatic regret over having reproached him.

"What? Why not?"

"Because I'm not at home," he clarifies.

"Oh, well, give me the number, then," I say, with fast-restored balance.

"This payphone says it doesn't receive incoming calls."

"You're calling from a payphone?"

"Yeah, I'm around the corner from you," he explains, matter-of-factly.

"Nice try."

"Yeah, Kleinster," he continues, using his pet name for me. "I'm in a place called, let's see… Vesuvios."

"Okay, so you called every hostel in San Francisco until you found me and then you found a link to Vesuvio's on-line. I know you," I say, referring to his penchant for pranks.

"Let's see, it's a *gezellig* little bar, I'm sitting upstairs, there are framed pictures of Jack Kerouac-*off*, whoever that is, all over the place and, oh, okay, from where I'm standing now I can see a fire engine going right on Broadway, I would guess toward your place."

"You're not here," I state, nonplussed.

"Kleinster."

"I'm supposed to believe that I've been asking you to come visit me for a year and now, without any advance notice, you're around the corner?" I ask, dubiously, as I perceive the distant drone of a fire engine growing nearer and nearer.

"I'll be there in five minutes."

****

I fly down the stairs and out the front door. After a year of phone calls and e-mails, always holding on and holding back out of fear of increasing the distance, wanting to see Gotthard has become almost more of a reflex than a desire.

Still, my heart pounds steadily, and as I pass by the stubby doormen and seedy strip joints, with the trace of his Dutch inflection lingering in my ear, none of it touches me. I am high on the vicarious thrill that comes from being in close proximity to Gotthard.

As I go by Black Oak Books, everything appears more vivid. Even the piles of worn paperbacks sitting in the window, waiting to be stocked, seem vibrantly aglow. For a moment I lose myself in memories of careless hours spent hunting through the narrow aisles of used bookstores in New York, feeling hidden and protected from the world, in the hours before I'd meet him for dinner.

Everything was so great then. Gotthard, my full-time partner and part-time soul mate, was one of those super achievers, doing an internship at Sloan-Kettering. He looked like a young Alan Alda. I was totally hooked. He was hooked, too. He thought I was funny, smart, beautiful. Then he split.

Tearing down Broadway, my excitement, tempered by a sort of ambivalence, starts to dwindle. Something doesn't feel quite right. Something doesn't feel safe. For one thing, I know I won't be able to keep up my English accent under any kind of scrutiny, least of all his. And, why, after trying for a year, in vain, to get him to come over here, has he come now, once I'm finally in a situation where having him around would actually complicate, rather than ease, my circumstance?

My features twist in trepidation, as I ponder the unpleasant possibility that he might actually have his bags with him. He might think we're going back to the Purple Parakeet together.

Nevertheless, I continue coasting, hanging a left on Columbus and flying past the Chinese restaurant, City Lights, and the Psychic and Tarot Card Reader, until I finally arrive in front of Vesuvio's. From the street, through the clouded rectangular windows, I spot Gotthard, sitting there in the upper gallery. And taking in his stunning silhouette, all disappointment is fast converted back into excitement.

I make my way through the saloon-like front door, feeling valuable in a way I haven't felt for a while. As I ascend the winding steps to the balcony, I am overcome by feelings of affection. These sympathetic feelings, resurfacing in full, moderate my ego and my frustration, so that by the time he sees me my expression has balanced into one of humble confidence. He looks reassured by how much the same I appear, having no way of knowing how many incarnations my countenance has been through between the last time I saw him and now.

His hug is long and warm. It settles me and feels like home. I stand back to admire my Hawkeye look-alike of a boyfriend.

"I can't believe you're here!"

He shrugs his shoulders and flashes a look that assures me that he and I are never *really* over.

"I can't believe you're here!" I repeat, as I settle into our little corner table.

"Don't you find the people here lame?" he replies, skipping all pleasantries.

81

"In this bar?"

"No. In San Francisco."

"Well, yeah," I grant. "But I don't really have to deal with them. I've been at the hostel pretty much the whole week."

"It's a total wimps town," he states. "I just saw these fags down by the water going swimming in wetsuits. Can you imagine? There was this seventy-five-year-old grandma doing laps in a bathing suit, and these three fags are in wetsuits."

I readjust to his particular rhythm and brand of candor.

"That's the problem with America," he continues. "The people here have *no* shame. In Holland, you would *never* see someone with so little shame. Never."

"I know, Holland rules. People are self-conscious, in the right way," I say, quoting him. "And, you'd never have to see somebody speed-walking."

"Exactly. People all just ride their bikes. It's all very *nuchter*. Very *gezellig*. How does that Brecht quote go again?"

"There are times you have to choose between being human and having good taste," I recite.

He reaches over to squeeze my thigh. "Right, and that's exactly the thing that's missing here. People are too human, in the *wrong* way. And then android where they *should* be human."

"Android is awful," I agree. "It's like *The Invasion of the Body Snatchers* or something. Set here, incidentally."

"Anyway," he continues, "so you're staying at The Purple Parakeet. How's that, Kleinster?"

The speed of our conversation renders our first meeting in over a year even more surreal than it already is.

"It's good," I reply.

"You're kidding?"

"No, it's all right," I say, with less emotion. I sense my liking the hostel too much, for some reason, will turn me into a target.

"I can't believe you like it," he marvels. "I hate hostels. They're full of lower-middle-class youth. Very unoriginal. There's nothing more unoriginal than traveling. What's cool is to go somewhere and *do* something."

I admire the bump on his nose. "I know how you hate the travelers, Kleinster," I say, addressing him with our shared nickname.

His gaze narrows. "So, how long are you going to stay there?" he asks.

"I don't know," I say. "The situation is a little complicated."

"Yeah, right," he returns, looking around for the waitress. "It always is."

Eager both to assess our situation and to change the subject, I ask, "Anyway, where are you staying?"

He leans back in his chair and stretches out his long legs. "Some dive by the wharf."

"Are those the same cords from the day at Bethezda Fountain?" I ask, recognizing my favorite pair of his pants.

He catches the waitress's eye and signals for two more hot chocolates. "Same model, different generation," he answers.

"Oh. So, how long can you stay for?" I follow up.

I am already trying to figure out how I'm going to explain to him that he can't join me at the hostel without it increasing his will to do so.

"It's just a one day stopover," he says. "The people in this town really have no bite. Don't you find?"

"*What?* One day? Why only one day?" I ask, as processing the fact that he's not here to see me gives way to a sense of practical relief.

"I'm taking off for a while before the residency," he states. "Going to Hawaii."

"You are?"

"Yeah, I'm going to teach windsurfing."

"Really? You can do that?" I ask.

The sting of surprise and rejection catch up with and begin to overshadow the initial sense of relief.

"Why not?"

"I don't know, I just thought you had to go right on to your residency."

"There's room for variation," he starts, as if preparing to make a speech he's rehearsed before. "On a theme, that is. There is an opposite to conventional. But it's free-spirited, not insane."

"Great, but why'd you only come for one day?"

He takes a breath and holds it. "I almost didn't stop over here at all," he explains, exhaling dramatically.

I purse my lips in dreaded self-defense.

He places his long, pale fingers over my hand. "Kleins," he says, softening.

"What?" I return, pursing them harder.

"Tell me one thing. Why were you talking in that accent?"

"What do you mean? I sent you like a two page e-mail. I couldn't get a bed there without doing it."

"No," he says, looking at his watch. "Rebecca, I don't think you get my question. Why are you doing this to *yourself?*"

I feel myself sinking and long to escape into the deceptive warmth of his almond shaped eyes.

"What do you mean? I *had* to," I explain. "It was the only way I could get…"

I break while the waitress places two cardboard Guinness coasters and two hot chocolates down in front of us.

"This is the problem," Gotthard resumes, slowly, while waiting for her to walk away. "There's *always* some drama with you, isn't there? Always some excuse for why you *have* to take the low road."

I feel the color in my face seep outward toward my ears.

"*What?* But this doesn't even affect you. Why should *this* bother *you?* Why are you trying to turn this into a crisis?" I demand.

"It damn well does affect me," he says, taking a sip of cocoa. "I've been thinking and doing a lot of reading."

I brace myself for what's coming next.

"I think you're bipolar," he says. "You have all the symptoms."

He drops a lump of sugar into his hot chocolate and stirs it delicately.

"Oh, really?" I ask, with sneering concern.

"Yes," he says, "and bipolar is a serious condition if it's not treated."

For a split second I entertain the possibility of just yielding to him. I don't want to fight. But I glance out the window and gather myself instead.

"I should be so lucky if I could whittle it down to two poles," I joke, attempting to defuse him a little.

"Kleins, you're not well," he explains. His frown is sorrowful. "You have all the symptoms. I've read over it several times now."

Determined to keep his pathological diagnosis out of my space, I stay neutral. "Hmm."

"Sidney has it too. We recognize some of the same behavior patterns in you," he continues, staring at me opaquely. "She says meds have really helped her a lot."

"*We?* You're discussing *me* with Sidney?"

"Yeah, why not?" he returns, blithely.

"Because this is *my* life!"

"What?" he challenges. "I can do whatever I want. It's no problem to discuss things with our friends."

"Wait," I start. I am overcome by a sudden feeling of horror. "But, you didn't tell her that I was pretending to…"

"Yes, I did," he owns.

I am dumbstruck.

"I told everyone," he continues.

"But, I explained to you in my e-mail that I didn't want anybody to know about it right now. If anyone, I wanted to be the one to explain it to our friends," I moan, uselessly, struggling to rush myself through the stages of powerlessness.

"I'm not going to censor your life for you anymore," he asserts.

"But isn't there a difference between not censoring and telling everyone everything?"

"See, this is what I mean. This should be a moot point. If you weren't sneaking around pretending to... Never mind. It's ridiculous. This is ridiculous. Actually, I'm not even going to discuss this with you anymore unless you agree to start taking medication."

I pause as a dreadlocked Italian I recognize from the hostel passes by our table on his way out. He gives me the international peace sign and an easy smile.

"I don't quite know what to say," I return, forced into temporarily resuming the accent until the hosteller is out of earshot. "I mean, I cer-tain-ly do appreciate your con-cern."

"This has gone too far!" he explodes.

I reach across the table to tug on his chin. "Don't yell at me when I'm off my meds, please," I tease. "I'm very fragile."

"Why can't you just lead a *normal* life?" he asks, in a voice even darker than usual. "Of *course* I can't be with *you.*"

I feel the familiar lump growing in my throat.

"What's the big deal?" I demand, his tragic spin triggering an unsettling righteousness in me. "It's a *lark!*"

He slams a hand on the table. "A *lark?*"

I catch a spoon from falling over the edge. "Yes! At least it's part lark," I bargain. "I mean, I'm thinking maybe I could even write a book about this month. It'd be about how at the end of the day..."

"At the end of the day? Do you even hear yourself? You're not even aware of it, are you?"

"Gotthard, listen to what I'm saying!" I finally shout, losing control of the volume.

"What are you saying?" he challenges.

My eyes dart down and across the bar to ensure the exiting hosteller hasn't heard any of this.

"I'm saying that eventually I'm thinking of writing this book."

He interrupts, sarcastically, "And what would that be? Your debt to conscience?"

"Well, no, it'd be a book about challenging cultural assumptions. About how superficial... I don't know, it'd just be about how people put, like, so much stock in these affectations that pass as nationalities."

I am trying to persuade my best friend and myself, perhaps, that I have a larger vision here.

"I like straightforward, Rebecca."

"I do too, though."

"This is what you call straightforward? Lying to people in the eye every day?"

"It's not like that. You don't understand. I am being me with the people there, too," I plead.

I yearn to convey to him that in my heart my sham is not so at odds with the truth, or even with my own spirit.

"You're being you? Kleins, are you really going to sit here with a straight face and say this to me?"

Taking a labored breath, I strive once more to make myself understood. "Look, I'll grant you, the disguise *is* devious. And scheming. But, Kleinie, I don't think it conceals a dishonorable motive. Or one I think I have to be ashamed of. My purpose for staying there, I think, is... pure. I do regard the people there. I consider them every day."

"Scamming people is scamming people, Rebecca, regardless of your intention."

I begin to lose steam. Debating the merits of what I'm already ambivalent about is the last thing I feel I can afford to be doing.

"I mean, you can always dress things up and make them sound better, Kleins," he continues. "But sooner or later you have to face the facts."

"Facts? What are *facts?*"

His eyes roll slowly into the back of his head.

"Why can't you see this as me playing a part for a while?" I reason, struggling to defend myself. "All the world's a stage," Shakespeare said. And our *real roles* are *roles* too, aren't they? So, I've just chosen an alternate one for a while. Is it really so awful?"

"Not this kind of nonsense, Rebecca. This abstract, pseudo-philosophical nonsense."

"It's not nonsense. It's true. Maybe you just have no sense of fantasy."

"Maybe you only have a sense of fantasy!" he exclaims. "Try reality! Try being genuine!"

"Surely, a mere accent, alone, doesn't compromise the entirety of my sincerity," I return, unable to help sounding like a character from a BBC production.

"Are you kidding? You're ill!"

"You just have no imagination!" I blurt out, going for his jugular.

"Don't euphemize your screwing people over and try to make it seem colorful. It's sick, Rebecca."

I pull out my most versatile of trump cards. "Well, Deepak Choprah says that reality is an interpretation."

"Well, Deepak Choprah, whoever that might be, can go fuck himself. How about that?"

There's a short silence and we both release a little laugh.

"You know," he starts. "It's probably not even your fault. The problem is you grew up in America."

"What does that have to do with anything?"

"People aren't serious here. It's only about entertainment. I like serious. You all watch too much TV. You don't seem to get that life is not a movie."

Opting to forgo hackneyed theories about art imitating life, I conclude, "Well."

"Kleins," he continues, standing up and leaning in over me. "I don't want to *be* with some kind of alter ego evangelist. You live in a dream world. It isn't real. It's not normal, it's not healthy, and you can stay here – but without me."

"Gotthard."

He pushes his chair back in. "You can do better, Rebecca," he says, solemnly.

I shuffle for anything.

"I don't even watch TV," I try.

But, he is already walking away from me. I take a sip of my cold, hot chocolate, in an attempt to control something. Then, I watch in dreamlike disbelief as his long legs carry him away from me down the winding staircase.

****

"Well, that's nonsense," my mother's voice assures me, minutes after Gotthard has exited the building. "Nobody flies from Europe to California if they really don't want to see you anymore."

"He was on a stopover, to Hawaii."

"Oh."

"People do make stopovers, even if they really don't want to see you anymore, don't they?"

"I suppose. Do you mind if I put you on speakerphone? I just need to open a can of tuna."

"Speakerphone? Mom!"

"I know, sweetie, but you're calling on my lunch break. I almost didn't even pick up. I'm so rushed. Except I thought it might be you."

"Okay, go ahead," I say, dejectedly.

"You know, sweetie," she starts, as I try fusing with the pub's phone, suspecting Gotthard's ear was the last one to have had contact with it, "I think it's good that he came, even though you didn't get what you wanted. Meeting up, after such a long time, it was bound to make or break it with you two."

"Uh huh."

"There's nothing worse than being in limbo. And now you can start to move on," calls my mother, to the tune of the electric can opener.

I watch dolefully as our waitress clears the only evidence of our last meeting from the table.

"Please, no more platitudes," I say.

"What? I couldn't hear you. I was washing my hands," my mother calls back.

"I said, please, no plat-i-tudes!" I shout. "I feel like I'm going crazy!"

"Sweetie?"

"What?"

"Are you aware you're actually still using that accent, with me?"

"What? No, I'm not."

"You are," my mother insists.

"Mom, you're not helping."

"Really. I don't think you're aware of it but…"

"Would you stop? You're adding insult to injury!" I snap.

"You're right, I'm preoccupied. I have a client arriving in about two minutes and now Charky is crying. He heard the can opener."

"Oh, Charky," I whimper, working myself into an emotional frenzy. "If only I had Charky here…"

"He's sniffing around the little speaker. I think he must recognize your voice," my mother observes, finishing me off altogether.

"Take me off speakerphone, then, immediately!" I demand. "Don't just let him suffer!"

"Honey, Charky is fine," returns my mother, picking up the receiver. "I think you might be projecting a little there. But, I can talk after six o'clock. Shall I call you back after I finish work?"

"No, of course not! Mom, you're my *English* mother! Remember? What do you think they'd think if you called in an American accent? You *can't* just forget these things. You *can't* call me at the hostel. No matter what! Okay?"

"What if there's an emergency?"

"Mom!"

"Okay, sorry, I'll just e-mail. If there's an emergency."

"Fine. And, also, don't tell *anybody* else about this either. It's all top secret, okay?"

"Okay. Mum's the word."

"Mom?"

"Isn't it Mum?"

"Why are you doing this to me?"

"Sorry, sweetie, just a little levity. Do you want to call me back later tonight?"

"I don't know. I can't make any plans. I need the open highway. Maybe."

"Well, if you want to talk, we can talk again later. Lydia and I are going to a theater for the deaf tonight. There's a special troop in town. But I should be home around nine o'clock."

"A theater for the deaf? Who's deaf? Never mind. Fine."

"And, honey, I know you don't want to hear this, but," she starts, sympathetically, "several of my clients swear by those Anonymous meetings. They use them as a supplement to their counseling with me. It might be a great source of extra support. I've never heard a bad thing about them. And they're free."

"What?"

"Oh, you know what I mean, Alcoholics Anonymous, Over-eater's Anonymous, they have them for everything. Why don't you try just sitting in on one sometime – any one, it's all the same stuff. See if it doesn't make you feel better?"

"Jesus, Mom," I return, scornfully, as I come to my senses. "I'm not *that* bad!"

An Attitude of Gratitude

"Hello, I'm Rebecca."

"Hi, Rebecca, welcome," they return, clapping in unison.

I am a little caught off guard by the ovation they give me, which to my ear sounds like a stadium. Yet, while I'm still attempting to assimilate the impact of this, an elderly woman sitting to my left is already reaching over to pat me on the shoulder, while the sharply dressed man sitting to my right is offering me a spirited smile and a hearty handshake. To complete the triangle of encouragement, the woman sitting in the row ahead of ours turns around as well, makes poignant eye contact with me, and whispers, tenderly, "You're in the right place."

"Any other newcomers?" asks the secretary who's seated at a little metal desk in the front of the room.

No other hands go up.

"And do we have any visitors from outside of the Bay Area?" the secretary continues.

"Hi, I'm Reynolds," a man replies. "I'm an alcoholic from San Luis Obispo."

There's more enthusiastic applause. The man sitting to my right, now balancing a cup of coffee on his knee, calmly taps his leg with his free hand, in lieu of clapping.

"Great. Let's have a moment of silence to do with as you wish, and then we'll say the serenity prayer," explains the secretary.

"God," they recite. "Grant me the serenity to accept the things I cannot change, the courage to change the things I can, and the wisdom to know the difference."

While most of the people in the room lower their eyes in reverence, presumably, for the words they are saying, I busily glance around the place and try to assess the scene. The room itself is dreary, with plastic utilitarian furniture and dusty old shades soiled with thumbprints along their lower perimeters. This bleak backdrop is juxtaposed, however, with an anything but dull-looking cast of characters, made up of a medley of ages and nationalities and faces whose common denominator, I suspect, has to do with having a story to tell and knowing how to tell the truth.

As soon as they open their eyes I shoot mine away, toward the far wall, where two large posters, constituting the room's only ornamentation, hang side by side. I study the posters, which are more like lists, citing the Alcoholics Anonymous principles and traditions.

Step one reads: *Came to believe that we are powerless over alcohol and that our lives have become unmanageable.*

Attempting a little alteration, to better suit my own situation, I reinterpret the step to read: *Came to believe that I am powerless over Gotthard's choices, and that my life has become unmanageable.*

Meanwhile, they're now reading aloud from a sort of AA bible being passed around the room. Some of what's being read catches my ear. Mostly, though, I continue to go back and forth between listening to what's being read and thinking about Step One, my own version of it, that is, until, after a few more minutes, the book makes its way around the room and reaches my lap.

I realize I'm a little bit excited about reading my paragraph. Mainly because, it occurs to me, I'm about to read communally, in my very *own* voice. This feels both like a privilege and like some kind of coming-out rite, only in reverse.

Unexpectedly, however, although I clear my throat, I notice habitual traces of the accent seem to linger involuntarily as I read my paragraph.

"More than most people," I read, "the alcoholic leads a double life. He is very much the actor. To the outer world he presents a stage character. This is the one he likes his fellows to see. He wants to enjoy a certain reputation but knows in his heart he doesn't deserve it."

I pass the book to the elderly woman sitting to my left. After about twenty more minutes of reading from the AA bible, or the Big Book, as they call it, the secretary then announces that the discussion portion of the meeting is open for shares.

At this, several hands shoot up. A young man sitting off to the left gets called on first.

"Hi, I'm Shane and I'm an alcoholic," he says.

"Hi Shane," we reply, all together again.

"I've really been struggling lately," Shane starts. His voice is heartfelt.

"I don't know what's going on," he continues, now to the tune of someone's absentminded knuckle cracking. "Just I've been feeling really thirsty lately. Real thirsty. I feel like, it's like I'm in this prison in my mind and I can't find the door. Hell, I can't even find the window. Everything is gray. Thanks for listening."

Oddly, after all the clapping and celebrating of each name and every introduction, now there is no form of feedback whatsoever. There's only a stony silence together with some soft snores emanating from the rear of the room.

"I'm Sheila. And I'm an alcoholic. Yes I am. Boy am I," begins the next woman to speak. "But, I'll tell you what. I've got an attitude of gratitude! I've got an attitude of gratitude… about the latitude! I'm just feeling grateful today! So grateful. For every last thing. What can I say? This program works. I feel happy, joyous and free now. And, believe me, it was not always like this. I was about forty pounds heavier, before I stopped drinking. I was afraid of people. I was afraid of everything. I was afraid of *life*. I was dying and I didn't even know it. Until I hit my bottom."

The meeting goes on in this way, with some people expressing doubts, others exalting over feelings of renewed hope, and still others packing up their things and departing, until finally the secretary breaks in again.

"That's about all the time we have, folks," he says. "If you didn't get a chance to share, grab someone after the meeting, or talk to me. Also, there's no smoking in front of the building. The kindergarten next door complains. So, if you want to smoke, just move down the street toward... the bars. But, don't go in."

A sage chuckle circulates the room.

Then we all get up, form a circle, and join hands. It'd be easy to spoof the scene. But the truth is, like my mother suggested it might be, there *is* something comforting about it. The feeling reminds me a little of the ski commune I stayed at one winter as a kid. It was one of those places where you stood in circles, held hands with strangers, and said what you were grateful for before they served you your lentil soup.

"How much time do you have?" asks the woman next to me, after we drop hands.

"Uh, it's four o'clock," I say.

"No, how much *time* do you have? It means how long have you been sober?"

"Oh," I say, not wanting to go into the story that I'm only here because of Gotthard. "Just today."

"Wow, good for you! It gets easier," she says. "Just keep coming back. Here, I'll give you my number. If you think you might pick up a drink, call me. Call me anyway, just to check in, if you want. It's good to stay connected."

"Thank you," I say. I'm unable to help feeling touched by her outreach, by the very concept, I think, of being offered support.

As we file out of the room, in fact, I feel so much better that I decide to take in the second half of another meeting already in progress across the hall.

****

After the meetings I wander over Russian Hill and slowly make my way back to the hostel. I think mostly about the passage I read, the passage about the double life.

Could it be so? Was the double life I was leading the same as the double life the alcoholic led? Was I doing it for the same reasons? Was it because *I* wanted to enjoy a certain reputation but knew in my heart *I* didn't deserve it? That was what the passage in the book seemed to be saying.

But, then, was the AA literature gospel? What about, for instance, those masked balls of the Elizabethan Court? Wasn't it also true that at those balls, the donning of masks was the very element that allowed people to communicate with each other, in some ways, on *more* authentic levels? Wasn't it having the mask which left people free to be more open, more honest, and *more* vulnerable, in some other ways? Perhaps *that* was all I was doing?

By the time I get back to the hostel I am still unable to make sense out of the conundrum. It occurs to me that what I want most is just to be able to stop thinking altogether. For this, I head directly to the rec room, which, being before six o'clock and already hopping, seems a reliable remedy.

As I cross the threshold, however, I notice I feel more conspicuous than usual, somehow extra uneasy. I mill around aimlessly for a few minutes, feeling more and more as if the minutiae of my many concerns are being broadcast across my brow.

Although I tell myself this is all in my head, that outwardly nobody notices anything different about me, I still attempt to make compensations for this by corseting my expression and features even more tightly than usual.

"Why so cross-looking?" somebody then shouts. This has to have been shouted at me.

I look around. Stacy, the Australian guy I met outside the bathroom last week, is looking back at me quizzically.

"Sor-ry?" I say.

"Why so cross? You look like you're in a right state," he continues.

"What are you *on* about, nut-ter?" I call back.

Carelessly, I make my way over to the pool table.

"You look like you've been sucking on a lemon or something," he explains.

"Can I get in on a game?" I ask, offhandedly, as if unfazed by his observations.

Stacy motions to a chalkboard on which to write my name.

"Can play winner."

As I add my name to the little board, the spell suddenly breaks. I am struck by how reassured I feel to be back amidst the uncomplicated conventions of the rec room after such a day.

"Can you even play?" he asks.

I take a seat on one of the stained chairs surrounding the pool table and breathe in the stench of stale smoke.

"Barely," I own.

"We'll play doubles," he says.

"Brill."

Hearing myself say *brill* is what makes me realize that I'm equally comforted to be back amidst my own facade.

Stacy flicks some ashes into an ornate, standing ashtray, already overflowing with butts.

"Where've you been anyway?" he asks me.

"What do you mean?"

"Where've you been? Haven't seen you around."

"Oh, I don't know. Out and about."

"Such a dark horse."

"Sor-ry?"

"Dark horse. You don't know that expression?"

"No, I don't," I confess, freely.

He stops and turns to me, having distracted himself from the game with the small talk. "Am I spots?" he asks, referring to the pool balls.

I observe an irritated-looking zit surfacing on his forehead. "I'd say so," I joke, recollecting spot to be the British expression for zit.

"Wait a minute, I'm not sure I get it," interjects a thickset American spectator. "So then what are spots?"

"Same as solids," I offer, sharing the information I acquired earlier this morning.

"Then what are smalls?"

"Australian for spots," I explain.

"Then bigs are stripes?" he deduces.

"Yes," I verify. I'm dazzled by my own recall. "And stripes are stripes."

"Okay, I got it. But, so then what's the deal with snooker?" he asks.

For a split second I freeze. But then it quickly occurs to me that I'm no more culturally indebted to know the ins and outs of snooker than I am to know the details of American football.

"You're on your own there," I tell him. Then I draw my attention back to the game, where Stacy's opponent has just missed his penultimate shot.

Stacy offers a conciliatory, "Unlucky!"

We all zero in for the big moment.

"Okay, hate to be flash now," Stacy announces, as he wraps the pool stick behind his back in an attempt to sink the black. "But you know where it's going and... *Yes!*"

"Rack 'em up!" Stacy then yells, much to the chagrin of his opponent, as he rides the pool cue around the table in a gesture of victory.

"So, then, am I up yet or what?" whines someone with yet another English accent, rising from a nearby table.

"You can play now. We'll play doubles," Stacy tells him.

The guy offers him his hand. "Beresford," he says.

Stacy shakes Beresford's hand, assigns him an immediate nickname, and tells me, "Right, Becky, so you're with Baz."

As pool protocol necessitates, Baz nods at me and offers me his hand too.

"No, no, actually, Baz and Ian. I'll play with Becky. I'll need to carry her, no doubt."

Removing the pool stick from Stacy's hand I pretend to be confident. I hug my fingers around the green felt as Will showed me in the morning and let my body weight hang from them. Then, nice and easy, I smash the triangular assortment of balls all over the table, sinking a green six and a purple four.

"Smooth," mutters Baz.

I walk around the table for my next shot, which I also manage to make, albeit together with the cue ball. Then I disappear off into the kitchen in search of my leftover pizza.

Rifling through the overflowing fridge, I am surprised by how satisfying it feels to be considered as a pool player. Upon finally locating my food, I am even more surprised to discover that someone has taken an enormous bite out of my slice and then *returned* it to its box.

"Eww," I cry, aloud.

"Bunk," commiserates a passing Angus.

I grab a knife and chop off the first third of it. "To-tally," I concur. "Hey, do you know where all the mugs went? At breakfast there are like a hundred and by din-ner there aren't any."

"I know, I'm pretty sure they lock them up, after breakfast," explains Angus.

"Oh," I reply, as I reach for a little saucepan from which to drink.

Angus pulls a paper bag from the fridge.

"*You've* got your own stash? I can't believe *you* have your *own* food," I marvel.

"No, it's not mine," he verifies. "I always use this bag though. This bag always has the best stuff and a steady supply. Block me a minute?"

My selective morality kicks in, and I look at him disapprovingly.

"You cheeky lit-tle monkey," I scold. Then I shift my position slightly, nevertheless, as unspoken pal-policy requires.

He removes some sourdough bread and gruyere from the bag and begins spreading the bread with some I-Can't-Believe-It's-Not-Butter margarine.

"Should be called I-Can't-Believe-It's-Not-*My*-Butter," he muses.

I point to the chopped off pizza remains still lying on the countertop.

"You're probably the one who took that bite out of this pizza," I suggest.

"No, I never!" he assures me.

I sink my teeth into my pizza just as Stacy walks over to me.

"Your shot, hustler," he says, handing me the cue.

"What am I again?" I ask, with my mouth still half full.

"Apart from a pig?" he asks.

Ignoring him, I make my way back over to the pool table. In keeping with native nonchalance, I contrive to overlook the need for a plate and slap the slice down directly on the edge of the bacteria-laden pool table. Baz immediately grabs for it and helps himself to a huge bite. But, instinct tells me to let this slide. Hostel society, with all its peculiar customs, is very nuanced, I'm learning. As a social faux pas, any display of tension trumps bad manners, by a long shot.

Surveying the arrangement of balls, I assess my most promising shot.

"Rebecca?" sounds Alan's familiar voice.

"Yes?" I reply, as I continue to focus in on my next shot, trying to let myself sort of feel the angle.

"We're having another party tomorrow."

"I know, I heard."

"Well, I need someone to supervise the cooking. You think you could handle it?"

"Oh, sure, Alan. With pleasure."

I like the thought of being put in charge of something.

"You sure?"

"Yup."

"Because I'm going to have to go deal with deliveries and I can't do everything."

"Right."

"I have to start delegating. I'm getting a little sick and tired of having to be the butcher, the baker *and* the candlestick maker *every* single time."

I zero in on the blue two. "Uh huh."

"You won't forget?"

"Nope, won't."

"Okay, thanks."

"No prob," I return, softly, as my ball goes right where I want it to.

"And whoever's slice of pizza this is," he adds, "get it *off* the fucking table! I *just* had this table recovered!"

After a few more hours of pool, I decide it's a good idea to tackle the laundry I've been postponing since arriving, due to being able to wear the same outfit over and over without any social repercussions.

En route to the laundry room, I stop at the internet zone. I'm now ready to read Gotthard's inevitable e-mail after what happened earlier today. Yet, my inbox is… empty. Empty. A conditioned response kicks in. And I feel my insides begin to drop.

Yet, this time, instead of spiraling all the way down, I manage to catch the fall. I remind myself that I am powerless over what Gotthard thinks or does. And I continue upstairs to the laundry room.

****

Determined not to backslide into any despair over the empty inbox, I concentrate entirely on the task at hand, transferring my wet laundry to the dryer without any of it falling to the floor, when suddenly I'm interrupted by an ominous-sounding American accent.

"Aren't you Rebecca?" asks the American.

A little warily, I twist around.

A gawky young woman with pig tails and that rare type of blonde-green hair that can result from too much chlorine in the swimming pool is leaning up against the laundry room door.

"Uh, yeah, I am. What's up?" I reply, coolly.

"I just want to introduce myself. I'm Frances," she says.

Her smile is euphoric.

I look at her suspiciously. People in the hostel don't introduce themselves to each other in this formal sort of way. Or smile like that. It makes me nervous.

"Hi," I repeat.

"You're a friend of Bill Wilson's, aren't you?" she continues.

She is staring at me even more peculiarly, now, almost as if there's something she's searching for with those perceptive grayish-blue eyes.

"Bill Wilson? No, I don't know Bill Wilson," I reply.

She places the well worn duffle bag she has over her shoulder on top of the other washer and persists, sphinx-like.

"Sure you do."

"Bill Wilson? I don't," I repeat, stooping down to pick up the inevitable pair of fallen underwear off the dirty floor.

"Okay."

She dumps out her own laundry and begins separating her darks and lights. "But, don't feel like you have to pretend around me," she adds.

I maintain my composure while shifting nervously into an American-British hybrid version of my accent in preparation for the worst.

"I don't know what you mean," I say, unsettled.

"Listen, I know," she explains. "But, don't worry. I'm not going to say anything. It's your own business."

Standing perfectly still, I study her face out of the corner of my eye in an attempt to figure out where she knows me from.

I remind myself that the only way I can lose is if I lose my nerve.

Then, attempting to rule out high school and college, I ask, "Whereabouts are you from?"

"Canada. Saskatoon."

"Oh, I thought you were American," I say. "Did you study here? In the States?"

"No. McGill."

"Right. I thought maybe I recognized you from college here."

"You went to college *here?*" she asks.

"Yes, I moved here at nineteen. My dad's American," I proclaim, with too much defensiveness.

"Oh, okay."

I rack my brain for another minute. Then, convinced we don't know each other, and unable to imagine how not knowing someone named Bill Wilson could put me in any kind of jeopardy, I finally demand, "Anyway, what are you *talking* about!?"

"I'm in program too," she explains. "I saw you there earlier today. I'm not trying to break your anonymity. I just think with both of us trying to stay sober while living here we could really help each other."

"Oh, right!" I say, as the name Bill Wilson rings a bell. "You mean Bill Wilson from the AA literature?"

She smiles knowingly.

"Yes, I did go to a meet-ing today. In fact, I went to two in a row. But," I reveal, sheepishly, "to be hon-est with you, I'm not exactly an alcoholic."

She scatters a cup of washing powder evenly over her wash and adds four quarters to the machine.

"Believe me," she says, looking at me sympathetically, "the last thing I'm going to do is take your inventory. But, nobody finds their way to AA by accident."

"No, actually I went to try to get sort of some... emotional sobriety," I elaborate.

She nods her head.

"Emotional sobriety is definitely one of the benefits of abstinence."

Sensing the need for a disclaimer, I clarify, "I don't actually *have* a problem with alcohol. At all."

A meditative look comes over her face then as she leans one leg up against the washer.

"Denial is a necessary shock absorber for the soul, sometimes, until you can face the reality," she says. "But, at the same time, awareness around the denial is a really important first step."

"Right," I say. "I agree with what you're saying. It's just that… it doesn't actually *apply* to me."

She stares at me with compassion. "I told myself the same thing," she explains. "It's actually emblematic of the alcoholic – the too-special/less-than duality. Don't forget, the disease is cunning and baffling. And the ego is part of the disease."

"That's interesting," I say, in an effort to stop creating what I'm defending against.

"And I totally don't mean to preach," she says. "It's just that I've been getting really clear lately. And I'm just excited. Everybody gets it in different ways at different times."

"That's cool. How much time do you have?" I ask, resorting to program-speak.

"Six months," she announces, with pride. "And I'm no different from anybody else."

My thoughts begin to spin, flipping back and forth like an out of balance rinse cycle.

"We're all the same," she emphasizes, supportively. "But it doesn't mean that I don't, well, that I can't imagine how much harder it is in a way to be coming from the UK."

I feel obliged to wear an expression of appreciation.

"For instance," she continues, "there's so much alcoholism in Ireland, Scotland, and even England, that it can be *even* harder to identify it. That's the thing. You just have a completely different yardstick."

Attempting to reflect a sufficient understanding of my own culture, I concede, "Perhaps that's true."

But she's just gazing at me now.

"Anyway," I conclude. I can feel my face growing rigid.

"Just try to keep in mind," she offers, confidentially, as she takes a step toward me and places a branch-like hand over my right shoulder, "it's not a choice."

"No," I say.

"It's a disease," she continues. "Like diabetes. And that's *nothing* to be ashamed of."

"Yes, right, I think…"

"I wasn't quite through, actually," she says. "All right if I just finish what I was saying?"

I nod.

"I was just going to say that the people in the rooms aren't there to judge you. They're there to help you get well. But we have to do our own part," she warns. "In AA we stop *all* the lying. *All* the hiding."

Sensing she could be making this point for a while, I remain focused on her mouth. The space between her two front teeth reminds me of the one I used to have, and spit summer swimming pool water through, before I got braces.

"Before we get well," she continues, "we have all kinds of irrational shame. We don't want others to know us. It's typical. But it's also what keeps us sick. Can you picture what I mean?"

Once more, I try to break her of her denial over my denial.

"Yes, I can. Easily," I say. "The only thing is, it's like I said, I'm afraid I'm not actual-ly hiding a prob-lem with alcohol."

"Except I was there," she cuts in.

"Sor-ry?"

"I saw your shame," she says. "I mean, well, I heard it."

Like seeing a police siren in a rearview mirror, this last sentence catches my full attention. I slam on the brakes. "What do you mean by that?"

"I think you know very well what I mean," she says. "The phony American accent you were putting on at the meeting?"

American accent? She thinks my real voice is the front?

I take a moment to process the reprieve.

"Oh, that?" I ask.

107

She smiles wryly. "What's insincere tends to stick out a little in AA."

"Okay, I admit," I say, eager to reinforce the misunderstanding, "once in a blue moon, I might pepper in a bit of an American accent. But I suppose that's only when I'm feeling real-ly uncomfortable being... myself."

Gesturing her hands in the air as if she's trying to catch a football, she pauses. "Significant," she whispers.

"Do you reckon?"

A look of triumph washes over her face. "Yes. Because it was the shame that was making you uncomfortable, see?"

"Oh," I reply.

"Nobody wants to be known," she stresses. "Not before we get well." She shakes her head enthusiastically. "But that's the paradox. Because letting ourselves become known for who we really are is *how* we get well."

"I see."

"Do you?" she asks. "I know it might be hard to believe, but in AA it really is safe to be yourself. No matter who you are."

"That certainly sounds... lovely."

She looks at me optimistically. "It is. You won't believe how freeing that kind of acceptance can be."

"Hmm."

"So, just don't feel like you have to hide anything in there. All right?"

I nod compliantly.

"Okay?" she asks, more emphatically.

"Yes, okay, thank you," I reply, deferentially, before, like a drug trafficker, I take the speeding ticket from her hand, put up the window, and pull safely away, with my trunk full of illegal stash still undiscovered.

Owning It

At eleven the next morning I arrive at Bagby. Without delay, I squeeze my hands into the pair of tight, rubber gloves I find beneath the sink and begin, lobster-style, scrubbing out the stove of the house's communal kitchen.

Although at first I just focus, single-mindedly, on the task at hand, after a while, as I work, my mind starts to drift. For some reason, of all things, I find myself wondering what the kids from my high school would think if they could see me now.

As I scrape some burned cheese off the bottom of the oven with the aid of a metal spatula, I cook up a mock update for the high school alumni newsletter:

Rebecca Lamb, Class of '89:

Following a checkered academic career that spanned ten years, Rebecca Lamb eked out a degree and a half and almost made it into conventional society. Ultimately, however, her doctor boyfriend of four years decided against her, deeming it an unsuitable match, due to her past promiscuity and budding bipolar disorder. Today, at thirty, Rebecca scrubs out ovens and changes sheets for the equivalent of $7.25 per hour. Her modest earnings all go toward securing her accommodation, a small room located above a parking lot which she shares with three other women and the occasional bedbug. In 1999 she switched over to soy milk.

Then, pressing the play button on the CD player sitting on the counter, I start listening to the copy of *New Skin for the Old Ceremony* someone left sitting in it, and begin mopping the floor. The music makes me feel calm, as if I'm exactly where I'm supposed to be and none of it even matters. In some way, that doesn't make any sense, everything seems to fit.

"Hi, how are you going?" asks a sleepy-sounding Australian accent.

A young woman with golden-brown curls and classic Modigliani features is leaning up against the kitchen wall.

I put my mop aside. "Hiya. Not bad, thanks. How are you... going?"

"Great. Okay if I come in?" she asks, glancing down at my freshly mopped floor.

"Oh, absolutely, am finished," I assure her.

She crosses the room, showcasing an athletic figure beneath an Indian block print halter dress, "Great day, isn't it?"

"Yeah, defo."

"We've been roughing it for a while now. We're pretty pleased to have a kitchen," she says, as she removes a big head of lettuce, a cucumber, and a bottle of fig-tahini salad dressing from the fridge.

"To-tally, I know what you mean."

"It's not a bad hostel, is it?" she asks.

"Yeah, no, I really like it here," I concur.

She leans over the sink and begins rinsing her lettuce.

"How about you?" I continue, noticing a little tattoo of Madagascar over her left bicep. "How long have you been here?"

"We're here about a week," she says, gesturing to her unshaven, barefoot boyfriend just entering the room. "We're both looking for work, too."

"G'day, how are you going?" the guy asks me, with a thick accent and a warm smile that exposes a chipped front tooth.

"Yeah, great," I say.

He opens the fridge. "Be'ah?" he asks.

Even though I still don't like beer, especially first thing in the morning, I'm somehow too interested in conversation with them to risk refusing.

"Oh, cheers," I say, taking a Heineken from his hand.

"How long have you been working here?" she asks, running an affectionate hand through her boyfriend's long, stringy hair.

"I just started today, actually."

"Really? It seems like a pretty cushy job, though, working here."

Compensating for my new status, I attempt to inject it with the grandeur of choice and leisure. "Yeah, no, definitely. Right now, even, I'm just waiting for the sheets to finish drying, you know? Pretty cush."

"Yeah, great! I'd like to get one of those fake social security cards," she continues, rendering what's left of my plebian complex irrelevant, by her seeming obliviousness to it. "A girlfriend of mine got one when she was here and worked here for like six months. I need to ask her where she got it from but she's on this sort of retreat thing in Daramsala now. And she's gone just completely out of contact. Do you know anyone who has one of those?"

"I don't know," I say. "But someone up at the main hostel must have an idea. What kind of work are you looking for?"

"Oh, pretty much anything. Cleaning, waitressing, babysitting. Dusty's looking for some moving or painting. Whatever's going really."

"Oh, right," I say.

"I'm Micah, by the way. That's Dusty."

Deciding my new nickname is official enough, I say, "Becks."

"Yeah, some moving yakka would be totally great," resumes Dusty, grabbing a seat. "Tryin' to get down to Fiji for September. Good money, moving."

"How long have you been looking?" I ask.

He leans back in his chair and crosses his legs, easily, like some old gentleman.

"Well, today's my first day, really. I've been a bit too hungover to look the other days. But, now it's time," he says.

He removes a boiled egg from the front pocket of his faded old jeans and reaches across the table for the salt shaker.

"Why don't you see if there's any work going here?" I ask.

"Well, I was thinking of it. You know, until something else comes through, just to cover our rent. Fifty-four dollars a night is pretty dear, especially on the Australian dollar," he says, cracking his egg against the wall. "But isn't the manager over there a bit of a prick?"

"Oh, you mean Alan? I did hear someone else say he was a bit of a *knob*. But he seems to be okay so far. Why? Did something happen?"

"Yeah, well, he asked me the other day if I washed. I thought it was kind of an odd thing to ask. So I just answered him, 'Sure, every week.' But he gave me this really crazy look. I'd thought he meant, you know, like wash my clothes. But now I think he might have meant wash – as in shower. The funny thing is I shower like three times a day. Never use shampoo, though, just water, otherwise my hair just goes completely flat."

"Huh, that does seem like a strange thing to ask someone."

"Yeah, I don't know. I mean, when *we* say wash, we mean wash our clothes, don't we?"

"Yah," I assure him, in Commonwealth solidarity, without remembering ever having found it necessary to distinguish between doing laundry and taking a shower.

"Do the Americans mean shower? I should find out. Whatever. Anyway, maybe I'll rock on over there in a few minutes and have a word with him about doing some painting or something."

"Yeah, you should. I should be getting back myself. I don't want them to think I'm taking the piss on my first day," I say.

I wonder whether if I really were half American, I'd have mentioned it in relation to the washing mystery by this point.

"Well, hang on a minute, Becks. Lemme just throw on a shirt, we'll wander over with you," Dusty says.

I point to my beer. "Do you have any paper bags for these?" I ask Micah.

"Huh?"

"Yeah, you can't walk down the street with an exposed beer bottle. It's against the law. We need paper bags."

"Really?"

"Yeah."

"You're joking!"

"No, seriously, you can even get arrested."

Dusty reappears in an old T-shirt with an illustration on it of a poppy and a marijuana leaf.

"Okay, ready to roll?" he asks. "Pun entirely intended."

I read the words on his shirt aloud, "Same, Same. But different."

"Pretty funny, isn't it?" he asks. "Found it in the free-bin yesterday. Must be from Thailand."

Picking up my sack of recycling, I nod my head, in knowing agreement. "The free-bin?"

"Oh, it's up at the main hostel. You know, lost stuff they find in the rooms. Micah has found quite a few things in it, haven't you, babe?"

"Oh, yeah, the free-bin. Can be pretty lush!" Micah says.

"Right, the free-bin, of course."

"Hey, Dusty," she adds, "did you know you can't walk down the street with a beer here? It's illegal."

"Yeah," Dusty says, turning around on the stairs to meet Micah's incredulous eyes. "I read that in the Lonely Planet. Bizarre, eh?"

I catch a glimpse of myself in the window. I look utterly at ease with a black garbage bag full of other people's stale recycling slung over my shoulder.

"Is pret-ty bizarre," I say.

If You Can't Take the Heat

Whenhen we get back to the main hostel, Dusty and Micah disappear to find Alan, and Zoella, the Australian woman with the crow's feet, flags me.

"Hey, Rebecca, what are you up to?" she asks.

"Why?"

"Have a minute to do some hoovering?"

"Actually, Zoella, I'm just back from Bagby and I'm supposed to go shopping for food for the... party," I say, in an American accent. (Pronouncing *party* with an English accent is where I've decided I draw the line.)

"Party – in an American accent?" she teases. She wears a mocking little smirk that tells me my casual attempt at trying to speak like an American sounds affected.

Meanwhile, I'm, of course, just reassured that when using my real voice she, like the girl from the laundry room, considers me to be an English girl impersonating an American one rather than the other way around.

"Anyway, I'm supposed to find someone called Isaac to come with me," I continue, resuming my accent. "Do you know who Isaac is?"

"He's here. I just saw him a second ago. Ike!" she calls.

In another moment a reedy man of about 6' 6" emerges from the internet zone. "Someone call me?"

"Isaac, this is Rebecca," Zoella introduces. "Alan wants you to go shopping with her for the stuff for the party tonight."

"Great. Okay. Hi. Are you cooking that same thing they cooked last time?" he asks, as he pulls a clip out of the front pocket of his overalls and secures his long, dirty blonde (dirty as in dirty, not as in dark-blonde) hair into a low pony tail.

"Wait!" Alan interrupts, materializing out of thin air. "*I* did it. I did the shopping myself, Rebecca. I'll show you where I put the stuff."

"Sure," I reply.

"And Isaac," he continues, "I want *you* fixing the bathroom next to room twenty-three. It *still* doesn't flush properly."

"Oh, all right," replies Isaac, passively. "I was just looking forward to going out and getting some air, but I guess I can wait."

"Getting some air? I saw you sitting out on the steps in the sun for the first three hours after you got here today," accuses Alan.

"No, no," Isaac chuckles. "I was waiting for the paint to dry."

They squabble for another minute while I think about how Alan is the very *last* person with whom I want to be alone.

"Right, Rebecca, I'll show you where I put the stuff," Alan says.

Isaac, now busy pinching the dark, tanned skin on his arm, exclaims urgently, "Hey look! I have old-man skin. I can't believe it! You know what I mean? *Old-man skin?*"

Alan looks at me, rolls his eyes, and gestures for me to follow him. Traipsing behind Alan, through the rec room and into the kitchen, I feel more like I'm floating, practically as if in a state of physical disconnect or something.

"Thanks for doing the shopping part," I say, aiming to redirect my thoughts.

He leads me down a few more stairs off the side of the kitchen into a small sprinkler room that leads us into an even smaller sort of storeroom or pantry.

"It was good for me to get some fresh air this morning" he replies. "Getting here in the morning is not what I call relaxing."

"No?"

There's no reply. We're concentrating on stooping down to squeeze past the sprinkler room's low threshold exterior without knocking our heads. A few more steps and we've arrived, together, inside the little dungeon, where it's not only tiny, cramped and pitch-black, but also about ten degrees colder even than the always freezing rec room.

"Hang on," says Alan.

He pulls a Zippo lighter out of his shirt pocket to illuminate the tiny grotto, which is so overstuffed with groceries that there's barely room to move.

"No," he continues, still not losing the thread, "I've just been having *such* a hard time with the Asians."

I try to hover closer to the flame of his Zippo for warmth. That's how cold it is.

"Oh?" I ask.

"Yes, they don't know how to walk," he continues. "I mean, I've had to start coming up Montgomery because there's just no way I can come up Stockton anymore."

"Oh, really?" I return.

He looks at me disbelievingly. "Are you *kidding?* I would *never* take Stockton."

"No, of course not," I concur.

There's a short silence. I try to hint at my interest in getting our ingredients and getting out of the sprinkler room.

"Blimey, I should've brought a jumper," I say.

Ignoring this, he looks meaningfully at me, oblivious to the temperature, the lack of air, and my growing claustrophobia.

"I really had a hell of a weekend last week," he says, parking a green All Star sneaker on top of a monster can of tomato paste.

I reply, as coolly as courtesy will allow. "Really?"

"Yeah, I did."

"That's a drag," I offer, noncommittally. I'm determined not to encourage any confiding.

"It's Maureen," he elaborates.

Extreme caution is called for. I'm all too aware that any increase in his trust in me will only result in an exacerbated sense of betrayal should my own secret ever come to light.

I mean, he'd be mad *enough* to learn I am not an English traveler, but rather an American interloper in disguise. How much angrier would he be if, on top of that, I'm holding any of his skeletons?

Leaning back on a giant bag of bagels for support, I wonder if in some way it's my very desire not to be confided in which is making me privy.

"Maureen?"

"My *wife?*"

"Oh, right, sorry, I didn't realize you were married."

"Yes, I am *married,*" he snaps, with exaggerated annoyance. "Why wouldn't *I* be married?

"No reason."

"Well, last week I found out that my wife of *fifteen years* wants to… she wants to try a… separation," he divulges.

Trying to strike that balance between concern and skepticism, I reply, calmly, "Oh dear. Is that real-ly bad news?"

"Well, it's not great," he returns.

He sounds less disturbed than I would have expected. I try to match his lack of distress.

"Well, I guess it could be worse, right?" I ask.

"That's true," he concurs. "Could be because of an affair. That'd be worse."

He begins grabbing five pound bags of penne off the shelf and tossing them at me until my chin is holding the last bag in place.

"Don't tell anyone, though," he then warns, looking at me suspiciously. "I don't want anybody knowing yet."

"No, I won't tell anybody."

"And that *includes* Angus."

I switch into as unEnglish a voice as I can get away with, and assure him, "No, of course. You can trust me."

****

With all of my necessary ingredients finally extracted from the sprinkler room, I make my escape to the kitchen, where I feel relieved to be back in the comparative safety of community.

Just as I begin to calm down though Alan's voice sounds again.

"Becky?"

I'm surprised by this. It's the first time since my arrival that he is addressing me by a nickname.

"In here," I call back.

With a young hosteller in tow, Alan enters the kitchen.

"This is Sam," he announces. "He's going to help you. Tell him what you want him to do."

"Oh. Great! Cheers," I reply.

"Hey there," volunteers Sam. "Put me to work, boss."

Aside from being, inevitably, English, Sam appears to be the ideal assistant, which is to say his very presence reeks of adolescent indifference, an overall lack of curiosity.

"Hiya," I return, warmly.

He shoots me a confident smile.

"Right, if you could dump that bag of carrots into that metal colander, start by giving them a good rinse, and then grate them, that would be smashing," I say, with moderate authority.

I sense immediately that this layering of roles is a good thing. Any form of texture is bound to have a camouflaging effect.

"I think I can handle that," he says.

"Cheers."

"So, how many hours equal a free night, then?"

Over the erratic drone of the faultily repaired faucet, I shout, "Every three hours buys you a free night!"

"How long do you think we can drag this out for?" he asks, familiarly.

"At least until seven o'clock. We'll need help cleaning up, too, if you like."

"No, that's okay, I'll be pissed by then."

I hand him a grater and a metal bowl. "Of course you will."

"What part of England are you from?" he asks, a minute later, as the novelty of grating wears.

"Oh, Arundel," I say, casually. I observe that the lying *is* growing less grueling with practice.

"Oh, you're kidding," he says. "I'm from Pulborough."

"Oh, real-ly, how funny!" I exclaim. I, of course, have no idea where this is.

"Yeah, it's funny, I was just saying, I've been away for six months now and already the most blatant things are starting to slip my mind."

I dump five bags of tomatoes out on the counter and begin dicing. "Right, I know what you mean."

"Of course it's not the ganja we've been smoking."

"No, of course not," I say.

"What's the name of that restaurant, the one right on the water, for instance?"

"Doesn't ring a bell."

"You know the one, it's in Arundel. Everyone knows it, with all the picnic benches on the bank?"

"Hmm."

"You don't know it?"

"Not sure."

"Or, what about that three-story night club near the roundabout? Have you been there?"

"Oh, it's been a long time. I don't remember that, real-ly."

"You don't?" he asks.

"No, not quite."

He is staring at me in a peculiar way.

"No, no, hold on, I think I do remember it, vaguely," I try.

"You do?"

"Yes."

"It has a Union Jack awning?" he asks.

"Yes, that's right, yes," I affirm.

He looks at me curiously. "Wait a minute."

I'm spooked, but I manage a reply. "What is it?"

"You," he says, placing down the grater. "I don't think... you *are* from Arundel."

My voice begins to wobble. "I'm not?"

"No, you're *not*."

His expression is shrewd, his posture accusing. The boy is a bloodhound.

"I'm not exactly sure why anyone would lie about being from Arundel," he continues, "but you are definitely not from there. So, why don't you tell me where you're *really* from?"

Stunned by the confrontation, and the idea of it all ending right here, just like that, I conceal a slow swallow. I didn't see it coming. Having no idea what to say, I start fumbling.

But he cuts me off. "You must be from somewhere even *more* obscure," he laughs. "You're from *Bogner Regis*, aren't you?"

Tongue-tied, I stare at him. I am registering the sensation of having been shot at and missed.

"You are, aren't you? That's it. Bloody hell, I got it. Oi, nothing wrong with being from Bogner!" he says, amused.

"Fine, maybe I am, okay," I say, lying about being a liar in order to conceal my lying. "But then don't go tel-ling everybody I'm from Bogner, all right?"

He looks at me with a little smirk.

At this, I snap, like someone miffed over being busted might.

"And stop looking so bloody chuffed with yourself, would you?"

"Oright, lass," he says, laughing. "Never mind. Your secret is safe with me."

"Cheers for that. You wouldn't want to admit to being from Bog-ner either," I continue. "Not that it's *so* bad."

"Probably not."

"At least I'm not from Bournemouth," I add, remembering Will, from the pool table, who told me to keep that knowledge under my hat.

"True. Good consolation."

Eager to change the subject, I look down at his grated carrots.

"That was fast."

"Well, I'm a quick kind of bloke."

"I guess so. You could peel those po-ta-toes next," I suggest, attempting to reclaim some weight.

He shudders at the sight of the giant pile of spuds. "What else could I do?" he asks.

"Rinse the lettuce?"

He appraises the twelve heads of flourishing California romaine.

"Or," he proposes, "what about having a quick fag break?"

"That'd work."

"Fancy one?" he asks.

"Actually," I say, still unsettled both by the close call and the latest lie, "if I could pinch one off you, that'd be brill."

He hands me the open pack.

"Cheers," I reply, believing, naively, that this incident is as close as the close calls are going to get.

****

By the time I finish with my kitchen duties, Sharon and Angus have already started eating. They're seated neatly around the little marble table in the reception area, dining off chipped china, amidst the backdrop of check-ins. I pull up a chair.

"How is it then?" I ask.

Sharon finishes off her last bite. "Gorgeous!"

"Is it?"

"Look at the way she's fishing for compliments," observes Angus, disapprovingly.

"Please, sir, can I have some more?" asks Sharon.

I manage to catch her reference, courtesy of eighth-grade British literature. "Defo, there's loads," I reply.

"Wait!" an eavesdropping Alan interjects from behind the front desk. "*Until* everyone has gone through the line once. And too much salt, Rebecca. Remember you can always add it, you *can't* take it away."

Omitting the fact that I followed his own recipe to the letter, I say, "Okay."

"It's also too hot. Less pepper next time, please," he adds.

"Got it," I reply, submissively, as a passing hosteller knocks me on the shoulder with his surfboard.

"Yeah, too hot," chimes in a hovering Stacy. His expression is deadpan. "Almost as hot as the cook."

Me?

Angus kicks me in the shin under the table.

"It was so smoky in there, I just had to get away," I start, apropos of nothing. I'm determined to deflect his compliment in order to preserve it.

"Smoky and freezing," Sharon adds.

"Yeah, why's it always so bloody Baltic in there?" Angus asks.

Alan glances down at the sauna sign-out clipboard. "Well, there's always the sauna," he says. "But I'm not going to turn the heat up in here. Not one degree."

"Aye, good idea. Who's up for a sauna?" broaches Angus.

"They have *no* idea what our electric bills are like here!" Alan continues, to nobody in particular.

"That's a good idea," Sharon says. "I could do a hot oil treatment while I'm at it. All the bloody American air conditioning is really doing my ends in. It should be called Amer-conditioning."

Angus turns to me.

"I'm in," I say.

"I'll sign the key out for nine o'clock. Sauna at nine, then!" he exclaims.

From the Frying Pan into the Fire

At nine o'clock I knock on the sauna door. "Fire."

There's no answer.

"Fire," I say, louder, knocking harder.

A nervous-looking traveler emerges from a darkened dorm room across the hall. "What? Did you say *fire?*" he asks, urgently.

"Oh, no, there's no fire," I assure him.

"You said *fire* didn't you?"

"I did, but there isn't one," I say again, as I catch a glimpse of an approaching Angus, sashaying down the hall in a ratty blue towel. He holds up a long metal serving spoon attached to the sauna key.

"Got the key!" he announces.

"So, *there* you are," I call.

He unlocks the door. "Looks like you're the first one here," he teases.

"What's that mean, then?"

"Means there's nothing like being too keen, honey. But I would be too. What of that comment anyway? *'Almost as hot as the cook.'* I'm sure he'll come."

I tug at his towel. "I'm here because I'm cold," I insist, coyly.

"Yeah, right. Well, I'm warning you, I've got my eye on him, and I'm going to fight you for him, Becky. Every inch of the way."

"Sounds pret-ty ardent," I reply. "Anyway, we need to change the password."

"Why?"

"Some bloke out there thought there was a fire."

"Okay, then to *ice,*" Angus says, pushing open the chunky cedar door. "Ice!"

I look around the little wooden room, kick off my flip-flops, and settle in on a lower bench. "God, this heat feels great," I say.

Angus looks at the temperature dial and scoffs. "It's not even on yet."

"Oh, well, turn it on."

"What do you think I'm doing? Sometimes you can be really bossy, Rebecca. Do you know that?"

"Don't get into a strop."

Angus lies down, stretches his arms out over his head, and lets out a sigh.

"Like my pants?" he inquires, referring to his "Having a ball! Or two!" boxer shorts.

"Classy."

"I know, they're perfect for me, aren't they?" he asks.

I look over at him, lying there on his back, unarmed, with all the natural expectation of confidence, and think about how topsy-turvy everything is. Now that I finally feel like I know and trust Angus enough to tell him about me without risking his telling Alan, I've passed the stage where a confession to him would be bearable, or even sensible. It's as if there was a particular point where it stopped being a ruse and turned into something else. And I've passed it.

"Yeah," I say, inattentively.

"My best mate, Logan, had them made for me for my going-away party," he says.

I console myself with the idea that telling him the truth would only be unburdening myself at his expense anyway.

"They threw you a going-away party?" I ask.

"Aye, it was magic," he starts, as someone knocks on the door.

"Password?" Angus calls from his bench.

"Fire," says Sharon.

"Okay, okay."

Angus hauls himself up to open the door. Sharon enters wearing a bright blue bikini.

"New password is *ice,*" I say.

She places a bottle of water, a bottle of oil, and a jar of hair cholesterol down on the floor beside the other lower bench.

"Excellent!" Angus exclaims, as he dives into the hair cholesterol and slathers it over his head.

"Fire," Stacy's voice calls from the hallway.

Angus flashes me a wide-eyed glance and then lunges for the door.

"New password is *ice,*" we say to Stacy in unison, as he enters.

Stacy looks at Angus's hair. "What happened to you?"

"Just shut up and lie down," replies Angus.

The four of us then just lie there, sweating in silence for a few minutes, until Angus moans, "God, a massage would sure feel nice about now."

"Yeah," we return.

"C'mon Stacy, I'll just do your shoulders," Angus says.

"No thanks, pal. But, Becky, you can do mine."

"Thanks," I reply. "I'll pass."

"I can't believe no massages are going to take place in here!" exclaims Angus, indignantly. "Everybody gives massages in saunas. What a bunch of boring bastards!"

"Massages in saunas? What are we, swingers?" I rally my energies to retort. "I detest obviousness."

"Yah Becky. And Stacy," continues Angus. "I can't believe you'd let her give you one and not me. You're just a little *homophobe!*"

Stacy flashes Angus a satirical smile. "Don't take everything quite so personally. Bitch."

"Okay, that's it. I've had enough," Angus says. "I can see this is not going to be any fun. I'd just as soon get down there and show off this radiant complexion before it fades."

"I'll come with," offers Sharon, standing up. "It's too hot in here."

****

"Ice," I call, still wet from my interim shower.

Stacy opens the sauna door and lets me back in.

"Actually, you kind of remind me of an ice bear," he starts, looking me over, as he lies back down.

"Sor-ry?"

"You know, a polar bear."

"Hey, thanks," I say, as I reset the timer on the sauna for another twenty minutes. "You remind me of a flamingo."

He turns over on his side. His relaxed features, beaming with sun-kissed health, seem to brighten up the barely lit space.

"C'mon, old girl, it's a compliment. Polar bears are the cutest ones out there."

"You think?"

"Oh, for sure."

"Nah, penguins are."

"Oh yeah, forgot about them."

"You want to hear a story?" I ask, hoping I have the stamina to get through a whole story in the accent.

"Go on."

"Well, some of my fam-ily live in Connecticut."

"Where's that?" he asks.

"By New York."

"Above or below?"

"Just near it," I dismiss.

Then I pause for a moment, processing the fact that I hardly know the exact location of my own state. I realize, therefore, it might follow that I am afforded more geographical leniency as a Brit than I've allowed myself, too.

He looks at me dubiously. "Have ya spent much time there?"

"Yeah, well, I grew *up* in Connecticut," I emphasize, though, in order to successfully assimilate this unlikely new information, in the most English accent I can rally.

"You grew up in England. There's no mistaking that accent."

"Well, I grew up both in America and in England," I say.

Yearning to tell the truth, I almost manage to persuade myself that a few trips to England as a child and my year abroad could, in a sense, constitute growing up there.

"Anyway."

"Right, anyway, this one set of cousins, their oldest son is slightly retarded. But he's high-functioning. In any case, one day their whole fam-ily went to the local Aquarium."

"True story?"

"Yes."

"Carry on."

"Anyway, and they lost Leon. They looked everywhere and nobody could find him. Finally they found him, and he was all wet. They tried to get him to tell them where he'd been, but he just kept sha-king his head and wouldn't tell. In the car, on the way home, the whole car stank. When they got home my aunt was like, 'Leon, now you go take a shower.' A few minutes la-ter she went into the bathroom to check on him. And he was in there, in the shower, with a baby penguin."

"Bull!"

"Yes, I swear," I say, registering the privilege of being able to swear the truth.

"You're joking," he insists. "How'd he get it home?"

"In his backpack! That's why it smelled so awful in the car," I explain.

"That's ace. What a little larrikin!" says Stacy, standing up.

"I know, pret-ty funny, eh?"

Stacy replies by slowly moving toward me until his mouth is inches away from mine. He bares a cocky white smile. Yet, his cockiness is the right kind, the open, self-connected kind, not the fear-based, posturing variety.

"Is this too obvious, by the way?" he asks.

I feel relaxed and attracted. Stacy's body is all easy confidence; his energy feels pure.

"Yeah," I affirm, acquiescing. "I'd say so."

He pauses for a moment, then, and I prepare myself to repel some kind of a dig. Instead, however, he moves slowly closer still, holds my face affectionately, and looks at me as if he's known me for a long time.

I gaze back into his uncluttered blue eyes, at the even mix of deep blue and white rays in his irises.

"All jokes aside, you're gorgeous," he says.

The heat gives way to a strange sense of permission.

"*You're* gorgeous," I reply.

"Nah, I'm just an old Australian crocodile. But, you, look at you," he says, pulling me closer and kissing me gently.

My hand slips up his shoulder to the back of his head, meeting a rawhide necklace tied tautly around his smooth neck.

I almost kiss him, but hold back some, too, worrying that on some cellular level he'll be able to perceive that the intonation of my kisses are not in keeping with the intonation of my voice – that the sincerity of my kiss will, by contrast, reveal the insincerity of my accent.

Stacy moves back a little, glances at the outline of my body under my wrap, and sets his square hands around my waist.

"Your body knocks me *out*," he says, in a low crackly voice. "You act as if you don't even know it. And nothing is hotter than…."

"You're a smooth one," I cut in, though never so annoyed by the sound of my own tones.

"Only smooth thing around here is your skin," he jokes, laying it on even thicker.

I smile and decide to stop talking altogether.

His arms reach around to my upper back, and he softly presses me closer to him, as my tan linen wrap and his red-striped trunks begin to feel like too many layers.

"You're definitely the most fascinating specimen in the laboratory, Becky," he continues, flexing his arms. "Seriously."

"How do you mean?" I ask.

"There's just something mysterious about you. I like it."

"Oh," I reply, more reluctantly.

Slipping down underneath him on the warm wooden bench, I let his heavenly body press against mine. I want to bury my face in the crook of his shoulder.

And yet, at the same time, while I long to give into the tenderness of his embrace, I am also careful to resist moving any closer. Although I'm *almost* me, I guess, if I'm honest, that *almost* represents a lot.

"Are you okay?" he asks.

I push myself back up into a sitting position. "Yeah, thanks, I'm fine," I whisper.

"Becky," he says, picking up on my uncertainty, "we don't have to have sex or anything like that, you know? I mean, sex would be ideal, but I really, literally, just want to kiss you."

"I know, but, I think I ought to stop," I say, realizing that allowing myself to get close to him without his being convinced of my sincerity would be crude, meaninglessness.

"Huh?"

"I should go, I should go," I lament.

"Oh, no, Becks, don't go."

"I've got to go," I repeat, more decisively.

"I'd be so stoked if you'd stay," he says.

"Yeah, I want to stay, too, but I can't."

I realize that perhaps it's my own sincerity I'm in need of being totally squared with before something can have meaning for *me*.

He strokes my hair. "You sure?"

"I am, I can't explain it. I wish I could."

"There's a boyfriend?"

"Well, no, not really."

"Hmm. I think there's a boyfriend in the picture."

"No, really, not," I insist.

Bending over, he kisses me on the cheek, then leans back against the wall. "No worries," he says. "I think I'm pickin' up what you're throwing down."

"No, you aren't," I say. "It's com-pli-ca-ted. I have this sort of... secret. But, I can't tell you about it here, not now. But maybe one day. I'd like to tell you some day. I'd like to tell everyone someday."

He takes his water bottle and dumps it over his head.

"It's really okay, Becks."

"It's not you, it's me," I ramble.

Standing back up, he gathers his wet hair into a sloppy pony tail and slips into his flip-flops.

"Let's rock on downstairs and have another game of pool?" he suggests. His tone is relaxed, detached even.

"Why?" I ask.

"You *are* in San Francisco," he explains.

"Sor-ry?"

He studies me a moment. "Gotta be the world's easiest place to come out, right?"

"Out?"

But Stacy doesn't answer. He just opens the door, shoots me a funny smile, and pauses under the threshold a moment.

"Shut the door, then," I say. "You're letting all the heat out."

"Nah, there's got to be heaps of hot air in here."

Layering the Uniforms

"I still think you're making too much of it," Angus says, the next afternoon, as we cross through Washington Square Park en route to Laguaria bakery to go *halvers* on some fresh baked focaccia.

"No, I'm not sure I am, actually."

"Why didn't you just tell him the truth?"

"I did. Well, I tried to. He'd only sort of implied it anyway."

"Just because you wanted to leave the sauna?"

"I guess."

Angus glances down at my corduroys. "Or maybe it's because of the way you look in those trousers," he chides.

"Some seventies cliché," I retort, though while considering how much tighter they were prior to embarking on my metabolism-jump-starting accent charade.

"No, seriously, Becky," he continues, "if not wanting to shag means you're gay, I'm the straightest boy in this city. Besides, I'll bet you anything he was just *pretending* to think you were gay."

"Really? Why would he do *that?*"

"Protecting his fragile little hetero ego. Blatantly."

"Really, you think? You're not just trying to make me feel better?"

"No, I'm sure he was just being a prat. But why should that make you feel better, anyway? What do you care if Stacy thinks you're gay?

"Oh, it's not that. I'm not married to being straight. Just, I don't know, just I might be a bit keen on him, okay?" I admit.

"I *knew* you fancied him!"

"Well, maybe a bit. I just don't want him com-ple-te-ly mis-in-ter-pret-ing me. That's all. You know?"

"*Knew* you fancied him," Angus repeats, as we approach the gracious ten foot windows of the nearby Filbert Street Inn. "You're so transparent, Rebecca," he laughs.

We both pause then in order to glance inside at the inn's lobby, which looks the same as it always does, spacious and airy, private and privileged. With its giant fireplace and the streams of sunlight spilling across the shiny wood floors, broken up by a few thoughtfully placed antique accents and well worn Persian rugs, the tone is one of safety and refuge.

"Wow, look at all of those hors d'oeuvres," I say, as I observe the long, skinny dining room table adorned with a teasing display of triple creams, olives, foie gras, and toast tips.

"Yum, how nice would that be?" Angus asks.

"This girl I used to know in New York used to go to this posh hotel on Madison Avenue every Sunday. She'd bring a suitcase and a newspaper and sit there eating the free brunch, without ever checking in," I recount. "She did it every Sunday."

"Dare ya," tests Angus.

I squint my eyes as I consider it.

"Double dare ya."

With no need for further encouragement I backtrack a few feet and boldly pull on the brass door handle. There's an unexpected buzz. Anonymous grazing will not be possible.

Instead, a graying manager type rises from a fussy little desk.

"Hi, can I help you?" he asks.

"Oh, hi," I improvise, affecting a more timid demeanor. "I was just wondering if..., if you're look-ing for help, by any chance?"

A second person, a lanky guy with tight brown curls and a possible chin implant, emerges from somewhere behind the manager.

"Yes, indeed!" he exclaims.

I realize a quick getaway is not in the cards.

"Oh. You are?" I ask.

"*Yes!*" Brown Curls replies. "We have an employee out on maternity leave for two months, and we need a fill in. Have a seat, my dear."

I lower myself onto the pale pink velvet couch. "Oh, thank you ve-ry much."

He points to the graying man hovering in the background. "This is Dennis Brennan, our manager. And I'm Elliot Liverlable, the jolly innkeeper." He grins.

"Oh, nice to meet you," I return.

He joins me on the sofa. "And you are?"

I freeze, like a deer caught in headlights and wonder why using my full name, in even the most ordinary of circumstances, always makes me feel like I'm up to something.

"Oh, sor-ry, Rebecca. Rebecca Lamb."

"Well, I *love* England," he starts.

"Oh, how nice," I reply, as if it's the first time I've heard it. "Have you spent much time there?"

"We were there for two weeks last year. In London. Everyone we met was just delightful."

"That's so nice to hear," I say.

"Great little country. But, you do know you drive on the wrong side of the street, don't you?"

I force a giggle.

"What part are you from?"

"Arundel."

"Arundel," he repeats. "Now where's that again?"

"In the south," I explain. "Near Brighton."

"Oh, of course. A lot of our guests come from England, you know. I'd say thirty percent."

"Oh my!"

"Yes, you'd be right at home."

"I should think so."

"I couldn't live without my Swaine Adeney brolly," he continues.

"No?" I ask.

"You must have one?" he presses on.

"Oh, uh, no."

He wears a self-satisfied beam. "But you're surprised I know what a brolly is?"

"Yes, indeed, it's ve-ry unusual that you should!" I congratulate him, recognizing that whether or not I know what a brolly is is not what matters here.

He rises and walks over to a closet, returning with an umbrella.

"Best umbrella there is. Swaine Adeney. Guaranteed for a lifetime."

"Indeed," I reply.

Liverlable places his brolly down gently across the glass coffee table, and looks at me suspiciously.

"You're legal to work here?" he inquires.

"Oh, yes, my father is American," I explain.

"Great! You'll train tomorrow with Dennis. Be here at four, or shall I say at... *teatime!*"

"Yes, sir, sounds good."

****

The rest of the afternoon is spent back at the hostel, playing Killer around the pool table and then looking at some pictures from Dusty's trip to Bhutan on his computer.

After dinner, Seamus puts *Trainspotting* in the DVD player, but I decide to skip the movie and go to bed. Tomorrow is going to be a long day. In the morning I'll clean Bagby, and then it's off to the inn, for my first day of training.

First Day on the Second Job

Due to an uncanny number of beer bottles I find strewn throughout Bagby the next morning, by the time I finish rinsing them all out and hauling them back up to the Parakeet it's already nearly 3:00 p.m. I then speed shower, change into something I find in the hostel's free-bin, and race off down Columbus to get to the little inn on time for my first day on the second job.

Although it probably goes without saying, expanding my make-believe world was not exactly part of the plan. Naturally, I'm not trying to make my life any more convoluted than it already is. It's just sort of what's happening.

And, anyway, I'm not entirely convinced it's a bad thing. In fact, I have this weird inkling that maybe it's all like mayonnaise. Ultimately, there *is* a point you hit with mayonnaise where more is not better. And, similarly, I'm starting to wonder if maybe, just maybe, there's a point you hit with lying where more isn't worse. At least that's how it's starting to seem.

In any case, by the time I get to the inn's front door, Liverlable, the self-professed *jolly innkeeper* I met yesterday, spots me right away and buzzes me in before I have a chance to ring the polished little bell.

"Well, hello there!" he exclaims, as soon as I enter.

"Hello there," I return.

"And how are you today?" he asks, with mounting enthusiasm.

I attempt to equal his level of cheer. "Very well, thank you! And you?"

"I'd be a lot better if my wife's mother were gone," he blurts out.

"Oh, really?" I ask.

I take a seat behind the desk to show I'm willing to start the training.

"She's been here for five days," he continues.

"And for how much longer will you have her?"

"We'll have the peasant until guilt is overcome by aggravation."

"Oh, I see," I say, taking off my coat and hanging it on the back of my chair.

"I can tell you, I did *not* get the best deal when I married my wife," he continues. "I got the peasant, and my wife's daughter, the Fat Bachelorette, from her former marriage."

"And you don't care for her either?" I ask.

"Care for her? Not only is she big and fat, she's an unmitigated, unrepentant slob!" Liverlable exclaims.

"I see," I laugh, extra amused by his bluntness, due to being English. "But, is your wife not entertaining your mother-in-law?"

"She can't!" he exclaims. "Donna checked into Betty Ford a month ago!"

"Oh, I'm sor-ry."

"No, it's better this way. She was really getting out of control."

"So, you're all alone with her mother, then?"

"No, because the daughter is staying with us, too, visiting the grandmother. Oh *brother!*"

"Yes, that does seem like it might be altogether rather too much," I offer, wondering where all of this is going.

"Are you kidding? I'm ashamed to be seen with that fat sack of shit. Plus that lunatic. Not even lunatic – that *nothing!*"

A woman seated by the complimentary hors d'oeuvres and wine glances over at Liverlable with a pointed expression.

"We have good wine, eh?" he calls to her.

Her smile is brittle. "I'm sure you do," she returns.

Liverlable appears oblivious to all tension. "Did I tell you I love England?" he asks me.

"Yes, I'm so pleased to hear it," I say.

"Yes, it's a great little country. I could talk about England all day."

"Indeed. And where do you live?" I ask, turning the tables.

"Sonoma. We just bought a home there. It's a wonderful gated community. Overpriced though."

"Yes, I can imagine."

"There are many people who worry about being in debt," he says. He looks at me triumphantly. "I, however, am not one of them."

The toy poodle chained to the sideboard lets out a yelp.

"Shut up!" Liverlable shouts.

The dog barks again.

"He always has to get the last word," Liverlable explains. "I should probably take him out and head home anyway. But the great thing about poodles is they don't shed."

"Yes, right."

"Okay, dear," he says, as he retrieves a maroon shoulder bag from the mantel. "Do you think you can hold down the fort until Dennis arrives to train you? He should be here any minute."

"Yes, indeed. I should think so."

"If anybody needs anything, just tell them to take a seat and wait for Dennis."

"Will do."

"Good. I'm off, then. We'll see you tomorrow?"

"Yes, I'll be here."

"Perfect, my dear. Pip-pip cheerio!"

"Yes, cheerio, sir."

Dennis Brennan, the manager, arrives fifteen minutes later. He seems frazzled and smells like he may have been drinking for days and weeks. With his wiry eyebrows, he reminds me of a terrier mutt. For a moment I am uneasy, worrying that the speed at which I'll be able to process his instruction will be so slowed by having to remain focused on so many extraneous details pertaining to persona, that I'll retain nothing.

But, as luck would have it, his fragile hungover state complements my own edgy condition perfectly. Slowly, slowly, Dennis Brennan shows me the ropes until the shift ends at ten o'clock. Then I head back to the hostel, ninety dollars the richer.

****

The first thing I do when I get back to the Parakeet is to peek into the rec room. Beyond the huge windows, like some kind of oil-painted stage set, the sky has turned all different shades of cherry and magenta. And all the players are in there, blissfully un-concerned, watching *The Life of Brian* and eating popcorn, with honey on it.

Quietly, I wander in and over to Sharon and Angus who are parked at our usual booth.

"She's back from her new job at the Filbert Street Inn!" Angus shouts, with exaggerated jubilance, as I make my way over.

"You're working *there?*" Sharon inquires.

I throw a pillow over the wires springing forth from the booth before sitting down.

"Yeah, well I just trained today," I return.

"How was it?"

"Yeah, okay. It'll be a refreshing contrast to here, I think."

She eyes me with an expression of hilarity. "I'd say so. Going back and forth from here to there. You'll be like Jekyll and Hyde!"

"Yes. Right."

"*More* like Jekyll and Hyde," adds Angus, arbitrarily, echoing my exact concern.

"How about you?" I ask them. "Did you work today?"

Angus nods his head, woefully. "I did, I did."

"Laundry?" I ask.

"Desk. And I felt really rough, Becky. Really rough."

"I'm not surprised, with the way you were caning that ouzo last night," I say. "But, at least you didn't have to do laundry."

"But, you know, the desk is starting to do my head in, too," he says.

"Really?"

"You know what really annoys me about desk?" Angus asks, sitting up on one knee. "When people make a reservation, they all spell out their obvious first names, but then don't bother to spell out their surnames. So it's like, 'My name is Dale Kloberdanz, that's D-A-L-E.' It's like, cheers, Dale, that's really helpful. Don't you find that annoying? What kind of name is Dale anyway?" he asks.

I pull the bottle of wine Dennis Brennan, the manager, gave me to try from my bag.

"Well," I offer, "how about some hair for the dog?"

Sharon tears off into the kitchen in search of glasses.

"I think you'll find," corrects Angus, as he inspects the label, "you mean hair *of* the dog."

"Whatever."

Sharon returns, placing a shot glass, a metal camping cup, and a small soup bowl down on the table.

"Sorry, this is the best I could do."

Angus lunges for the bowl. "That'll do," he returns.

"What about a corkscrew?" I ask.

"Bolted to the front desk," answers Angus.

"Here, I'll go," I say.

143

"Isn't there a corkscrew that's supposed to be chained to this desk?" I ask Alan, eyeing aimlessly around.

Alan knocks on the counter. "Here," he snaps.

"Oh, thanks."

"Sometimes I wonder how you people even manage to get here from the airport," he carps.

I begin twisting the screw into the cork. "Often by shut-tle. Why do you have it chained down anyway?"

"Because they keep disappearing. We've already lost three," he blames, in his customarily abusive manner. "It's the only way to control you."

"Oh, okay."

"Are you kidding?" he asks. "Did I tell you what we found the day after the last party?"

"No, what?"

"Somebody peed outside the laundry room door."

"Sor-ry?"

"Yup," he says, walking out from behind the desk for extra emphasis. "Right *there*."

"That's pret-ty crazy."

"I know. And I can just picture the logic. They, no doubt one of the Irish, or possibly one of the Australians, thought it was the bathroom."

"Huh?"

"Thought it was a *locked* bathroom!" he emphasizes.

"I still don't get it, I'm afraid."

"So, he's standing *here*," Alan explains, demonstrating.

"Right."

"And he has to pee, right?"

"Yeah."

"And so he says to himself, 'Gee, it's locked. So, then, I guess I'll just have to pee here, on the door.' Get it?"

The severity of Alan's expression triggers a look of amusement across my own. "Yeah, I guess. That's pret-ty bad."

"You know who it was!" he accuses.

I draw the stubborn cork out of my bottle of wine. "No, Alan, of course I don't."

"Are you *lying?*" he asks.

"No, real-ly," I assure him.

"Okay. Well, anyway, I'm getting cameras put in."

"You are?"

"Yup, this was the last straw. Actually the last straw was last month. Some guy, thought he was Ozzie Osbourne, crapped *all* over the throne."

"That's a really good idea, you *should* get a camera," I encourage.

"Camera? Cameras! It'll really be great. Once we have cameras everywhere, there'll be no more *pissing* outside laundry room doors!"

"Indeed."

He points toward the adjacent internet zone.

"I'll get one here, and one *there*," he roars, as e-mailing travelers look up and flash shut-up-please glances in our direction.

This is when I suddenly spot Frances, that alcoholic girl from the laundry room, peering at me incisively from behind her computer. She is observing the bottle of wine in my hand with an expression of alarm.

Although I pretend not to notice her, something tells me my identity is in danger of becoming even more complicated than it already is.

Slumber Party

The weeks pass faster and faster. Between working here and at the inn, playing pool, and hanging around with the other hostellers, I still haven't had any time to do the most basic on-line research about England and Arundel. I guess I haven't exactly been making it a priority though. So far I've been lucky. At the same time, I'm still reasonable enough to know that this luck has to run out. And I resolve to start looking into the British basics – government, geography, and high school testing jargon – after the weekend.

Meanwhile, as luck wouldn't have it, on Sunday night, before the weekend ends and I have a chance to do the on-line research, Angus decides we aren't getting nearly enough time together during the day and insists on a slumber party in my dorm room.

"Alan would have a fit if he found out you were sleeping in here, you know," I remind him. In the eleventh hour, I'm still hoping to escape the inevitable intimacy and subsequent guilt of even the most platonic pillow-talk.

"I know," says Angus, from the bunk below mine. "But I checked the bed-sheet. There's plenty of space. And Zoella's on desk. She knows better than to check travelers in with staff if there's space in other rooms."

"Thank God for that. I really could use a few days off from all these tarty lit-tle tourists."

"I'd still rather be sharing with a few tarty girls than with the lads who're in my room this week," he observes.

"No, you can't imagine what it's like," I start. "The insipid perfume and all the faffing with plastic bags, first thing in the morning. Ask Sharon. The last girls staying in here were real-ly starting to do our heads in."

"Where is Sharon?"

"Still at Specs, I think."

"Oh. Still, better than beer farts," he continues, as rap music begins blasting forth from a car idling in the parking lot below our window. "The beer farts are unbearable. How's that new job going?"

"Oh, brill. And you know that thing you said about taking reservations? It's totally true. Today I had Hansgeorg Mouat on Bath Road. 'That's B-A-T-H.' And Mr. and Mrs. Bacchigaluppi on Ward road. 'That's W-A-R-D.'"

"I know, what *is* that?"

"I don't know, but it's bizarre."

"Americans! I'll have to stop by soon for some cheese and cracks though," he observes. "What else do you have there?"

"Bickies, duck mousse pate, olives, smoked salmon, cornichons, red wine."

He claps like a seal. "Cornichons, my favorite! I'll def be by."

"Okay, but give me another week or so to get more used to it," I suggest.

"What's your schedule like, then? Are you on tomorrow?"

"Yes. I'm doing three days a week."

"Three days? Plus working here?"

"Yup."

"You're really going to rake in the wonga."

"Yeah, but it's only for two months. Until the lady gets back from her maternity leave, remember?"

"Still, it's not like you have to pay for food or anything."

"I know, I figured it out. In two months I should be able to save about $2,400. If I'm careful."

"Then you're taking a flat?"

"Uh huh," I return, reluctantly. I think about how much I'd rather stay on at the hostel, *if only* I could do it legitimately.

"How joyless!"

"Well, I can't just live like this forever," I explain.

The relentless whine of a car alarm joins in with the still blaring rap.

"So why don't you go traveling?"

"What do you mean? I'd still have nothing to come back to."

"Dusty said he got by in India on like sixty U.S. dollars a week. You could stay for like six months at that rate, after the ticket."

"Real-ly?" I ask, incredulously.

"Aye, defo. As a Scotsman I reckon I could do it on even less."

"Wow!" I return, as concern over having no funds to return to becomes swiftly irrelevant in the context of a possible six and a half months off.

"I know."

Inspired, I consider the actual feasibility of doing it. "I always wanted to go to India, too," I say.

"So, sod the flat and splash out on a ticket," he advises.

"You know," I say, sensing a new adventure might be just the right compensation for having to leave the hostel, "I think I will. I'm going to do that."

"Amazing, then we'll all be flying out of here at around the same time."

"Yeah."

"It'll be like a mass exodus."

"Total-ly," I say. Then I roll over into the fetal position and reflect. "I have to say, I'll miss it here, though."

"Same."

"What is it about this place?"

"The constant influx of new talent," answers Angus.

"As well. But…"

"No, it has been a really good laugh. But by then, it should be enough, eh?"

"Actually, I don't know if I could ever get sick of it here," I admit. "I mean, I just feel so, so, I don't know… so free here."

"Well, it is pretty cushy, as work goes," Angus says.

"Yeah, but it's more than that. This place is magic. For the first time, stuff is clear for me."

"Huh?"

"I just feel like I've always been bombarded with all this… advertising. It's like I've tried to get away from it, but I never could. And this is the first place I've been where it's like the advertising doesn't reach me. Like we're under the radar or something. And I can finally think straight."

"Right."

"Like suddenly there's an absence of static. And things are so much less complicated. It's like my life is finally, I don't know – it's not a drag. And I'm not bogged down by… details. I'm not even… I don't even care anymore about what people from school would think if they knew I was cleaning Bagby. Like that girl Anna, from Belgium, didn't care that she was cleaning the toilets. It's as if there's something more going on. It's such a weird life here now, but it's a life I can feel. You know what I mean? I can finally *feel* my life. It's like this is the first place I've ever been where I'm not waiting to live. You know?"

"Aye."

"Yesterday," I continue, "it was so strange, but I had this revelation.

"Um."

"It's just that I realized my choices – the choices I've always

149

made – haven't even really been choices."

"You mean like you've let your family decide things for you?"

"No, not like that. It's more like I've realized my choices – they've just been reactions. Reactions to the decrees of the advertising, and based, more than anything, on a sort of fear of ridicule. It's like I've spent all these years basically trying to avoid something negative instead of going after what's real for me. And now I start to see I don't actually even want what I thought I wanted. It's like something can be out of your reach and below your standard at the same time, you know what I mean?"

"Crikey, girl, how much did you smoke?"

"I didn't smoke."

"You didn't?"

"No, really, I didn't. Why?"

"You just seem really passionate. Plus you're practically in an American accent. All drama-queen, like. I only get like that when I'm stoned."

"Oh, okay."

"I can relate, though. At school, like I told you, I was called Fatty Paddy. And after my first week here, I remember just stopping and saying to myself, 'Fuck me, I'm *popular!*' you know?"

"Yeah, I do. That's exactly what I mean," I say.

Suddenly, I feel that it would be possible to tell Angus about me. If I do it right now. I'll tell him everything – about how Gotthard went away, about how I panicked, about how I put on the fake accent just to qualify for the hostel.

"Angus, there's something I need to…"

"What kind of school did you go to anyway, Becky?" he interrupts.

"Pardon?"

"What kind of school did you go to?" he repeats, ambushing my momentum. "I bet you went to public school."

Unwillingly, I am cast back into the dishonest dimension.

"No, actually," I say, remembering that public means private, but not able to recall whether or not private is the term used for public.

"Really? You didn't?" he asks, astonished.

I opt for the only answer that can't be followed up with any questions about A-level scores or the name of my school.

"No, actually, I was... homeschooled."

"You're joking?"

"No."

"What was wrong with the schools in Arundel?"

"My parents were odd," I return.

"That *is* a bit bizarre."

"What about yours?" I counter, miserably defeated to be focusing, again, on cunning, after coming so close to striking an equal footing.

"I get on great with my mum, you know. Things are okay with my dad, now," he offers. "But, he was kind of freaked out, like, when I told him I was gay."

"Really?" I return, apprehensively. I ask myself if he'd really want to be sharing this kind of personal information with someone whose very nationality was being concealed from him.

"Yeah, I'll never forget that afternoon. I was at my cousin's... You know, it's funny," he says, interrupting himself. "I've never really talked about this with anyone. Except my best mate, Logan, of course. But, it's weird, I feel like I can be myself around you for some reason. I guess it's because you're always so much yourself, Becky. Odd, that."

The Morning After

As daylight pours in through the lace curtains of our dorm window, light eclipses dark, and feelings of guilt, again, subside. I stretch my arms over my head, more than anything relieved that something kept me from spilling the beans to Angus last night.

It's funny, too, because at the time, lying there, in that moment, it seemed like revealing the lie would've been the best thing I could've done. Only now, with the brightness of the day illuminating my perspective, can I see what a disaster it would've been. Like a drunken one night stand, this morning would have been a hungover mess for both of us. How betrayed Angus would feel. And how strange and uncomfortable our interaction would be now.

Instead, Angus and I shuffle into the kitchen together, familiarly, exhibiting all the fluent shorthand and physical ease of solid friendship.

Taking in the length of the breakfast line, Angus instructs, "Get our fruit and tea, Becky. I'll get our bagels going."

"Sliver mine into three," I remind him.

He looks at me blankly.

"Too stodgy otherwise," I elaborate.

"Don't micro-manage me, Becky," he snaps. "I *know!*"

"Oh, naff off," I return, taking my place in the tea line, behind Stacy.

Stacy offers a halfhearted acknowledgement.

"Hungover?" I initiate.

"How'd ya guess?" he asks, looking at me sarcastically through bloodshot eyes.

I gesture at the two packets of sugar disintegrating in his tea water.

"Well, for one thing you just threw your sugar bags in unopened. Plus your shirt is on inside out."

Glancing down at his cup, Stacy tosses its contents into the sink.

"Oh. Yeah. I guess I'm fairly thrashed today."

I survey the various mugs in search of the least stained one.

"What'd you do last night?" I ask.

"Started out at this place. Triumph," he says, as he draws himself a second cup of tea out of the big aluminum vat.

"Where?"

"Triumph. Natoma and Eighth."

"Oh."

"It was pretty lame," he says, eyeing my hand-knit wool hat.

I try to distinguish myself as independent of fad. "It's not for fashion, honey," I explain.

"Figured that one out," he ribs. "Anyway, it's supposed to be a good place," he continues, "but as it turned out last night was gay or *mixed* night. I mean, which is cool, the music was good just, no offense, but you know."

No offense?

His delivery on this point seems so natural that for a moment it's almost hard for me to tell whether Stacy really does think I'm just into women or, like Angus said he was, is just pretending to think I am in order to lessen what he felt to be a personal rebuff that night in the sauna.

Regardless, determined to spell out my interest in him, I lean back against the wall and gaze at him super attentively.

"You know," he justifies, oblivious to my communication. "Just with the rest of the blokes being out on the pull."

Wearing a tacky little grin, I now resort to cheap flirtation in an attempt to emphasize my interest.

"The *rest* of the blokes?" I ask.

But he's too busy with his own marketing campaign to recognize mine. "Course, I don't go out to pull," he explains.

I reach for a spoon, contriving to be in need of milk stirring, in an attempt to draw out our conversation. "Duly noted," I reply, coyly.

But he just nudges me in the arm and wanders off, unaffected by my wiles.

****

Barely managing to balance the two cups of tea and the plates of fruit, I then make my way out of the kitchen and over to the long rectangular table in the middle of the rec room at which Angus is already seated. Isaac, approaching the table at the very same time, catches one of the fruit plates just as it slips from my hand.

"You're wearing too much cologne," Angus censures.

"Don't wear cologne," Isaac discards, mid yawn. "Don't even wear deodorant."

A self-conscious looking new arrival lowers himself onto a chair diagonal from ours.

"Sorry," he volunteers. "Could be me."

Angus gets up and crawls toward him, dragging his worn, carroty-colored moccasin across the table top in the process.

"Yuh," he verifies, sniffing him from about a foot away. "It's definitely you."

"Sorry," repeats the traveler, though with a tone now indicating some degree of indignation.

Angus settles back into his own seat. "No worries. Just I can't taste my bagel. Not that it tastes of much anyway. But kind of early in the morning to be all tarted-up, isn't it?"

"Well, I am on holiday," tries the abused visitor.

"Where from?"

"London."

"How long are you here for?"

Looking relieved to be off the topic of his cologne, he replies, "Depends. How long does it take to see San Francisco?"

"One day, really," returns Angus, flippantly. "Isaac, don't you think one day is long enough to see San Francisco?"

"Maybe two," considers Isaac. "Don't stay for twenty-six years though. That's way too long."

"But, don't bore us with your life story," barks Angus.

"Oh, right," concedes Isaac.

The traveler takes an unhurried glance around the room.

"This must've been a pretty nice space in its day," he comments. "Imagine if they fixed it up, like?"

"No, I like it this way. I like the faded glamour. The decrepit elegance," corrects Angus.

"You're quite the arbitrary contrarian today," I observe.

"It's because I'm fed up with mornings and the fact that I can never get a lie-in around here," Angus snaps.

"Ride the chaos. You can't try to resolve it," muses Isaac. "That's what you have to do. You'll never resolve it."

"Well somebody was riding something last night," Angus states.

"Oh, I know," I confirm. "It was totally over the top, wasn't it?"

"The people staying above Becky were shagging like *crazy* in the middle of the night," Angus explains. "Our bunk was even shaking – and it's attached to the wall! Then all of a sudden they both just stopped. It was totally perverted, like. Not to mention totally rude toward me and Becky below, to make us listen to that."

"Yeah, it's like, what did they take us for? Filthy little voyeurs?" I add.

A pensive look comes over Angus's face. "Yeah," he says. "It's almost as if they knew us so well already."

"Was it around 4:30 a.m.?" Isaac asks.

"Yes, why?" interrogates Angus, wildly. "Was it *you?*"

"No," returns Isaac. "There was an earthquake this morning."

"Seriously?"

"Yeah, it was a five."

"Oh, wicked. My first earthquake!" Angus shouts. "Was it really?"

"Umm, someone smells lovely," interjects Sharon, as she pulls up a chair.

A look of vindication steals across the new arrival's face. He even rises a little from his seat to claim credit.

"Morning," he remarks. "Nick."

Sharon makes a flirtatious little bow in his direction. "Yeah, really nice," she says.

"Definitely too early in the morning for this kind of tawdriness," declares Angus.

"You have toothpaste on your face," Sharon says, pointing to the corner of Angus's mouth.

"Please, are you that stuck for conversation?" he snaps.

She represses a patronizing smirk. "Touchy."

"Hey, doesn't that girl look just like Rebecca? Only with straight hair and without the double chin?" Angus deflects, pointing across the room.

"Dou-ble chin!? I don't have a dou-ble chin!" I exclaim.

"Well, not quite double, then."

"Sod off."

"Anyway, anybody up for MOMA?" Sharon asks, glancing around the table. "It's free today."

"What's MOMA, then?" asks Nick.

"Museum of Modern Art," she replies.

"Yeah. Why not? I'd be up for that," he says.

"Great! How about you lot? Becky?" Sharon asks, dutifully, so Nick won't think she's too interested.

"I have to work," I say.

"You do? Again?" she asks.

"Afraid so."

"You grafter, you!" she exclaims. "You work all the time, don't you?"

"I know, I'm going to go to India at the end of next month though. I've got to save," I announce.

"You are?"

"Yup," I confirm, as I notice, aside from having to speculate on what grafter might mean, that I feel like an official hosteller – at last.

A Glutton for Punishment

As I make my way through the thick San Francisco fog to my Filbert Street Inn job, I think, again, about how pleased I am that I resisted confessing to Angus last night. Everything is going so smoothly now. I mean, yes, there are near collisions every day, but I'm almost growing accustomed to their regular rhythms. And, moreover, I have two jobs, money, food, shelter, friendship, and travel plans. It's funny, it seems like the bolder I am and the more I embrace my facade, the *better* things are getting.

Still, in an effort to err on the side of vigilance, shortly after I settle in for my shift, as I promised myself I would, I pull a map of England up on the internet and attempt a quick review of the counties.

Within a quarter of an hour, however, my study is cut short. An English guy with a long nose and an extra long set of sideburns needs my help arranging a shuttle van to the airport.

"Cheers, appreciate it," he says, as he takes the receipt from my hand.

Though his accent is on the urbane side, his poor posture, together with the old sweater he's wearing, which looks about two sizes too small, lend him a regular air.

"So, where abouts' in the UK are you from?" he adds, familiarly.

"Oh, Arundel, West Sussex," I toss off.

"Oh, right," he says, smiling to himself. "I'd have said Surrey."

Bearing in mind the map and county locales I've just finished reviewing, I'm pleased to be able to supply something more specific than my stock "yes, right" reply.

"Not far off," I affirm. "How about you?"

He looks at me dryly, defying me to suppose he could be from anywhere else. "London."

His girlfriend collapses on the couch. "We've been shopping all day. We're just shattered," she chips in.

I wander over to the afternoon hors d'oeuvres table and load my plate up with cornichons and hexagon-shaped pieces of dill-havarti.

"Get anything good?" I ask.

"Lots of underwear," she replies.

"Right, that's always nice."

"It is! Especially because finding a bra is so hard for me. See, I have a big cup, but I'm just *tiny* around the back!"

Though feeling increasingly like the only proper English person in the room, I feel obliged to offer some kind of reply.

"Yes, right," I say.

She raises her right leg. "And I got the most fabulous new shoes. See?"

She's acting like an American.

"Oh, fabulous!" I indulge. "What else did you get?"

"Fantastic new trainers!"

"And where are they?" I ask.

"Up in the room."

"Let's see them," I encourage, wondering why I'm pretending to be so excited about this.

"Really, you want to see them? Okay," she says, jumping up.

"Bring mine down, as well!" the boyfriend calls behind her.

"Actually, I think I'll show you tomorrow," she suddenly decides. "I'm knackered. I'm going to turn in so I'll be in top form for *more* shopping tomorrow. What was your name, Miss?"

"Rebecca."

"Well, goodnight, Rebecca. Goodnight, Daniel, my pet."

"We've been on an around-the-world for the last nine months," he explains, blowing a goodnight kiss to his girlfriend. "We're a little excited to shop. Products! You know?"

"Yes. Definitely. I can imagine. Where were you?"

"Mostly India and Southeast Asia."

"Oh, really? How was it?"

"Great. Hard work. But great."

"I'm planning…"

"Bloody hard work."

"Why was it such hard work?"

"You know, the constant hassle."

"Right. I'm actually going to be going…"

"We were quite literally hassled the whole time."

"Real-ly?"

"Yeah, well, we've been going around the world for nine months," he repeats. "We go back to London next month."

"Are you ready to go back?" I follow up, surrendering to the one-way nature of the new acquaintance.

"No, not really. Actually, we'd like to stay in San Francisco. Love it here. I'm just trying to figure out how we could do it."

"Well, what do you do?" I ask, noticing a configuration of moles on his left cheek resembling the Little Dipper.

"We make documentary films. Well, I do. Chelsea used to."

"Oh, that's interesting. What sorts of assignments… or projects do you do?" I ask, tongue-tied. Suddenly I am feeling restricted by my presumed social status.

"Well, before I left I was helping to produce *Faking It*. Do you know it?"

"No, I'm afraid I don't," I admit.

He reaches for a cookie. "Oh."

"What's *Faking It?*" I persist.

"Oh, it's a documentary series. RDF Media for Channel four. It's kind of like a make-over spoof series. Basically, each program follows a volunteer from one walk of life who lives and trains with top practitioners, famous in their own fields, who tutor the faker. The volunteer is then given four weeks to master a skill well enough to fool a group of experts."

"How cle-ver."

"Yeah, it's quite clever, really."

"What's an example of an episode then?"

"Well, let's see. On one we took this sort of soft-spoken Oxford-educated chap and had him train with Tony Agastini, a kickboxing champion. Four weeks later he was hard enough to work as a doorman at the Hippodrome."

"Brilliant! What else?"

"We had this other episode," he continues, with a widening grin. "Reverend Nigel Done. Vicar to secondhand car salesman."

"So, you mean," I cut in, delighting over the notion of a plot within a plot within a plot. "It's people who fake being someone else entirely?"

"Right."

"Sounds pretty pioneering."

"Yeah, well it is. Though a mate of mine on the show and I are actually trying to introduce a splinter version of the series, wherein we cop onto something real, some kind of genuine con, already in progress, and follow that. I think that could be pretty mental. Blimey, if I could find something going on in San Fran, I might actually be able to stay on."

"Isn't that interesting?" I say.

"Yeah, it's okay," he allows, a little dismissively.

Feeling typecast as an uncreative fawning inferior struggling to sound clever enough, I sneak in a creative-by-association reference.

"Someone I know just graduated from the doc program at Berkeley," I say. "She just graduated and is already finding a lot of work."

"Really?" he asks.

For a moment his glance seems to suggest that perhaps I'm not quite so regional as I seem.

I angle for authority. "Yes, there's a lot of work going, I'm sure."

He scribbles his information on the back of a napkin. "Here, get him to e-mail me some good doc companies. Give him my e-mail address."

"Her. Sure," I say, taking the address from his hand.

"Right."

"So, meanwhile," I continue, "you're looking for a scenario where somebody's conning or faking something, right?"

"Yes, but it isn't exactly something you just come across. It takes a lot of asking around, observing, staying somewhere for a while, networking, scouting."

"I'll keep an eye out. I might know of something," I say.

He bites into a macadamia nut chocolate chip cookie with a look that suggests he won't be holding his breath.

I smile back, pride dented. "No, actually, I think I do know of something," I add.

His expression is condescending. "Oh yeah?"

"Yeah, as a matter of fact, I *do* know of something."

Putting his cookie down, he pushes his sunglasses up onto his forehead and leans forward.

"What's that, then?" he asks.

I like his showing a little interest in me. Or more to the point, I like being treated as less overtly inconsequential.

"It's just that I...," I begin. But, as usual, the fear of repercussions narrowly outweighs the craving for release, leaving me as impotent as ever.

"Oh, I don't know," I say, pulling back.

He stands up and withdraws his attention. "Right."

"I'm faking being an alcoholic," I blurt out.

"What do you mean?"

"I mean I go to AA meetings."

He laughs out of his nose, a half-amused, half-perplexed sort of laugh. "Why would you do that?"

Surprising myself a little, I go on, in earnest, to disclose to him the whole AA-Gotthard correlation, to which he replies, "Well, that's *sort* of endearing but I'd need something a bit more…"

"I also fake…"

"What?"

It's a stalemate. A lose-lose. If I don't tell, this pretentious cad gets to write me off. If I do tell, I vindicate my pride, but at the expense of my own discretion. Yet, just as I conclude that I can't justify telling this guy everything just to spare myself from feelings of momentary mediocrity, an unlikely third option comes into view. And, once again, I find myself standing at the threshold of a very bad idea.

"Being American," I answer, walking through. "I fake being American."

"What are you on about?"

"I fake being American, at the AA meetings. At the hostel, where I stay, I just fake being an alcoholic-in-recovery."

"Why on earth would you fake being American?"

"Good question. Just for fun, I guess."

"You're batty, you know that? A real nut. But, I like it."

"Thanks?"

"What about faking being an alcoholic-in-recovery at the hostel, though? I mean, I can get the whole thing with your ex-boyfriend, I guess, and why you like those meetings, but why would you bother doing it where you live as well, if you aren't really one?"

I'm a little confused about how to best answer him since, of course, in fact I'm *not* faking being an alcoholic-in-recovery at the hostel, despite the fact that Frances, the true alcoholic-in-recovery there, believes I'm an alcoholic-in-denial.

"I don't know," I reply. "Just something to do, I guess. But, I just thought, since you're looking for something going on now, I'd…"

He has a far-away look in his eye, as if he isn't listening to me anymore. I begin to shrink. Just as I do, though, suddenly, like a composer preparing to conduct a symphony, he throws his arms into the air:

"Girl, as English as tuppence, successfully fakes being a Yank-in-recovery in the Golden State," he commences.

"I like it," I say.

"No, scratch that," he says. *"Brit-abroad gets into recovery – American-style. A Yank prank in the Golden State."*

"Even bet-ter."

"Brit backpacker fakes sobriety at debauched youth hostel," he continues.

I nod along enthusiastically.

"You know, I think there actually might be something here."

"Do you real-ly think?"

"I do. I think we could be onto something. What I'll need to do is get some sample footage in the next few days. Get some of you at an AA meeting and some of you at the hostel. Then, I'll run it by my commissioning editor. See if he's interested. If he is, I mean, believe me, everything takes ages in my field, but if he likes it they may very well let me come back to shoot it with a proper crew. That could float me in America for at least a couple months, by the time we finish the editing. And who knows what could open up by then, if I get some contacts here. I could actually make some money off this."

"Sure."

"But, hang on, Rachel. Let's hear you first?"

"It's Rebecca."

"Well, Rebecca, then," he snaps. "Talk. In the American accent."

"Hi Daniel, what brings you to America?" I say, in my own voice.

"More."

"There's an AA meeting tonight at ten o'clock. We could go as soon as my shift ends. I mean, you wouldn't be able to film at the meeting, naturally, but you could get the flavor," I propose.

"Now *that's* not a bad American accent," he observes. "Not bad, indeed."

Keeping it Real

Following my shift, Daniel and I set out together along Bay Street to catch the second half of the ten o'clock AA meeting. The fog is so thick tonight that as we walk along we knock into one other constantly, apologizing more often than green tennis players.

"How far is this place? I don't know how much longer I can walk side by side with you," he says.

"About twenty more minutes. Why don't you walk on the other side of the street, then?"

"Listen," he starts, changing the subject, "the more I think about this thing, the more possibilities I think it has."

Through the dark haze I glance over at him. He's one of those people whose thoughts are right there on his face. At the moment he looks even more cunning and scheming than I feel. And it's calming to feel the less calculating one, for a change.

"Like what?" I ask.

"Well, I'm thinking, what if... I mean..." He looks at me conspiratorially. "What'd *really* be full-on is if you were actually faking being American at the hostel, too. Can you picture it?"

"But they already know I'm Eng-lish," I remind him.

"Yes, but what if you checked into a *new* hostel, where nobody knew you? You could actually fake out the other Brits themselves. I mean, wouldn't that be a gaff? Imagine it! You'd be among your own, and they wouldn't even know it!"

It takes some restraint to contain myself. At least in theory, I'm dying to divulge to him that said gaff is already in progress, only dissimilarity being I'm *not* one of the Brits, but they think I *am*.

"I suppose."

"But, do you reckon you could ever actually maintain it around the clock?" he challenges.

"Exactly, I don't know that I'd have the cheek for *that*."

"I imagine it'd be an issue of stamina, not cheek," he suggests.

"Perhaps."

"Right. Never mind, the way it is is good enough for now. But, speak in the American accent until we get there, would you? Let's get you warmed up. I want this to be perfect. Where'd you pick it up anyway?"

"The accent?"

"Right."

I relax into my own voice. "Oh, the movies mainly, I suppose."

"Movies," he imitates, with an amused chuckle. "You *really* do a bloody good job with it. Sounds very natural."

"Do you really think?" I ask.

Listening to my real voice again, after such a long time, I notice it sounds a little unusual, even almost – foreign.

"Definitely, it's spot on, isn't it? I mean, you should hear mine."

"Really?"

"Do you want to hear mine, then?"

"Go on."

He stops walking and turns away from me. Then he swallows dramatically, as if preparing to spit to the other side of Bay Street. In a bizarre Southern drawl, he exclaims, "Hey you guys, how's it going?"

"That's not bad," I say.

"No, it's crap. Give me a pointer or two."

"Well, I think it's a different intonation, is the thing."

"Give us an example?"

"It's more disjointed or something. It's like 'Hey you guys' with the emphasis on *you*. Get it?"

"Okay, okay. How's this then? 'I'm going to fucking blow you up, Jack!'"

"Yes, that's more it, but less simpering. It's like…"

"You mother fucker!" he shouts over me.

"Nearly, if you…"

But he's on a roll. "You lookin' at *me?*"

As Daniel continues to spew hard-hitting lines from the standbys, I reflect on the inherent silliness of everything. As if a reality show about faking it isn't absurd enough, faking that I'm faking it really promises to keep me on my toes.

After a while, though, he goes quiet. He has that scheming look on his face again and I suspect his thoughts are now tied up with putting together his proposal for the episode or something. So I stop talking, too, and we meander together through the streets of San Francisco in silence, for a while.

Out of the silence, some inevitable self-censure, of the *what am I doing?* variety resurfaces for me. It's not the latest lie, as such, that triggers this, but just the whole web in general that trips me up in the moments I have to myself.

It seems the best way to avoid coming up against my own conscience nowadays is just to not stop talking. And to not stop inventing. Stillness, I think, is the biggest threat to the delicate eco-system of the lies.

But to manage the inevitable worries that *do* slip through the cracks, I also must constantly rationalize why going overboard, in some twisted way, makes perfect sense.

I consider this rationale as akin to borrowing $80,000 in student loans. Then borrowing $40,000 more, because another $40,000 doesn't actually make a whit of difference once there's no way I can make the minimum monthly payments anyway.

With the debt, it's illogical, but the higher it gets, the *less* fear I'm in, because paying it, at all, becomes less and less of a possibility. The loans then become almost just a concept in the backdrop of my reality. Therefore, in a funny way, the more out of control things get, the more they fall back into perspective.

So, this is my rationale for the moment. Because with this, too, despite all of the risk involved, I can tell you, there is also a certain element of freedom that comes from being completely, rather than partially, in over my head.

In any case, by the time Daniel and I arrive at the meeting house, it's already 10:30 p.m. Although we've missed the main-speaker portion of the meeting, we arrive in time to hear the shorter individual shares from the rest of the room. As we scurry to find seats, several hands are already up in the air.

"Let's hear from the guy in the green hoodie," says the secretary.

"Hi, I'm Alex, alcoholic," begins the guy in the green hoodie.

"Hi Alex," returns the room.

"Yeah, I've been feeling really easily triggered lately," he continues. "It's just difficult to cope sometimes with all the demands I feel there are on me. I just feel really tapped-out lately. Pardon the pun. I've been building up a lot of resentments, too, which I know I can't afford. And what I really need is to check-in with myself more. To put my program, my meditation, first. I guess it's like the wheel of a bike. My program *has* to be the hub, and the spokes go out to the rest of my life. But if I don't take care of the hub, the rest of the wheel doesn't roll."

Immediately, I am drawn in by his share. It's not only the content that attracts me, but some peculiar aptitude everybody in here seems to have for speaking openly. The fact that each person who speaks actually seems comfortable in their own skin is awe-inspiring to me. And light years away.

"I wasn't an alcoholic. I was just this unlucky, depressed guy who threw up on people," jokes the next person.

After about fifteen minutes Daniel, who apparently has not been receiving the same hit from the shares that I have, leans over to me and whispers, "I'm going to step outside for some fresh air. Meet me outside afterwards."

I signal to him that I've understood and to stop whispering. Then I listen carefully to each share until the meeting draws to a close.

As we did last time, we then stand in a circle and hold hands. Only this time we say the Lord's Prayer. The earnestness in the voices around me, and in my own, is killing. I find I even have to go so far as to brace my voice from audible quivering. On some level I guess it's like I'm just so far away from myself, from who I was meant to be. And for some reason saying the prayer out loud makes me feel it, if only for a moment.

****

When I get outside, Daniel is nowhere to be seen. I'm annoyed. He may have just slipped off to get a slice of pizza. But another side of me suspects he may have split. And this possibility serves to confirm, big time, that I made the right choice in not trusting him with the true lie.

In the meantime, two circles have formed outside the meeting house. Roaming around the outskirts, I try to figure out where I might be able to mix in most casually. Although the fellowship seems integrated, one circle seems to be made up more of newcomers, puffing away on cigarettes, while the other is made up of people with some "time" under their belts.

Feeling more like a newcomer than a veteran, I wander over to the first group. Without any angling, I am welcomed into the fold.

Unlike at the hostel, where there is a mandatory hazing period, here I feel accepted right away. And the general lack of pretension proves contagious. Before long, I am talking freely about my own struggle with "alcohol," secretly referring to Gotthard as I do, and receiving all kinds of applicable feedback.

When I see Alex, the first guy who shared tonight, I walk right up to him. "Hey," I say, "I really liked what you were saying in there. I could relate."

He offers me his hand. "Oh, thanks. I'm Alex."

"Rebecca."

"So, what's been going on for you?" he asks.

"Well, just getting the hang of it."

"So, you're doing okay?"

"Yeah. For me, it really comes down to total abstinence," I say.

"Right on, it's so simple, but it's so key to keep it simple. *Just* don't pick up."

"Yeah, I definitely can't afford to pick up," I say. Naturally, I am referring to the phone, and to my decision not to call Gotthard anymore.

"It's really that simple," he says.

"Yeah, for sure. Because once I do, it's a slippery slope. The disease is subtle but it's insidious, and it's always so tempting. It's like each time you think it's going to work, and each time it lets you down. It's always just an illusion of security, of salvation. And actually it brings the opposite. It's like trying to fasten yourself onto a tornado, for safety," I riff.

"You've got it in a nutshell. Awareness is the key. It's a simple program. We're granted a daily reprieve, based on the maintenance of our spiritual condition. Not a complicated deal."

"Well," I start, "I really dug your metaphor about the wheel."

"Whoa!" he shouts suddenly. "Something just moved!"

"What?"

171

He points. "Over there, in that bush. I think there's someone in that bush!"

I whip around to see some reflective glass moving within the bush at which Alex is pointing. Immediately I know who it is.

"Scuse me folks," starts Daniel, stumbling out from behind the shrub with his camera perched on his shoulder. "I know this is meant to be anonymous, but you wouldn't mind if I got just a little footage here, would you? I couldn't get the right light from back there," he explains.

Feeling, to some extent, like an honorary alcoholic, my first inclination is to safeguard my community from the obnoxious intrusion.

Employing an English expression to ensure the clearest possible communication, albeit in a fully American accent, I state, firmly, "Daniel, this is *not* on!"

"Okay, okay," he concedes. "Calm down."

The rest of the group seems equally taken aback.

"Rest assured everybody," he placates, "*some* of your voices were *vaguely* in the background, but only she was on camera. I only had the camera on Rebecca, I swear."

But his justification doesn't fly.

"Why is this man filming us, or you?" a woman asks me.

Like someone who fires before aiming, I answer before thinking.

"Oh, I actually do a small reality show for British television," I improvise. "It's about ex-patriots. Like me. Living in… England."

"I'm not sure I'm following," she replies. "Why is this guy here, filming us?"

The only thing I can think of that could possibly explain the situation (aside from the truth which is, of course, always out of the question) is, "I guess you could say, for the lack of a better phrase… that I'm a little bit of… well, of a minor celebrity there."

She looks at me doubtfully, and I am suddenly convinced that sober people may be better than regular people at discerning lies.

"I'd say more, but I'd prefer to remain anonymous," I reply, pretending to interpret her skepticism as added interest, in order to bring the conversation to a close.

She turns away from me. "Paparazzi at an Anonymous meeting," she comments. "Now that's rich."

Meanwhile, I figure Daniel will quit while he's ahead. I figure he'll offer a token thank-you wave and veer off the free exit ramp. But, I'm wrong. Rather, he blathers on. And on.

He is attempting to smooth things over, presumably in order to preserve relations for future filming opportunities.

"Folks, no disrespect intended. Really," he persists, obsequiously. "My auntie's husband is an alcoholic. If ever there was one, that man knows how to put away the lager. Not that he's in AA or anything, like you lot. But he probably should be!"

The worst part, of course, is that as Daniel is offering his version of an amends, he is also continuing to fiddle obsessively with his camera, still trying to adjust the light.

Finally, Alex walks over to Daniel. "Excuse me, man," Alex says. "But this whole shtick doesn't really work for us. We're trying to keep it real, you know?"

"Oh, believe me, I know all about that."

"Huh?"

"That's what *I'm* trying to do," explains Daniel. "I'm trying to keep it real, too. Look, if you must know, my show is a virtual *reality* show, okay?"

"Sure, brother, that's cool. But, some of us aren't feelin' the being filmed part. I know I'm not. It's all cool. But, if you wouldn't mind just kind of stepping off, that'd be appreciated, okay?"

Backing Alex up, I try to shoot Daniel a look that tells him I'm not going to play at being American anymore if he doesn't stop.

Catching onto something in my look, Daniel finally surrenders.

He switches off his camera and with words that don't suit him replies, "Okay, peace, brother."

Then, like a couple of vampires, Daniel and I vanish together back into the vapor.

****

"You real-ly shouldn't have done that," I say, once Daniel and I are out of earshot. "It was bang out of order."

"I know, mate, but I couldn't resist, I'm a filmmaker. I could say I'm sorry, but I wouldn't mean it. It's what I do. Nothing is sacred. And that's the way it should be. If you want the truth."

I think about how much saner it must be, in a way, to have both feet in, the way Daniel does, rather than one foot on the brakes and one foot on the gas all the time, like I do.

"Well, you ought to have some scruples, you know?" I say.

"Fine, but I don't. Anyway, you started this whole thing."

"True, but I told you not to film there, didn't I?"

"Anyway, let's change the subject. What's done is done. More importantly, I have to say, you were really on-point back there. I think you've got a real knack for the American accent. I really do."

"Stop," I protest.

"No, seriously. I mean, *I* can hear just the slightest tinge of self-consciousness in your voice, you know a sort of, 'Am I really pulling this off?' But rest assured, only *I* would ever pick up on it."

"Oh, really?" I ask.

"No, I'm just very attuned, that's all," he explains. "It's only because I've been with the series from the beginning. My ear is hyper-sensitized to the con. But, believe me, don't worry. Nobody else would ever catch it."

"So, you real-ly reckon I can pull it off, then?"

"I do. It's a skill, frankly."

"You think?"

"How many English do you know who can nail it that well? Hell, the Americans themselves couldn't tell the difference, could they? And that lot was stone-sober."

"Yes, I suppose you're right. We do have a hard time with the American accent, don't we?"

For a moment our exchange hits me as sheer comic absurdity. But then something else occurs to me. Oddly, after such a long leave-taking from my real voice, speaking *American* actually *is* requiring some effort on my part. And this effort is probably what Daniel is hearing. Fortunately for me, however, although his instincts are sharp, his conclusions still lead him off course.

"Can you do the Brooklyn accent?" he resumes.

"No, I shouldn't think so. I just do the generic American mostly."

"I actually quite like your version of the Yank accent, in particular," he says.

"Thanks."

"Yeah, some of them are really awful, don't you find? Especially here, in California. Have you noticed how loudly the people speak? What's going on with that?"

"I have, yes. Especially when they're on their mobiles. It's like they're all trying to be famous."

"Precisely. They do seem generally more confident than we do though, don't you find?"

"Americans?"

"Yes."

"I don't. No. It's more like more like they're generally more unconscious. It's a fine line."

"I just think it's great here. It's like see what you want and take it. It's the American way. No apologizing, no beating around the bush, like we do, just out with it."

"No, I disagree, I think that's precisely the problem here. That's why I like AA. People in the rooms are how I imagine Americans used to be. You know, in 1940's movies or something."

"Yeah, the place just reeked of Vivien Leigh, didn't it? Just what I was thinking."

"No, I'm serious. What I mean is they're kind and considerate of each other in there. And isn't that what glamour is, in the end? 'The whole of heraldry and chivalry lies in courtesy,' said Emerson, I think. In general, the prob-lem with some of the Americans now is that they're to-tal-ly self-centered. They're not attuned to anybody else. It's like they're always impinging on your space, to-tal-ly unconsciously. I'd say their *presence* impinges on my space. But it's not even that. It's more like their *lack* of presence does. It's like they're not here, but their pollution is, you know?"

"Yeah," he says. "I really want to be a part of it."

"It's not just that," I continue, parroting a theory I overheard, in an attempt to persuade him against the Americans. "What's also really annoying is the way people here have this self-conscious overemphasis on irony. It's a cynical perspective. So much of American contemporary culture is based on the ironic reference. Especially in California, I see so many people, things that are not authentically ironic... There's this need to sort of shoe-horn them into an ironic experience. But it's a very low level ob-ser-va-tion... that's forced... and is like, it's just, it's inauthentic... in its low level."

"I'll agree with you there. If what you're saying is that its worst point is its best point," he replies.

But I don't even know what I'm saying or talking about at this point. And as we approach the inn I just smile inwardly, because I realize Daniel seems to be finding some form of freedom in modern American culture the same way I'm finding it among his compatriots.

"Look, so I think I got some pretty good footage tonight," he says. "What I'll need to do is come by the hostel, tomorrow, too. I think tomorrow late afternoon would be good. Say at five o'clock. Get some more. Footage of you not drinking, surrounded by your pissed mates, for instance. Of your pulling off being in recovery. You know, to prove you're leading the double life you say you are."

Take Three

The next morning, with plenty of legwork to be done before Daniel arrives, I head downstairs for an aberrant 7:15 a.m. breakfast. My first order of business will be to set the (new) record straight with Frances, the real alcoholic-in-recovery. And I figure the surest way to check that one off my list is to stake out the rec room. The problem is that three hours and four bagels later, Frances still hasn't made an appearance.

By two o'clock, after checking her room, the rec room, the internet zone, the laundry room, and the sauna, at regular thirty-minute intervals, I finally conclude Frances must be off at Alcoholics Anonymous doing one of her meeting-marathons, as she refers to them.

Half giving up, I pass the rest of the afternoon playing Scrabble with Angus, while sporadically glancing out the rec room window to the street, in hopes of catching Frances's return.

"So, explain it one more time then," Angus asks.

"I told you, he's a doc-u-men-tary filmmaker, and he's doing a piece on youth managing to stay sober in par-ty-environments."

Angus is quick to mock.

"A *piece?*"

"Or, a show," I snap. "What-ev-er you want to call it."

"And so basically you're pretending you don't drink just so you can get on tele?"

I choose not to confuse matters more by telling Angus the show is actually about faking it. And that Daniel *knows* I'm faking being sober, but that Angus and the others aren't supposed to… and that *that's* the story.

"Yes, in a nutshell."

"You must have a lot of time on your hands, Becky."

"I know it sounds a bit bat-ty. But just play along, all right?"

Angus shuffles his letters around and peers up at me with a wily grin.

"Okay?" I press.

He quietly places all seven of his letters down on the board.

"Xenophobe," he announces.

"Well done, well done," I say.

"I'd say so. Forty-six points well done, that is."

"Yes, the only thing is," I continue, "I don't exactly know *how* he's going to go about get-ting the clips. So, just, the im-por-tant thing is not to let on, okay?"

Angus is busy recording his score on the inside of the box's worn lid.

"I'll see."

"Oh, c'mon, please?"

"Okay, okay! Just stop *pestering* me!"

"Cheers, you're a real mate."

"Don't mention it. I'll pretend I don't drink either. It's about time I got on tele, frankly."

"Sure," I say. "I mean, Frances, do you know Frances?"

"Zany green-haired girl who never drinks?"

"Well, yeah, I was just going to say she's sober, too."

Angus glances out the window absentmindedly. "Look at *that* one. He's a bit of a dish, isn't he?"

I squint to get a look at a scrawny guy with mirrored aviator glasses and messy black curls wandering in circles on the corner.

"Oh pants! That's *him!*"

"Who?"

"Daniel. The filmmaker. The guy who's coming here. God, is it already five?"

"It's not even half four."

"Shite," I reply. "What is he doing here so early? I haven't even got-ten a chance to talk to Frances yet."

"Well, it doesn't look like he's massively in a hurry," Angus points out.

I look back at Daniel who, indeed, is just sort of idling around on the Montgomery steps, lazily playing with his phone.

"No, I suppose you're right. Maybe he's waiting for someone, or something."

"He's quite dishy, though, in his own way," Angus observes. "I go for that skinny rat look. Anyway, I'm going to go change out of this shite. If I'm going to be on tele, I'm damn well going to look better than *this.*"

****

Right after Angus exits the rec room, Frances enters. Just in the nick of time.

"Frances!" I shout. "I've been looking for you *all* day."

She makes her way over to my booth.

"I know, Zoella told me to come find you as soon as I got in. Why? What's up?"

"Look, can I talk to you for a minute?"

She nods her head.

"Well, why don't you sit down," I say, motioning to the freshly taped-up plastic booth. "It's a bit serious."

Like a crab, Frances inches herself sideways into the booth, until we're face to face. "What is it, Rebecca? You look so anxious."

"You know," I start, "how we met in the laundry room?"

"Huh?"

"The first time? You know, after you'd seen me at the AA meeting?"

"Yes?"

"Well, I haven't been letting on, but the thing is, since then I've actually giv-en quite a lot of thought to what you said that night."

A satisfied expression overtakes her face.

"I *am* an alcoholic," I preempt.

Without missing a beat, she applauds, as if I'm announcing myself at a meeting.

"I'm Rebecca, and I'm an alcoholic," I repeat, echoing her joke.

"Hi Rebecca," she replies. "But, seriously, that's great! Now you can start treating your disease. Because one leg in and one leg out is the definition of hell."

"Too right, Frances. Anyway, so I'm sober. I have been for days. But the rea-son I wanted to mention this to you ASAP is because, well, there's this guy com-ing here today. He'll be here in about fifteen minutes and he's making a doc-u-men-tary about the challenges young people face staying so-ber in depraved drinking environments. And so I just thought I'd tell you so you'd under-stand why he's here and why I'm saying I'm so-ber. Because, well, I am."

"Wow! That's really exciting, Rebecca. It's amazing, actually. Just like that. But that's the way it happens, you know. It's like a divine intervention. One day you just wake up and you're sick and tired of being sick and tired. Congratulations."

****

A half an hour later I am summonsed to the lobby for the guest sign-in ritual. It's a pretty random piece of bureaucracy if ever there was one, considering the fact that once they're signed in they can drink, puke and affront until their heart's content, without ever receiving an ounce of flak.

In any case, there I collect Daniel, waiting patiently in quarantine, and officially vouch for him.

"Hi, mate, sorry I'm late," he starts. "Had a ridiculous amount of details to deal with and got all caught up on a conference call. You know, the usual tedium. Such is life as a part of the media, I guess."

"Funny, I could've sworn that was you out there pacing back and forth for the last half hour on the corner. Was that not you?"

"Oh, sod off," Daniel replies. "Let's just get on with this, shall we?"

I touch his shoulder tentatively before we adjourn to the rec room.

"Listen, I have some other friends you might want to talk to, as well, okay?"

He talks under his breath. "Are they faking it, too?"

I tell him all about Angus and Frances, about how he is and she isn't, and hope I can at least manage to help Angus get his two minutes.

Back inside, after a token round of introductions, Daniel is eager to begin the interviews. Although his rush-rush pace seems a little put-on (considering the fact that he hung around outside for over a half an hour before even bothering to come in) his agitation is also infectious. In another minute Frances and I find ourselves tripping over each other for air time.

"It's a unique sort of challenge," explains Frances. "But, you know, I try not to get into self-pity around it. I mean, I'm relocating to San Francisco from Canada, and for one thing, this is where I can *afford* to stay. The second thing is I've realized I have a *right* to listen to music and have fun and be social. The only difference is *I* don't drink. I'm new at it. And being here, it *is* a challenge, but the thing is, the more days I get under my belt, the more confidence I get that I can keep doing it. After all, it *was* how we were meant to play – soberly, that is."

"That's brilliant," Daniel replies. "Very inspiring. Tell me more about that right to party without partying."

"Well, but I *do* party. That's the point. I just don't have to *drink* to dance or have fun anymore. *Alcohol* does not a party make, it turns out. But, paradoxically, you don't grasp that concept *until* you stop. If you want to know *why* you drink, by the way, stop drinking, and you'll find out."

"And why exactly don't *you* drink, Frances?" he asks.

"Why don't I drink?" Frances asks, repeating his question. "Because I'm not in scarcity, and alcohol makes me think I am. That's the main reason. There's nothing wrong with drinking in and of itself. But it's not right for me. When I drink, I stop growing in other ways. And I stop knowing I can grow."

"Fantastic. Just fantastic. And what about you, Rebecca? What's your take on this lifestyle?"

"Yes, I agree with Frances. She's kind of been like a spon-sor to me, I guess you could say. Umm, it *is* a challenge, liv-ing here, soberly. But, in a way, it's like learning to ski on the East Coast. After that you can ski anywhere, and you're the best one on the slopes. It's like learning to drive standard in San Francisco. After that you can drive up any hill, anywhere. It's like learning to surf with one leg. Imagine how good your balance would be if…"

"We get the picture, thanks," says Daniel, panning the camera back over to a flattered-looking Frances.

"And how did you and Rebecca realize you were both, in fact, sober?" he asks. "Was it like a Freemasons sort of thing? Or were you both pretty out in the open with it?"

"Well, let's see. We met in the laundry room. Quite by chance I had *seen* Rebecca at an AA meeting earlier that day. Well, she wasn't ready to admit, *yet*, to being an alcoholic. She went into this whole made-up story about why she'd *really* been there. It was poignant. I mean, we've all been there, haven't we? Anyway, only recently has she come forward with the truth, that she is an alcoholic and that she, too, needs help. Now, I finally have some hope for her."

As Frances and Daniel discuss my initial denial, I reflect on my latest venture, trying to distinguish the nature of this lie from that of the main one. What strikes me is that while lying, even lapse-lying, to my friends feels sleazy, like I'm violating something vulnerable and important, somehow lying to Daniel feels more like a practical joke.

As I think about it, it dawns on me that my friends here are totally trusting. That's the trouble with it. *That's* what makes it feel so lousy. Daniel, in contrast, is sly himself. He doesn't necessarily deserve nor need the truth the way I imagine the others do.

I remember once hearing someone say he didn't feel bad lying in instances where the conversations themselves were lies anyway. He explained that if the conversations themselves are lies, then lying into those equations doesn't really corrupt anything.

"And Rebecca?" continues Daniel. "Do you *miss* the drinking, the smoking?"

"Well, Daniel. I'm thir-ty years old. I figure I've had a pret-ty good run. I miss it a lit-tle, but I'm abstaining now. I believe it was the American bloke, Pete Seeger, who said, 'To everything there is a season.'"

"Yuck, beer. I don't touch the stuff myself," chips in Angus. "Just totally bloats me out."

Daniel turns off his video camera. "Good, I've got everything I need for now."

"And as for pot," Angus mumbles. "Smoking pot just turns me into... into... a human being."

"Is that it? That's all you need?" I ask.

"Yup. This is more than enough for now. You can't invest too much before you know if they're even interested. All we need now is enough to give them a sense of the material. And we've got that. But I think we've got a good chance here."

****

Twenty minutes after having signed Daniel in, I am already ushering him back out through the lobby. Stopping for a moment to reorganize his jumble of camera equipment, he opens his mouth, but no words come out.

"Rebecca, listen," he finally manages, "that Frances girl is a real gem, isn't she?"

"Yeah, she's pretty cool, I guess."

He looks at me with a mix of suspicion and hope. "She isn't faking it, too? *Is* she?"

"Afraid not," I assure him.

"Too bad. She was just so inspiring, did you not think?"

"Oh, yeah, I did."

"Something in her face. *So bloody* realistic or something."

"Hmm."

He gives me a knowing wink. "Well, as long as you're still *sober.* We still have you."

"Quite."

"And we still have the bit with you as the American. If anything, I reckon that'll be the dealmaker."

"Shhhh!"

"Sorry."

"You're all right, just careful, eh?"

Daniel lowers his voice to a stage whisper. "You do a good deal better job with that than with this, though, by the way. No offense. But never mind, this is still worth a submission."

"Well, thanks, I'm glad you think so."

"So, then?" he asks.

"So, then, I guess nice meeting you and all that. Enjoy the rest of your stay in America," I say.

"Cheers."

"Where are you off to next, anyway?"

"Well, we're off to Vegas for a week, then to Tahoe, then to Baja. Then we'll be back for two nights."

"Oh, right."

He gives me a mechanical pat on the shoulder. "Anyway, sit tight. I'll be in touch if I need anything else. Or if there's any news, okay?"

"Okay, then."

And with that, Daniel rushes off down the stairs.

"He was a bit of a tosser, wasn't he?" Angus asks, as Daniel traipses down the front steps with a cord to something or other trailing after himself.

"A bit."

"I mean did you see how he put the camera away when *I* started talking?"

"I did, pal. I did. That wasn't ve-ry nice. But, think of it this way, it means you're a bad liar, which is probably a pret-ty good thing, in the end, right?"

A Traitor in Our Midst

The next morning, with Daniel safely en route to Las Vegas, I feel lighter, as if back to only three hundred pounds. Bringing in the whole separate subplot was a foolish move. Though, as I think about it, it wasn't even so much a move as it was a reaction.

There Daniel was treating me like some kind of lowbrow dolt that first night I met him at the inn. And there I was, so determined to control his perception of me, that I just leapt right in and took the sucker punch, without so much as a second thought to possible outcomes.

My conclusion from the experiment is that I need better impulse control. It's one thing to lie for the sake of survival, like I've done by coming to the hostel. But creating new lies for the sake of ego-survival is a little on the gluttonous side. It made my week interesting, but way too stressful.

Anyway, I'm just grateful things are back to normal now. Normal-ish, that is. At least for a minute anyway. Which is usually about how long back-to-normal-ish lasts. It never sticks. What seems to stick nowadays is the abnormal: the adrenaline, the crises. Which has, in a way, become the new normal.

But even that, like the fog on the San Francisco bay, always evaporates sooner or later. And its departure neither relieves nor encourages me so much anymore. I know it'll be back. And then it'll go again. And then it'll be back.

In a way it's like I'm prepared for pretty much everything these days. Like heading down Highway One to the ocean. There, I never know exactly when a big wave is coming, but since I know I'm in the ocean, I'm always expecting one, and I'm always ready to jump. Well, here too, I never know exactly what the jump is going to be like, or when it's coming, or how big it's going to be, but I can pretty much count on there being *something* all the time. Most importantly, I understand that however calm things may appear on the surface the surf can swell at any moment. And this morning is no exception. This morning the tide is definitely coming in.

Although it starts out typically enough, with my getting up and then heading downstairs to the kitchen for breakfast, today, unlike usual, before I make it to the rec room, Alan cuts me off, grabs me by the arm, and pulls me into his office.

"Do you know?" he demands. His manner is urgent, accusing.

For a moment I wonder if he's trying to ask me in some roundabout way whether I know *he* suddenly knows I'm not really English – but quickly rule this out as cumbersome thinking. It could be any number of things. And, knowing him, with his taste for drama, I can't even say for sure it's with *me* he's angry.

"No, I don't think so," I reply, uncertainly.

"You haven't *heard?*"

"No. What?" I inquire. I am now half expecting to hear about how, perhaps, the laundry-room-door-urinater has struck again.

"Two planes have gone into the World Trade Center."

"Huh?"

"The World Trade Center!"

"Oh, that's ter-rible," I answer, automatically. I am still too dazed to gauge how big a deal the news is.

"It's unbelievable."

"How did it hap-pen?"

"We don't know, yet," he says.

"Huh?"

"I have to check on some friends and get back to the news. You should do the same."

Instinct tells me to follow his orders. "Okay, I will."

After stepping out of his office, I rush over to the phone booth and close myself in.

"Hi Mom. It's me," I whisper, to my mother's answering machine. "I'm just calling to say I'm safe. Don't worry. I'm fine. Talk to you later."

Then, I make my way back through the lobby into the rec room. Uncharacteristically missing are strains of music or even victory shouts coming from the foosball table. An eerie stillness permeates the air.

The whole hostel is gathered together in front of the TV. Only as I glance up at the screen to view images of planes crashing into two skyscrapers does it occur to me that the World Trade Center is not the same thing as the Transamerica building in San Francisco. The World Trade Center is in New York. It's the Twin Towers. And I grasp the magnitude of the event.

Together we watch replay after instant replay of the incident in silence. It becomes clear that the crashes were not an accident. The quietness takes on a new significance.

From my position, engulfed by the concave purple couch, I look around the room and take in the multitude of thoughtful, sensitive faces that surround me. I am overwhelmed by feelings of gratitude. Gratitude over being incubated, day after day, especially today, by so much care and community.

Alan interrupts my reflections. "Rebecca, the dishes are piling up in there," he admonishes.

"I know, I saw," I reply.

"And?"

"And, what?"

"So, please make an announcement that the TV goes off until all dishes are done."

I look up in amazement. "Sor-ry?"

"They've been watching the same thing for hours. The dishes still *have* to get done!"

His insistence is so emphatic that it doesn't dawn on me to dispute this.

"Well, why do *I* have to tell them?" I nitpick, instead.

"Because you're in *charge* of the kitchen now!" he explains with an equal amount of emphasis. "And *they* know that."

"What about Tamika?"

"I have no idea where Tamika is. Anyway, she's from Brooklyn, and I'm not going to make her do *anything* today."

Deciding it would take more energy to go on bargaining than to just fulfill the request, I finally say, "Well, okay."

"One free night."

"What?"

"I'll make sure you get one free night's credit," he offers.

"*One free night?*" I ask. I'm taken aback by the thought that turning off the TV will be the equivalent of working for three hours.

He misinterprets my surprise for a lack of appreciation.

"Yes," he returns, irreproachably. "It's not like you'll be pulling the plug on the World Cup."

"Right, of course."

He vanishes. And I slowly make my way toward the front of the room.

Apprehensively, I step up onto an upside down milk crate.

"Hello, everyone," I start.

"Shhhhhhhhh!" they return in unison.

"Is it okay with everybody," I continue, "if I turn the TV off now?"

Expectedly, the query is met with indignant pleas for silence and embellished sighs.

"I'm really sor-ry, gang, but I think we've all seen the same thing now," I say. "And it looks like it'll be a while longer before they…"

An anemic-looking girl with pursed lips observes me pointedly.

"Are you kidding!?" she interrupts.

I shake my head uncertainly.

She laughs through her nose. "What are you *on?*"

"If you'd all just…" I start.

"Do *dishes?*" someone calls, chucking a fully-loaded ashtray at my milk crate podium.

"Look, I know doing dishes may sound a bit banal, with everything hap-pen-ing, but we real-ly must…"

"It may be just more news for *you!*" snaps back the first girl. "But, *I. Am. American!*"

There is a clamorous cry of public support and I have no idea how best to respond.

"Right, well, again, I'm sorry if that sounded flip," I say, "but we simply have to get on with the day *here,* too."

"Unbelievable!" someone observes.

"That's enough," I say, more righteously. "This affects *all* of us equally!"

"Yeah, right!" scoff a few.

Taking some charge, I shoot my arm up to the TV's control panel and strike the off button.

"It can go back on after all the dishes are done," I conclude.

"Who does she think *she* is?" the American girl asks the room.

Stepping down from the crate, I take a moment to locate my knees and then beat a hasty retreat. But as I exit the rec room, the last words I hear before the door swings catch my ear:

"Her name is Rebecca," someone explains. "And she *hates* Americans!"

"You were classic earlier. Your imperialist roots really came out," observes Angus, a few hours later, referring to my turning off the television.

"Yeah, right," I say, as I reach across an abandoned egg-encrusted frying pan for the kettle. "Cup-a-tea?"

He dumps our lunch dishes into the cavernous sink. "I have to start my shift. Bring it to the desk?" he asks, as he bends down to steal a speckled breakfast banana out of the fruit-stocked cupboard beneath the sink.

"Sure."

"Thanks, pet. I wonder if we'll even have any check-ins with all this drama today."

"Anybody else?" I offer, glancing around the kitchen, in accordance with observed practice prior to *putting a kettle up*, though whether out of value for courtesy or efficiency I haven't yet figured out.

Frances appears out of nowhere. "A cup of tea would be really nice," she says. "I was just about to make some."

"Milk and sugar?"

She disappears momentarily into the adjacent pool area to retrieve a stool. "Just milk, thanks," she calls.

Making my way over to the sink, I resist the impulse to fill the kettle up with illegal, already-hot water.

"Always time for tea," I muse.

"I still just cannot get my mind around any of this," Frances begins, as she reenters the kitchen.

"I know," I say, meeting her eyes. "It's just crazy."

She perches herself atop the wooden stool. "How are you doing, anyway?" she starts.

"Well, it's cer-tain-ly a bit destabilizing, but I suppose I'm doing okay," I return, singeing some eyelashes as I light the gas stove. "It's pretty shocking, though."

"I know."

I feel my lashes to make sure they're okay.

"I kind of wonder what's going to hap-pen next."

"Me too," she says, seriously. "The only thing to do is just take it one day at a time though. To stay in the day. Even today."

I can't help asking, "As opposed to?"

"Future-tripping," she elaborates.

"Oh."

"Future-tripping just makes everything crazier."

"Right."

She glances over at the greasy little clock on the stove. "Is that clock right?"

"I think so."

"I'm going to the three o'clock meeting if you want to come?"

"Oh, thanks, but I'm okay."

In fact, it occurs to me that I could use the comfort of that support group today. But I don't want to show my face there again after what happened following the last meeting I went to with Daniel.

"Well, this is definitely a time for me to stick close to the program. I know that," she confides. "It's not going to be easy to get through any of this sober, even if we're not American."

"I am, actually, half," I say, correcting her on only that part.

"Oh, that's right, you said, eh? It hits you even closer to home then," she acknowledges.

I have some hope that my dip in popularity since this morning will not be permanent.

"Right."

"Anyway, it's a whole new thing to feel feelings like this. To feel fear like this without drinking over it, you know?"

"Umm."

"It's so second nature to just sort of numb the feelings."

I nod, leaving some space for her to finish her thoughts.

"I just keep thinking," she continues, "if I just don't pick up, you know? If I just don't pick up. It's gotten me this far."

"And you're doing great," I remind her.

"Thanks. I really appreciate your saying that," she says. Her gray-blue eyes begin to well up a little. "Sorry, it's all just so overwhelming today."

"I know. I feel the same way," I say.

The kettle begins to whistle. I lift it off the gas flame and pour the boiling water into a round little tea pot with three bags of Tetley's.

"Just milk, right?"

"Yes, thanks."

Opening the fridge, I realize I don't have any milk.

"Actually, do you have any milk?" I ask.

She points toward the top shelf of the refrigerator. "Sure."

Then a solitary tear gives way and streams down her cheek.

"No, it's okay," I cut in. "I can get the key and use the hostel's."

"No, it's not the milk! Of course you can use my milk!"

"I know. I was kidding."

She releases a slight smile.

"Oh. It's just… it's sad."

"And scary," I add.

"It triggers something for me."

"Well, it's upset-ting in itself," I point out.

"I know. It just feels so… out of control or something."

"Definitely out of control."

"Do you? No, never mind."

"Sor-ry?"

"Nothing."

"What?"

"No, it's awkward," she says.

"What is it?"

"Well, just, my sponsor tells me it's okay to ask for hugs if I need them. And I really could use one. Would it be too weird if…"

"Oh, sure," I say.

She offers a retraction. "No, it's okay."

Extending my arms, I offer her an embrace. "No, of course," I insist.

"Thank you." Her voice sounds relieved. She wraps her arms around me, and adds, "It's actually just what I need."

"Sure, me too."

"Becks?" intrudes a familiar voice from afar.

"In here!" I call.

"Oh!" Stacy exclaims, seeing me and Frances. "Sorry, ladies. Angus said you were in here. I hope I'm not… interrupting something."

I attempt to disentangle myself from Frances, who, in turn, starts sobbing and clings tighter.

"Of course not," I answer, stroking Frances's back. "We were just…"

"It's cool. No need to explain," he says.

"I wasn't explaining anything."

"Just, Becks," he continues, rifling through the bottom of the fridge, "where'd you stash the Heinekens we were on the other night? We didn't finish the lot, did we?"

I look at him sharply.

"Oh, that's right. You don't drink beer, do you?" he asks.

"No, I don't. Did you not hear that I'm sober?" I ask him.

"Good on you, mate. Didn't know the Brits have a separate name for it, when you only drink rum. God love the Poms."

195

Atlantic Allies

The next morning when I wake up, I feel so overwhelmed by how convoluted things have become that I can barely manage to drag myself out of bed. Not only am I half English now, but also an American-hater, an American *imposter*, a lesbian, an alcoholic-in-recovery, and an alcoholic-in-denial. It's a lot to keep track of.

I have five new characteristics with which to contend. Besides that, there's the feeling of being knocked off balance after what happened yesterday, with the terrorist attack.

The point being there's not a lot of room left in my psyche for further complications. It's for this reason that today is the day I finally decide to roll up my sleeves, hunker down, and secure some actual information about England.

More than anything, I abhor the idea of having the lie exposed through imperfect knowledge. And being up on the country's particulars, I'm hoping, will at least bring the point at which I publicly revert to my authentic self under my own control.

Within a few hours of making this decision I am busy printing out various maps of my region off the inn's computer, while at the same time scrupulously surfing the web for tidbits about A-levels, O-levels, the British monarchy and the health care system.

This proves immediately reassuring. And I sense the endless preoccupation with possible pitfalls under which I've been agonizing all this time is about to be wiped out in one fell swoop.

Yet, just as I start getting really into it, the door bell, followed by a potent cloud of amber-y perfume, communicates to me that my efforts will have to be deferred for at least another few minutes.

"We're here!" exclaims a buxom redhead, now looming overhead.

I flip my freshly printed map of West Sussex and its neighboring counties onto its back.

"Yes. Hel-lo. Your last name, please?" I ask.

"That'll be Begnaud."

I hastily pull her reservation card. "Yes, here you are," I say.

I am eager to rush through her check-in and get back to my all important study. But the expectant expression on her face tugs at me for more. Always more.

"Did you have a nice trip?" I ask, with strained hospitality.

"Well," she starts, as she removes a silk paisley scarf from around her neck, "we were just coming from Sacramento, when the attacks started. But, yes, it was actually okay. I'm just glad we didn't have to fly. We would have had to cancel."

"Indeed."

She shakes her head incomprehensively. "But, then, I suppose we should consider ourselves lucky," she starts.

"I know."

She frowns. "Those poor people who perished yesterday."

"It's so shocking," I say.

"And their poor families."

"It's really ve-ry, *ve-ry* tragic," I add.

I want to let her know that we are of the same mind, despite our being from different sides of the Atlantic.

"We'll get through it," she assures me, acknowledging my camaraderie. "I think we're all pretty much just in shock right now."

"It's all just so surreal."

She places a handsome Hermes clutch on the counter.

"The biggest challenge, I think, will be not to dwell on it overly," she says.

"Quite right."

"We all have to go on," she continues.

"Yes, we do," I agree, as she begins tenderly searching my features.

I flash a warm smile. It has become an indispensable prelude to the lie, disarming all guests, or, at least, because I believe it does, relaxing me.

"So," she starts, predictably, "where are *you* from?"

"Arundel, West Sussex," I say.

My eyes smile too, and my head nods, in agreement with myself.

"Really?"

"Yes." *Really.*

She gazes at me. "You know, I thought so," she says. "Your accent is so regional."

"Do you think?" I reply. "I suppose one never thinks of oneself as having any kind of accent a'tall."

"Well, I've spent a fair bit of time overseas, and I do think yours is really the nicest regional," she says.

I exhibit a queer strain of reserve that stems from living in a constant state of fear, rather than from humility.

"Oh, well, thank you," I say, softly.

"I imagine you're altogether more used to this sort of thing over there."

"Sor-ry?"

"With the IRA," she elaborates.

"Oh, yes. Cer-tain-ly one never grows *used* to it, as it were," I reply, a drop indignantly. "But, indeed, you're right."

"Of course. But, you know, *we've* just never had anything like this happen here before."

"No, I know, you haven't."

The doorbell rings again. A disgruntled manservant of a husband enters.

"Honey," Mrs. Begnaud says to him, "did you find a place to park?"

He drags the rusty wheels of three suitcases across the cumaru floor.

"Nope. Couldn't decode the dang parking signs. I just went to the garage. May as well be written in Chinese," he replies.

"I'm Barbara, by the way," she says, cordially, offering me her hand. "That's Walter."

I affect an equally gracious air. "Well, it's a pleasure to have you both here," I say. "I'm Rebecca. Oh, and I need to give you your keys, don't I?"

"Oh, right!" Barbara laughs.

Placing the set of keys in her palm, I say, "He-re you are. You're in room sixteen."

"Which is?" she inquires.

"You're on the second floor."

She looks at me playfully. "Do you mean the first floor?"

"No, it's the second floor," I confirm, confused.

"Because our first floor is your ground floor and our second floor is your first floor, isn't that right?"

"Oh, right," I reply.

I try to process what she's getting at amidst the dizzying back-drop of my own cultural dyslexia.

She looks at me. "That is right, isn't it?"

"Yes! And, conveniently," I deflect, going for the cheap segue, "there's a lift."

"But..."

"So, no need to take the stairs at all," I bulldoze, less Englishly. "Just step right in and press two. You're bound to get quite enough exercise walking around town!"

Barbara glances unsteadily at me, her bearing no longer so lighthearted. My erratic manner has ended the conversation and ruined the playfulness. Although I know I may have her enmity, I also know she's not going to press on any further. And, as usual, for my safety, this is a price I'm more than willing to pay.

The Mystic Assistant

Following my shift at the inn, I hurry off to the farmer's market to get the ingredients for the party, before returning to the hostel. With a shopping cart of overflowing produce in tow, I then make my way up the steep steps that run alongside the building toward the rec room's back entrance.

One step at a time, I drag the bursting cart up the hill until, just as I am arriving at the door, a cantaloupe goes overboard. Nervously, I watch for a moment as it rolls eagerly down the steps, stopping only as it reaches the busy intersection at Montgomery and Broadway. A car swerves. I hope my fugitive melon won't cause anybody to crash, but I'm just too tired to go back down to get it. Turning to the rec room's back entrance, I fiddle with the combination lock and let myself in.

Back inside the hostel, I wheel my cart into the kitchen. Isaac, the hostel's carpenter, the one with the self-professed old-man skin, is the only one in there. He's busy slicing a black banana into his blender concoction.

"We're going to need this space to start cooking in a lit-tle while," I say.

"Oh, right, okay."

"It's just that I went straight from work at the inn to the farmer's market," I justify. "I'm pret-ty shat-tered and now I've got to cook lasagna for one hundred and fifty people by half seven."

"Well, I'll make it quick," he says. "Want some smoothie?"

"Where'd you get the fruit?"

"Chinatown."

"No thanks."

He looks up, inquisitively.

"They put something called thiabendazole, whatever *that* is, on their fruit," I explain. "I saw it written on the side of a box of bananas under *ingredients.*"

He drops in a handful of burgundy-colored figs, and chuckles, "Oh, okay."

"You don't worry about that?"

"Not really."

"You should."

He shrugs his shoulders.

"Ever been to that restaurant in Berkeley, Alice Water's restaurant?" I ask.

"Chez Panis? Oh, no. I can't even afford to *say* it," he says.

"Well, she, apparently, believes in using whatever is in season, and it's always organic," I lecture, boring us both with worn-out all-natural orthodoxy.

"Ah."

"Anyway, that's how I want to live. If nothing else, you should be eating organic."

"Maybe, but it's too expensive," he says. "If I did that, I'd never get to eat any fruit. Ever."

"Less expensive later, though," I suggest.

"Well, maybe. I believe in the innate power of my spirituality in governing my health anyway," he says. "Plus, you never know. Might not be a later."

I glance over at the big screen TV still showing instant replays from Tuesday morning's terrorist attack.

"True," I grant. "It's still so hard to believe, isn't it?"

He peels the fuzzy skin off a kiwi. "Oh, I wasn't even talking about that."

"You weren't?"

"I was thinking more along the lines of a fatal skiing accident, getting attacked by a shark, taking an overdose."

"Oh."

"I mean, you never know what's going to happen. You can't worry about later now. If you do, you end up missing now and are ultimately left with nothing," he continues.

"What a morbid way to live," I observe. "Basing all your decisions on a sort of expected future ruin."

"No, it's great! That's the great thing about certain risky behavior. It forces you into a state of presence."

"What do you mean?"

"To be able to deal with high risk, like a ski jump, you have to be totally present," he explains.

I contemplate his comment, considering it in relation to my own charade and the heightened sense of awareness I've been experiencing since arriving here.

"So, you're not freaked by 9/11?" I ask.

"Oh, I'm freaked out. But I can't worry about wars," he says. "I have to worry about how to pay the rent."

"What are you on about?"

"Well, yeah, charity begins at home. If you don't have a home, then you *are* the charity, right?"

"I guess."

He presses the blender buttons back and forth. "No, it's not really that," he reflects. "I just try not to engage."

"Why? You don't believe in self-defense?" I ask.

"Nah, more in a sort of high philosophical anarchy. What's the difference between *chop* and *pulse?*"

"What's that?"

"I don't know, I'm asking you."

"No, high philosophical anarchy?"

"Oh. You know, no sides, rise above the battlefield. None of it's real anyway."

"Not real?"

"Not real, relative to what's more real, what's eternal," he expounds.

"Huh?"

"This is more of a sort of big dream of dented pride, all over the world. Flip sides of the same coin. Never ending circles of, I don't know, shared hallucination. The only way to win is not to play."

"Huh," I repeat.

While I try to assess whether he's coming more from a position of naïveté or enlightenment, Isaac is busy evaluating his smoothie.

"Yup, this is exactly the consistency I was after," he says.

Lifting the pitcher off the blender base, he looks perplexed by the sight of the secured lid, as purple liquid starts spilling out all over the metal counter top.

"Oh. Whoops," he remarks.

I identify the cause. "The bottom! The bottom fell off it!"

Just then Australian Dusty saunters into the kitchen.

"Broken blender?" he asks, removing a rolled cigarette from his mouth.

"Yup," Isaac replies. He giggles as he scrapes all the liquid off the counter and into a glass with a plastic cutting board.

"I'll try to bring ya a new one from work," says Dusty.

Calling to mind a term I heard Dusty use once before, I say, "You found *yakka?*"

"Yeah. Been doin' some moving work. The finds have been totally primo."

"Finds?"

"Yeah, the people who move just throw out all this gear."

"I can imagine."

"No, you wouldn't believe it though. We've been getting everything: CDs, TVs, skis, furniture. Got a grand piano yesterday. We're going to replace that one with it," he says, pointing across the rec room to the old green piano. "I'll catch a blender in no time."

"Cool."

"I know, it's great. Ya gotta love the Americans."

"It's funny," I observe. "Seamus brings that beau-tif-ul pastry from his bakery, you're bringing a new piano. And I've had more money living like this than ever before."

"It's a minimum of responsibility with a maximum of perks," comments Isaac, as he sips recycled smoothie out of a chipped pint glass. "All the advantages of being out of society without any of the disadvantages. The best combination."

"You're *drinking* that?" I ask.

"Yeah, why not? It's good."

"It was just all over that filthy counter," I point out.

"Speaking of which, Isaac," interjects Dusty. "That chicken curry you made the other night?"

Isaac wipes off the offending counter with an even more offending sponge.

"Yeah?"

"I meant to tell you. It was actually just like the stuff I had in India."

"Thanks, that's the best compliment I've ever…"

"Gave me serious diarrhea," finishes Dusty.

"Oh, wait," catches Isaac, with a slow smile.

"I'm telling you, it's that Chinatown produce," I caution.

"Nah."

"Which reminds me, I've got to get going for tonight's *do*," I say. I am niggled by the trade-off that allows me to replace *party* only with the easier-to-pronounce, but more affected-sounding, *do*.

"Yeah, I might not be the best cook," starts Isaac. "But I know this guy. *He's* like *the* best garbage chef."

"What do you mean by that?" I ask.

"Like salvaged-food chef."

"Eww!" I exclaim.

I begin tossing various bags full of farmer's market vegetables from my cart onto the metal island.

"Oh, no!" he continues. "He's the best forager. Wild edibles too. And he even knows the best spots to go with the food, like to a cliff in Malibu."

As I dump eight bags of spinach into a colander, I stare at him, amazed, more than anything, by his lack of self-consciousness.

"Yeah, like a picnic," he continues, now with a chuckle. "Like riding off into the sunset."

"Ve-ry romantic," I chide.

"No, but seriously," he says. "He was the first guy I met when I moved to LA. Taught me how to dumpster-dive."

I shoot him a doubtful look.

"No, really. I was ready to do something drastic, steal something, or do something illegal."

Reaching back into a far recess of the refrigerator, I locate my stash of fresh oregano. *"Dumpster-dive?"*

"Yeah, it's great," he says, breaking into peals of laughter. "You can really find a lot of stuff. Sometimes there's diapers and cat litter, but it's worth it, if you're like I was."

Glancing at the clock, I change the subject. "Right, well I've got to get started. You two want to help out until Alan brings me my prep cooks?"

"Sure, for a little," returns Isaac.

Dusty drifts away toward the pool table.

"Chop or wash?" I ask Isaac.

"Uh, chop."

I pass Isaac some eggplant. "Okay, chop this aubergine, then," I say, placing the knife's edge where he should make his first cut. "About this thick."

"Wait, are you *English?*" he asks.

"Well, yeah, I'm half," I reply, astonished that he's been able to separate me from my accent this whole time.

"Oh, okay, I didn't notice until I heard you say aubergine. We call it eggplant," he explains.

"Yes, right. Eggplant."

The Celebration

Once everyone has started eating and I pop the last lasagna into the oven, I find Angus and collapse next to him in our booth.

"Lasagna is tutta bene, regazza," he says.

"It is?"

"Aye!"

"Good. I've been smelling it all afternoon. I can't taste anything anymore."

"Way overcooked noodles, Rebecca," an approaching Alan admonishes from behind.

I twist around and affect a tone of concern. "Real-ly?"

He puts a heaping forkful in his mouth. "Totally," he says. "It's ruined."

"Well, sor-ry about that."

"It's one of the reasons I can't use English hostellers for cooking, generally," he starts.

"How do you mean?"

"You guys overcook everything. Typical British. Big problem."

I try to look miffed. "No we don't!" I exclaim.

"You have to *undercook* lasagna noodles. See, because they cook more when they bake," he explains.

"But, I..."

"I can't discuss it now. I have to make the announcements," Alan says, as he rushes away from us toward a microphone set up in the middle of the room.

"Okay everyone!" he shouts. "I have two announcements! First of all, we re*cycle* these red cups! So please don't throw them away! Everybody hear that? We *recycle* these red cups!"

"Is that why there are bite marks on mine?" hollers back an English accent from the crowd.

The group laughs.

"No," quips Alan. "That's Braille. It says, 'Please don't throw this cup away!' Got it? And secondly, more seriously, I just want to acknowledge I know there is a war brewing, but I just want to say that in America we're not only about war. And I want to introduce a special guest. Usually she would be thought of as the enemy: she's Islamic and a Muslim. But she's our friend here at the Purple Parakeet. And I just want to welcome her!"

Alan gestures to a dark-skinned girl standing in the kitchen wrapped in a floral head scarf.

She waves awkwardly to the crowd.

"What's he like?" an Irish guy asks Angus, leaning over from the next booth.

"That's Alan. He's a bit of a dag," explains Angus, throwing in some Australian slang.

"I guess so," he replies.

"Hey!" Angus exclaims. "You wanna play Scrabble with us?"

The guy glances down at our table. "Scrabble?" he replies. "Yeah, why not? I'll have a quick game." He pulls over a chair.

Angus slams down his first empty shot glass.

"Whew Heeeeeew!" he shouts in a Southern accent. "The best little whore house in Texas!"

Then he pushes a glass in front of the new guy. "Help yourself, mate," he tells our visitor.

"Oh, cheers," he replies. "I'm Niall."

"So, you're coming from Ireland, by the sounds of things?"

"Right you are, right you are," affirms Niall.

"So, how long have you been away?" Angus inquires.

"Ten days."

"And where are you off to next, then?"

"Back to Dublin, I'm afraid. Dublin, San Francisco, a cup a tea, and that's about it."

"Shame."

"How about you?" returns Niall.

"Working holiday," Angus replies. "Front desk."

"And laundry," I say.

Angus looks at me, grits his teeth, and mutters, "Bitch."

"I think you'll find you're the laundry bitch," I whisper.

"Seven letters, right?" Niall asks.

Angus nods his head, reluctantly taking a pen and paper out of the box to keep score.

"Surname?"

"O'Reilly," Niall says.

Angus draws neat little columns on the pad. "So, that'd be N.O." Angus continues. "Not an indication of things to come, I hope."

"Come again?" asks Niall.

Angus chortles. "Oh, nothing. Though, I'd love to."

"Love to what?"

Angus slithers downward in the booth. "Nothing. My God, I'm triple O, Rebecca! Help!"

Just then, a petite blonde wearing an aqua tube top and heavy eyeliner approaches our table.

"Hey, Niall, give me my passport, would you? I'm going out to buy some drink."

Niall fishes around in his bag for the passport.

"Seems like you don't really want to play anyway, do ya?" he asks Angus.

Angus cackles. "Depends what you mean by play?"

Girlfriend takes heed.

"What's that supposed to mean?" she asks.

"Means what you want it to mean," Angus quips.

"Huh?" she asks.

"Look, we're just having a good time, lovey, don't go getting your knickers all in a twist."

He throws his hands in the air and begins chair-dancing.

"What are you talking about?" she asks. "What are you doing?"

"Isn't it obvious?" Angus snaps. He has a look of wild disobedience dancing across his features. "I'm *trying* to steal your boyfriend!"

She stares at him.

"Why?" he continues, hopefully. "Is there going to be a fight?"

"Please!" she shouts over the music. "Have *another* drink."

"Oh, c'mon, *kidding!*" Angus yells.

"Anyway," Niall intervenes, "we'll need a fourth. You up for a game, Maeve?"

She perches herself neatly on Niall's knee while reaching to take refuge in a shot of scotch.

"Well, I'd definitely rather play that than this, whatever this is," she says.

"So, you want to play in teams?" asks Niall. "How about me and Maeve, then, against you two?"

"Fabulous," Angus says. "Just fab. But, then no flirting over the letters, okay? Because that kind of thing really makes me ill, you know?"

"Rebecca," murmurs Alan, approaching me from the side. "I need to talk to you."

I rise from the booth and put my ear right up to his mouth in order to hear him over the music.

"What's up, Alan?"

"What did you think? Was my speech wrong?"

"Oh, you mean about?"

"Yes."

"There was something maybe a bit awkward about it," I concede. "But I knew what you meant."

"You did?"

"Yes."

"Thank you. Good. I mean, Seamus was so furious at me he left the party. He said it was outrageous!"

"No."

"I didn't think so either. The opposite. I just sort of stumbled over my words was all."

"Yes."

Just then Dusty bumps into us. He examines Alan out of the corner of his eye.

"Good evening, Becky. Alan," he says.

"Hello Dusty," Alan replies, warily.

Dusty gestures casually in the direction of Alan's hand, "Give us a smoke of that, would ya mate?"

"It's *pie* crust," states Alan, taking a bite.

"Oh," returns Dusty. He staggers back off into the crowd.

"Anyway," Alan resumes, "this party is going pear-shaped, Rebecca."

"Well, it's early, yet."

"We *have* to live up to "Best Parties." That's how it describes us on the website."

"We already do."

"Not tonight we don't. *Nobody* is dancing!"

"Well."

"Nobody's going to be talking about *this* after leaving here," he complains. "I can guarantee that."

"Give them time," I say.

Alan shoots me an annoyed look.

"No," he explains, "we can't take that chance. We've got to *make* it happen."

"Oh."

"You've got to get it started."

"Me?"

"Yes, get up on a table and start dancing! Like you guys did last week."

"But, that was spontaneous. Why don't you?" I pose.

"They won't follow me. They'll follow you."

I'm stimulated by the thought of being well liked. "You think *I* can get it started?" I ask.

"Yes! Please! Get it *started!"* he entreats.

"The tables haven't even been cleared yet though. What about all the cups and plates?"

"Fuck it! Just kick 'em off!" exclaims the same man who last week forbade me the use of lip balm at the computer, worried it could make the keys sticky.

"Real-ly!?" I ask.

I am thrilled by the idea of engaging in a recklessness that's sanctioned.

"Yes!" He hands me his cup and demands, "Get up there!"

I down a sip of what tastes like pure alcohol and pass it back to him. "Oh my God. What is *that?"*

"Tequila."

"Whew!"

"Get *up* there!" he insists.

I gesture once more for his drink and this time chug the whole cup down, Frances's sponsorship and my morning hangover be damned.

Stepping up onto the table, I then kick all plates and cups out of my way to make room for myself. This shocking act is well received by the crowd. All the more since they think it to be unauthorized.

"Thank you!" mouths Alan.

Then, someone, possibly doused by a cup full of kicked beer, shouts, "Fuck you, you fat cow!"

For a moment my confidence falters. Still, the satisfied look on Alan's face plus my own adrenaline manage to override the insult. And I start to move, slowly, in stark contrast to the fast-thumping music, allowing myself to access my own groove, as if I'm too relaxed to hurry.

That's when it hits me: Despite everything, I *am* too relaxed to hurry. Act-as-if has just about turned into *is*. I *do* feel comfortable, like I'm dancing at home, among friends.

Continuing to trust my own tempo, I connect with my inner rhythm, and am soon rewarded by cheers of approval. Cheers which, rather than tripping me up and embarrassing me, spur me on, and launch me into some sort of free space. At once I feel I am being known for exactly who and how I want to be.

And, that's when it happens. Suddenly my body is moving without my moving it. Every movement is flowing entirely of its own accord. I am experiencing, for the first time, either what it feels like to be in a state of divine grace, or what it feels like to have — fun!

"Go Becky! Go Becky!" calls Angus, as he leaps up to kick the rest of the place settings from the table.

I watch in wonderment as Angus claps his hands in the air, immediately locating his own groove, and casts a spell over me and the rest of the room. We begin matching our movements, mirroring each other in a sort of effortless synchronicity.

Energized, we pick up our pace and kick into even higher gear. We thump, pump and stomp in complete unison with each other and with the music. For me, the dancing opens up into a wild celebration of everything I am feeling.

Little by little the others join in, until finally around one hundred of us are dancing together on the tables. And as we disco together into the night, I register the joy of *Us*-ness. How much better it is than the *Me*-ness I've always tried, so doggedly, and so in vain, to secure.

That's when I catch sight of Stacy atop the giant speaker. We stare at each other. Somehow I'm confident I am finally managing to convey to him how I really feel: that I like him.

He reaches for his didgeridoo and blows into it.

"Didgeri-*don't!*" someone shouts.

Then, as the fine line between being afraid you can't possess something and being overwhelmed you might be able to disappears, I avert my eyes. I retreat to my own private rhythm, my own part within the larger frame, reclaiming the refuge of solitude within the sanctuary of community.

And this is the sweet zone in which I remain for the next hour until nature refuses to be ignored any longer, and I have to temporarily step down from the romp.

****

On my way back from the bathroom, I stop for a soda. Out of the corner of my eye I can see Frances approaching me.

"Rebecca?"

I keep my attention fixed on the soda machine.

"Rebecca?" she says again.

"Oh, hiya."

"You've got lasagna in between your toes," she observes.

"Oh, I know, from the table."

She closes in on me. "It's kind of like you're seeking spirit through spirits."

Once again, she sees me as a practicing alcoholic.

"Right," I reply, as I deposit four quarters into the soda machine.

"Getting mixer, eh?" she persists.

"Huh?"

"Mixer? You're probably out of mixer."

I'm determined not to let her waylay me any further. "How's your night going?" I divert.

"Well, thanks."

"Good."

"It's not a self-sufficient illusion, though. That's the main problem with it," she explains.

"Yeah, right," I dismiss, as two of my quarters don't take and drop back down to the change slot. "Shit."

"Irritable and discontent?" she inquires, softly. "The Big Book talks about that."

"Please! You're, like, the most strident... the most officious person I've ev-er met!" I exclaim, allowing myself to lose a modicum of self-control.

She freezes, as if too stunned to speak.

I'm stymied. Here I am, angry she's seeing me as someone I'm not – an alcoholic-in-denial. Whereas, at the same time, I'm playing someone I'm not: the British Rebecca, as well as an alcoholic-in-recovery.

Retrieving my can of Coke, I look at her confrontationally.

"What?" she asks.

"Are you even aware of it?" I challenge, disapprovingly.

My tone lacks kick, however. The constant consciousness of my own hypocrisy makes it hard for me to feel legit condemning anybody for anything anymore.

"When we act on our vices, even in small ways, it wears on our self-esteem, even unconsciously," she explains. "Then we don't have the self-assurance we need to stand up for ourselves."

"I don't fol-low," I reply.

"Sorry, that's because that bit doesn't exactly relate to this."

"Oh."

"I don't know what to say, exactly. Just, it's a program of honesty. Deep down, I know you want to be honest, too."

Unable to bring myself to deny this particular point, however out of context it is, I reply only, "And?"

"And I really only want to help. That's what the program is about: one alcoholic helping another one. It's what's going to keep me sober, too. I feel like I could help you if you'd just let me."

I recall a phrase from the meeting's introductory readings. "But, isn't the program based on *attraction rather than promotion?*"

"What?"

"It's supposed to be based on attraction, not promotion, isn't it? At least that's what I understood from the meetings," I explain.

"You know," she concedes, suddenly, "you're right. You're absolutely right."

I exhale in relief.

"Sorry," she owns. "I suppose I just wish someone would have cared enough to be so persistent with me. But, maybe that's not the way it works, is it?"

"Maybe not. And, moreover," I remind her, with tequila all over my breath, "I'm *already* sober. Do you not remember Daniel, the documentary filmmaker, who came here to shoot footage of just how sober I am?"

She looks at me mercifully.

"I am," I insist. "I'm just taking one night off. But, I can take it or leave it. That isn't the issue. So, please, just stop worrying about me, okay? Because, to be honest, I feel like I'm suff-o-ca-ting."

"Well, I don't know," she replies.

Just then Stacy walks by us. He observes the intensity of our conversation and shoots me a funny look. For some reason, whenever he looks at me, though, no matter what his expression, it always makes me feel special. Like I'm me. Only more so.

It's odd with him. All of his actions keep letting me know he's lost interest. But all of my instincts keep telling me he hasn't. It doesn't add up. And it's becoming annoying.

So annoying, in fact, that even though Frances is draining me fast, with what's left of my tequila-induced Dutch courage, I get an unprecedented urge to grab Stacy aside and tell him, directly, just how much I like him. I'm sick of his seeming not to know this. Of there being some kind of misunderstanding between us that I just don't understand. But something stops me.

"It's just that I think you might be confused," Frances starts again. "First I *see* you at a meeting. Then I meet you, and you claim you're not an alcoholic at all. Then last week you come up to me and say you're a definite alcoholic and that you're now committed to staying sober. And now, again, you're saying that you have no problem with it and that you can take it or leave it. It's one thing to have a slip. After all, the motto is *Keep coming back,* isn't it? But the one thing you can't mess with is the truth. Your truth. You just have to know that, that's all," she says.

"I do," I answer.

"Okay," she says. "I'm actually grateful to you for reminding me of that principle, by the way, the one about attraction not promotion, I mean. I'm still learning, too."

"Well, cool," I say, trying to wrap it up. I am now extra eager to resume my table-top dancing before I totally lose the mood.

"I feel like I owe you an apology, though," she continues, holding me captive. "I don't know why I get so controlling about it. It must be some kind of self-will residual. I'd really like to offer you an official amends."

"Thanks, but it's really not necess-ry," I say.

"It is, actually, it's essential," she pushes back. "See, I have to keep my side of the street clean – for *myself.* If I don't, my program doesn't work for me. It works if *I* work it."

"Well, then, like I said, what if you just dialed the supervising back a bit from now on? If you real-ly insist on making an amends, that could be like a… living amends?"

"Sounds pretty counter-intuitive, but if you really think *less* support is what might help you stay clean, I'm willing to give it a try," she agrees, as I strain to glimpse the action inside through the sporadically swinging rec room doors.

But what I see sobers me completely. Stacy is back in there dancing super closely with some girl. Some girl that isn't me.

Hangovers and Juggling Acts

The next morning I head downstairs, with the grandfather of all hangovers. Wandering into the kitchen, I take my place in the breakfast line behind a female hosteller (of the nervous-newcomer variety) and contemplate what a good mood I seem to be in, concluding, ultimately, that after a good night, a hangover is almost like a souvenir.

Expectedly, the girl standing in front of me does the clingy, little half twist in my direction, which I pretend not to notice.

Redoubling her efforts, she then turns all the way around and asks, "Pretty cold here, isn't it?"

Too hungover for coffee-talk, I offer back only the apathetic, "Yep."

"It wasn't this cold in Santa Cruz. Or in San Diego," she continues. "I wonder if I can expect it to be this cold in Yosemite."

"Hmm."

"I hear Yosemite should be nice. Have you been yet? What is it, about a ten hour drive?"

Her social anxiety is acute. It drains and pulls on me. It pulls on me like... like... I guess like *mine* pulled on everyone else when *I* first arrived.

That's when it hits me. For the first time since arriving here, I'm comfortable in the silence, in my own, and in the collective. It's no longer a matter of affecting detachment.

And it dawns on me what the stillness, the strange, unfathomable calm that's made me so anxious at times actually is. It's *hangover* silence. Not anything more mysterious than that. Just innocuous hangover silence.

"I didn't expect it to be this cold. Does it get much colder than this?" she forces.

To this I offer no response. As harsh as it seems on one level, I know, on a deeper plane, I'm actually doing us both a favor. It is now up to *me* to communicate to *her* that no rescue remarks will be offered. It's up to me not to enable. Knowing full well she, too, will learn to take the heat.

Just then Angus walks into the kitchen. "Morning, Tamika," he says.

Observing the sunglasses he's wearing, Tamika snaps back, "It's not that bright in here, man."

Turning around to take his place in line, Angus then spots me, and in that specific way friends do when they first see each other again after a night of depraved drinking, we both break out laughing.

As soon as we finish gathering our breakfast, we then hurry out of the kitchen, both eager to get over to our usual booth in order to rehash the highlights from the night before.

After reviewing every detail several times, we finally get back to the trivial.

"Tamika's pretty agro today," Angus remarks.

"No, she's not. She's the same as ever. You're just hungover and so everything feels like more, in con-trast," I explain.

"Sometimes you're really out there," he says.

Angus changes his position so as to be able to see any cute new arrivals as they enter the room.

"Must be from that homeschooling. Nutter," he continues.

"Hmm."

He reaches over onto my plate for a dollop of apricot marmalade.

"Did your mum have a homebirth too?" he jokes.

"No."

"Where were you born, then? *Arundel* Hospital?" he asks, mockingly.

Despite there being no practical danger in doing so, somehow I am unwilling to own this particular detail. "No, I wasn't, actually," I return.

"You weren't?"

"No."

"Where then?"

But I am hitting a predictable dead end. What was I thinking? Clearly, even a momentary foray into conscience has the power to undo everything. I rack my brain for an explanation.

"Well," I start.

"What?" he persists.

"Nothing," I say, biding for time. *How to keep up the ever-expanding juggling act?*

"So, where were you born?" he repeats.

The spot is a pretty tight one. Still, recognizing the necessity of now throwing him off the topic of citizenship altogether, my parallel identity manages, once more, to pull in diagonally. "I was adopted, actually."

"You were?"

"Yup," I confirm, dismayed by the way resisting the little lies inevitably leads to manufacturing larger ones.

"Oh, okay. Sorry," he offers, gently.

"Why?" I challenge, embracing my newest situation. "I'm not sorry."

"Well, then, sorry for saying sorry," he clarifies.

"It's okay."

At that moment Alan, a welcome interruption (being a common enemy, of sorts) enters the rec room. Storming over to us at top speed he trips over a cable and soars, headfirst, for about four feet until he crashes to the floor with a loud thump.

Enraged, he lifts his head. His eye immediately trails the responsible cord, until he reaches its source – an amplifier, surround by a group of guys, all of whom appear to be straining to conceal their amusement. The room becomes silent.

"Sons of *bitches!*" Alan screeches, malignantly.

This, naturally, has the effect both of breaking the ice and of making the group of guys give in and begin laughing in an unrestrained way which, in turn, makes everybody else start erupting too. All of which, of course, pushes Alan to the edge of his edge. To the kind of limit that has no words.

Finally, raising himself off the floor, Alan brushes a smashed cigarette butt from his pants, glares around the room, and begins.

"That's *it!*" he announces, attempting to enforce the greatest of consequences. "There'll be no more smoking pot in here. Until *after* 1:30 p.m. I'm not kidding! Everybody *got* that?"

"Yes," somebody sitting nearest to Alan consents weakly.

"Goes without *saying!*" Alan snaps back at him.

Then, having established himself, once again, as a force to be reckoned with, Alan makes his way over to where Angus and I are seated and collapses in the booth.

"I can't believe I had to come in today. My head is made of glass," he says, familiarly.

"Why did you?" I ask.

"Because someone has to receive the deliveries. Of course it has to be me. And to have to hear this shit first thing in the morning. I hate rap. It's just complaining. I have my own problems. I really hate this shit."

"Most of it *is* shite," Angus agrees.

"Whenever I'm in a bad mood, invariably it turns out it's because someone's put a shitty CD on. I'd rather hear *them!*" Alan adds, pointing fleetingly toward the group of musicians still surrounding the amplifier, without seeming to notice one of them standing atop a ladder and pushing the hands of the clock forward by three hours.

I think about how magical it would be if only time really could be pushed forward like that. Or backward, for that matter. If only I could push back time… I'd have had the wherewithal to simply say I was from Connecticut instead of the Bay Area when I called to make my reservation that first day. If only I had, this whole time I could've been staying here legitimately, as myself.

But, then, maybe everything happens for a reason. For one thing, if it would've happened that way I might've never been able to learn exactly where my threshold for stress does finally end. As, every day, I'm getting closer to finding out.

In the Dark

The weeks come and go and come and go. It's weird. I'm so engaged with the day to day goings-on, so involved with the mini-crises that crop up around the running of the hostel, so preoccupied with the post-9/11 tone of terror in America that, to some extent, the risk of danger concerned with my persona evaporates.

At the same time, the danger still looms. I've been mulling the situation over. I think because I became a hostel worker at the same time I became British, the two have gotten sort of woven together. Oddly, being British actually feels *as* central to my current identity as does being a worker. It really is bizarre.

By the time I get to my job at the Filbert Street Inn today, I still can't seem to make heads or tails of how I'd go about separating the two characteristics, even if I wanted to. But, like a kid playing with fire, I continue messing with it all anyway, in a half-intrigued, half-deranged sort of way, until, as usual, the first check-in of my shift rescues me from myself.

"Hello? Oh, hi Jack. Yeah, just got here. Yeah, middle seat. Yeah, all the way from Hawaii. Yuh. Not good," the new guest explains into his phone.

I put away my musings and produce an unassuming smile.

"Hi there, sorry about that," he says, as he snaps shut his miniature phone.

"Oh, that's okay. Your last name?"

"Pemberly."

Searching the computer unsuccessfully, I say, "Let's see, Pemberly. Hmm..."

"Sounds not so good," he observes.

"Wait, here you are. Looks like you were under Remberly, that's all."

Distractedly, he hunts through his wallet for a credit card.

"Huh?"

"You were incorrectly entered into our system, under Remberly," I repeat.

"I see."

Just then, out of nowhere, all the lights go out.

"Oh my God," he cries. The panic in his voice says everything.

We glance out the window at the rest of the darkened street.

"It's probably a blackout," I say. "We get them kind of of-ten here."

"Really?"

"Yes, I'd say so," I say, calmly.

But the look on his face still seems to fear the worst: a terrorist-related attack.

"Real-ly," I add, more authoritatively. "I'm sure it's nothing."

"Well, appreciate your reassurance."

His expression visibly relaxes then. It feels good to be in a position to reassure somebody of something. And I suspect it's the daily practice I have managing my own personal little reign of terror which in some way grooms me for the post. I'm used to the false alarm.

"Well, we can skip the paperwork and credit card authorization, anyway," I add, offering him his room key.

"Yeah right. Good thing you don't have those electronic keys here. How long do you think it's going to last?"

"I don't know, really. But..."

Suddenly, Reggie, the inn's houseman, emerges from the kitchen staircase. "What happened? What happened?" he asks.

"It's a blackout," I confirm.

"I was just in the back reading my Bible. All of a sudden I saw nothing. I thought it was another terrorist attack or a sign from Jesus."

"Yes, no, probably not either. Probably just a blackout. Let's hope, anyway."

"We had the same thing last month. It lasted three days! But, at least we got one of them, right?" continues Reggie, gesturing to the fireplace.

"Ah, no," returns Pemberly. "You've got to be kidding. Three days?"

"No, I ain't kidding," returns Reggie. "Three days. We had candles going and everything."

"Actually, Reggie," I cut in, "that's a good idea. Would you mind running out and seeing if Columbus is still lit? We could use some torches from Walgreens."

"Say what?"

"If you could get us some torches – or rather, flashlights?" I say, as if to correct myself. "I think we'll need them."

"Torches? Man, we both be speakin' the same language. But, man, you be using some funny words."

"Yes, so I've heard," I return, with counterfeit self-consciousness, as I hand him thirty dollars out of the petty cash drawer. "Just get as many as they have, if you would. I'm sure we can't have too many emergency supplies."

The Interview

Dennis, the manager, arrives just after all guests have returned to their rooms for the evening.

"Well, everything seems to be pretty well under control here," he observes.

"Oh yes, I think the worst is behind us."

Privately, I judge his presence unnecessary to the point of being annoying.

He places a white paper bag down on the coffee table in front of the book his arrival has required me to put down.

"Brought you a ham sandwich," he says, settling onto the couch beside me.

"Oh, thanks," I return. "I actually just ate, I'm afraid. But that was ve-ry kind of you." I choose not to explain that I've been a vegetarian since I was twelve.

"That's the great thing about England," he starts. "It's such a sandwich culture, isn't it? We're a burger culture here."

I recall the pleasure of packaged ploughman's sandwiches from Victoria Station on trips to and from Arundel. "Oh, absolutely," I concur.

"Gotta get back for a visit some time. I told you I visited Scotland a few years back, didn't I?"

"Yes, I think you did mention that."

"Beautiful place. Beautiful place."

"Yes, it is."

"You've been there?"

"No, I'm afraid I haven't, actually," I admit, before launching into requisite remorse at having lived so near for so long and never having taken the opportunity.

He seems to enter into a state of catatonia.

Eager to avoid the intimacy of silence, I keep jabbering. "I wonder when the lights will come back on."

"Hmm," he returns.

He stares at the fire, increasingly entranced by its bright orange flames. I, meanwhile, levitate a few inches above the couch, all my energies focused on resisting all tendencies toward familiarity. Still, together we sit, side by side, alone, in the darkness, in perfectly excruciating silence, save for a distant sort of beep emanating from the closet which mimics the chirping of summer crickets. And I curse the day I became English.

After about five minutes Dennis finally speaks. "Rebecca?"

"Yes?"

"There's something I've wanted to talk to you about," he starts.

Oh, no. Please no. Whatever it is, not now, not here, not without the buffer of light and electricity. No, no, no.

"Yes?"

"I've wanted to mention this for a while, but, well, it's a delicate subject."

"Sure, Dennis, what is it?" I am anxious with equal measures of curiosity and paranoia.

"Well," he starts.

Then he tortures me with more stalling, while I wait, helplessly experiencing, for the first time, the unknown dimensions existing within the space of a moment.

"I can put up with a lot of things, Rebecca," he resumes. "But, if there's one thing I don't respect, it's dishonesty."

My heart races. "Of course," I respond, as calmly as I can manage. The darkness, in which he can't discern my crimson face, is a precious gift.

"I won't tolerate a liar," he accuses.

"No, of course not," I say, my voice grave.

But he can't know. How could he know?

"That's why, and it may seem harsh," he continues, as I humbly prepare the phrasing for my feeble explanation, "but I've decided I'm going to have to terminate Nadine's position here."

"Oh. *Sure!*" I nearly cry out.

"It was that jury duty shit that really turned the tide for me. Saying she had jury duty. It was all nonsense. I mean, what does she take us for?"

I spur him on. "No, you're right. That wasn't right."

"No, it wasn't. And if I can be perfectly frank, Rebecca, that woman picked the wrong man to try to feed baloney to.

"Quite."

He laughs, affectionately. "You probably don't even know what baloney is."

"Oh, sure I do."

"Do you have baloney in England? I thought it was American."

"Mind you, it's been a while since I've lived there, but I should think you can get just about anything anywhere nowadays," I equivocate.

"Anyway, to feed somebody baloney... it's just another way of saying to try and pull the wool over their eyes."

"Right, I see. Never a very nice thing, that – is it?"

"No, it isn't. And the point is when she gets back from her maternity leave, I'm afraid she isn't going to have a job here."

"Well, perhaps that's for the best," I reply, selling Nadine and her newborn child down the river in the fever pitch of my own personal salvation.

He looks at me sharply. "Well, then there's your role in all of this."

"Oh?"

What on earth are you getting at now?

"And that's why I've wanted to talk to you. That's why I came in tonight."

Make your point already, would you?

"Right."

"Rebecca, with Nadine gone, we're going to need a new assistant manager."

"Oh, I see." It all falls neatly into place.

"I'm hoping you'll take over the post, Rebecca. You haven't been here long, but it's just that you're a great addition here. There's nobody better for the job."

"Well, thank you. That's very kind of you. I'm not sure what to say."

"How about *yes?*"

"Well, the thing is I've actually been plan-ning on go-ing to India at the end of next month. I thought Nadine was coming back and I already bought my tic-ket, I'm afraid."

"Oh, I see. Well, that'll be a real adventure for you. A real adventure."

"I expect so."

We sit in silence for a few more moments.

"You understand, now," he resumes, "that I don't like to see anyone lose their job, especially when they have children."

"No, of course you don't. That goes without saying," I assure him.

"I guess it does. But, Rebecca, lies and manipulation," he clarifies, with a critical look sweeping over his expression. "There just isn't room for that level of dishonesty here. I just wish there was some way I could talk you into staying with us."

An Unwelcome Invitation

Following the turbulent shift at the inn, I step out into the frigid night, where the whipping winds immediately begin harassing me from all directions. After all these months in San Francisco, I should know by now that no matter how hot it is, no matter how clear the sky is, no matter how still the air is one minute, the weather in San Francisco turns on a dime. It changes drastically from morning to noon, from noon to night, and from one side of the street to the other. Its fickle nature, I realize, echoes the climate of my own situation to the hilt, yet, although I have learned to come prepared for the constant and sudden swings in my own world, I have not yet trained myself to bring a hat and scarf with me to work.

In an effort to flee the elements, as well as to get somewhere private enough to process the day's episode before returning to the hostel, I start looking for somewhere to go. An empty Suet Lee's, the first Chinese restaurant I come across, fits the bill. I cross over darkened Stockton Street to the still-lit Columbus Avenue, and enter the unappetizing little joint.

As I peruse the menu, under the fluorescent lights which illuminate what looks like months of greasy buildup over it, I reflect on the whole range of curiosities, from my eerily increasing stamina for stress to the way Chinese restaurant menus in California never seem to include Lo Mein.

Immediately, a waiter is standing before me.

"Yuh?"

I settle for the similar sounding Chow Mein. "And I guess a glass of white wine," I add.

Approximately a minute later my food and wine arrive, together with my fortune cookie and bill.

Letting the Chow Mein cool down some, I gulp down the wine. Then I crack open the cookie. It reads: *Just because you're paranoid doesn't mean they aren't after you.*

What?

"Hey!" I call behind my waiter. "Can I get another cookie, please?"

"What you want?"

"Another cookie. Please?"

He points disdainfully at my little cookie mess. "You no eat that one!" he carps.

"But, this is not a fortune," I explain. "It's just a… modern quote."

"I charwge you," he warns.

"How much?"

"A quawtew."

"Okay," I agree. "And another glass of wine, please."

Downing a few mouthfuls of Chow Mein, I decide whatever fortune cookie number two reads will be the prophecy.

The waiter returns with my wine and hands me the second cookie on a black plastic tray. "Here."

I take another sip of wine and break it open: *Invest in a friendship.*

Invest in a friendship. Invest in a friendship. Yes. That's more like it. Advice I can apply. I lean back in my chair and let the words sink in. I picture Angus's trustworthy face.

"Eating your pudding before your dinner, lovey?" a syrupy voice drips over my shoulder.

233

"Oh!" I jump. "Zoella! Hi. You come here?"

"Just ordered some take-away. Electricity's out at the hostel."

"You're kidding? I'm just coming from work. It was out there, too."

She flops down in the seat across from me. "Oh, no. What was that like?" she asks.

"Pret-ty mellow, really. A few grumps. But most people, I think, found it kind of fun, in a way. How about there?"

"A real pain in the arse, frankly. People just take the first opportunity to muck about, you know?"

"Real-ly?"

"Yeah, it's like just because the lights go out everybody seems to think they can just sod their duties. You should've seen the way Seamus cleaned the loos tonight. He was just sort of dragging the same filthy rag from toilet to toilet. Not making any effort at all."

"Ick."

"It's actually a lot harder than you'd think to get a solid crew going at the hostel. You know, people who are fun, but who also take responsibility and want to *contribute*."

"Right, I know what you mean," I say, noticing it feels markedly less loaded to be conversing with Zoella out of context, on the neutral ground of Suet Lee's, rather than at the hostel, on her turf. Though maybe, too, the two glasses of wine consumed in under five minutes are playing a part.

She sits down and looks at me adoringly. "People like you. I wish there were more like you coming through."

I wear a sick grin, calculated to endear.

"I'll really miss having you around, you know. We'll have to stay in touch once you go."

"Definitely."

"Who knows, maybe I'll meet up with you in India. I have to leave the U.S. at the end of November to renew my visa anyway."

Suddenly it hits me. *Zoella is the highest common denominator. If I clear myself with her…*

I study her for a moment and decide to put some faith in my second cookie.

"Zoella, there's something a bit crazy I want to say," I dare.

She squints to read my discarded fortunes. "Yes, lovey?"

"It's about me," I start.

"What is it?" she asks, more seriously.

"Well," I proceed, "before I came here, I was a lit-tle different."

Her eyes look puzzled, and her pupils seem to retract some.

"Different?"

"Missed vegable and bwown wice," interrupts the waiter, as he hands Zoella a pink plastic bag and a bill. She takes out her wallet.

In this instant I flash back to something she said last week about an old boyfriend she'd had and about how being lied to is the one and only thing she really and truly despises.

"Thanks," she says, gesturing to our waiter to keep the change.

I pause, with a meaningful look in my eye, searching for something to offer in place of my confession.

"So, what are you on about, Becky?" she presses, the curtness in her tone validating my decision not to confide.

"It's just that I used to… cook more, you know?" I say.

"Yeah, sure, I do," she affirms, letting me off the hook. "That's not crazy!"

"I just really miss cooking stuff. You know, my own sort of dishes," I continue.

"Sure, I can imagine," she says. "I mean Alan really dictates to you what you have to cook. And there's very little freedom to be yourself. For personal expression, lovey."

"Well, exactly," I join.

"What kinds of things are you into cooking, anyway?" she asks.

"Oh, I don't know," I say, "maybe just more Thai and Indian."

As relieved as I am to be back on familiar ground, at the same time I'm discouraged by the predicament: If I dare to tell the truth, I'll be thought dishonest. If I continue lying, I'm believed to be true.

"Listen, do you have plans for Saturday?"

"No, not real-ly. Why?"

"Well, why don't you come over our place for the night? I'd really love to have you over to the cabin before you take off for India. And we'll cook."

Being boxed into a secluded day of cooking with Zoella promises to be nothing short of a recipe for disaster.

"Oh, really?"

"Yeah, I'm glad you brought it up. I've been meaning to have you over for ages now."

"Great."

"Yeah, we can cook some Thai food, or whatever we want. How does that sound?"

"Just fan-tas-tic!" I rally my energies to exclaim, before plunging, head first, into my plate of Chow Mein.

Fancy Meeting You Here

The second I open my eyes the next morning the dread of the Zoella date returns. Lately things seem to be becoming more and more unmanageable. More and more out of my control.

Idly, I stare out the window at the vine of bright orange bougainvillea that grows up the side of the building, and admire the way it survives all the fumes from the parking lot below without ever losing any of its vitality. It has much of nature's integrity and power to survive despite changes to its environment.

Perhaps what's natural has an inherent power to act and to endure, I determine. Whereas, what's not, what's fake (like a phony), is condemned forever to reacting, subject to the will of its environment. Which would explain why *I'm* now obliged to spend a whole day alone with Zoella.

Getting out of bed, I take a deep breath and remind myself: *One day at a time. One day at a time.*

I have to stop thinking about how I'm going to get through *that* day. All I've got to get through is *this* day. For now, it's only *this* day's show that must go on.

I slip on a pink and blue striped turtle neck and a worn pair of jeans, both compliments of the famed free-bin. The three pairs of pants *I* arrived with, which were then way too tight, are now way too loose. Compliments, no doubt, of my extra-nervous nervous system.

Tying my hair up into a high bun, I then catch a glimpse of my new body in the mirror. It's strange to look so light when, in so many ways, I feel so heavy. Still, it's nice not to be quite so weighed down physically, at least. I pick up a little sample of Givenchy perfume someone left behind on our sink and put a dab on each wrist and behind each ear. Then I leave the room.

Once in the hallway, I pause in order to observe a heap of cigarette butts that have been snuffed out directly on the floor beside the couch. I realize that I am witnessing, for the first time, the legend of the upstairs carpet.

Just then Angus crashes into me on purpose.

"Crikey mate! Steady on!" I snap.

"Feel like riding on a cable car?" he proposes.

I rub the sleep from the corners of my eyes. "Not es-pec-ially. I've only just woke up, haven't I?"

"C'mon, let's go."

"Look at that," I deflect, pointing to the cigarette butts.

"Hope the fire alarms work," he replies.

"Apparently Harrison got the rug used from a Las Vegas casino speci-fi-cally for this very virtue. It's immune to having fags put out on it."

"Crazy. Anyway, c'mon," he whines, holding up two Muni travel passports. "Someone left these passes behind. They expire tomorrow."

"I have to work."

"You don't have to work for two hours. It only takes an hour."

"Well."

"C'mon, let's go ride a cable car around town. You know you want to ride a cable car before you leave here," he insists.

"Not real-ly, not more than you want to see the Golden Gate Bridge."

"You're a misery," he says.

I hold my hand up like a backwards peace sign to give him the finger(s), just before he pulls me down the stairs, through the lobby, and outside under the blazing Broadway sun.

"Anyway, since when do you like to do tourist stuff?" I ask, giving in to Angus's agenda, as we set off together to ride our first cable car.

"I'm leaving in a few weeks. I always was going to. I just don't like doing it right away, you know?"

"Yah."

"Yah, yah," he teases.

Minutes later, as we approach Mason, Angus screams, "There it is! Hurry! Leg it!"

"No, it's too crowded," I lament. "Let's wait for the next one."

"*What?*"

"Yeah, let's wait," I try, weakly.

"Never! Crowded is perfect! How else will we get to rub up against all the hottie-tourists?"

We race up to the stop and take our place in the line.

"Oh, just jump on, push your way on, Becky," Angus gripes, as I hesitate fussily before the steps. "Act like you're on the Thirty-Stockton going through Chinatown!"

After hoisting ourselves up onto the jam-packed cable car, we manage to find some standing space in between (cultural clichés holding steady) an obese American family of four and a deodorant-free European couple. The cable car begins moving.

"Woo-hoo!" Angus screams, ridiculously.

I look at him in make-believe horror which makes him smile. That's when, suddenly, I hear an English accent call out my name. Turning around, in anticipation of meeting one of our fellow hostellers out of context for the first time, I am shocked to see, "Luke?!"

"What are you doing here!?" Luke returns.

"Riding the cable car."

He squeezes past the family of four, now huddled around their guide book like figures on a Chinese pincushion.

"Well, I can see that. I mean, you're still in town?" he asks.

"Yes, actually."

"Why haven't you *phoned?*"

"It's a long story."

"Huh?"

"I'll tell you about it all later," I mouth.

"Well, how are you?" he asks.

"Well, thanks. You?"

"Yeah, great. Oh, sorry, this is my cousin, Deirdre," he says, gesturing to a woman standing beside him who, with her dramatic dark eyebrows and square jaw, resembles a female version of himself.

"Hiya," she says. She bites her bottom lip a little.

With the erratic noise provided by the cable car, I figure there's a slight chance I can pull this off.

"This is Angus," I announce. "This is Luke."

With an uncharacteristic practical interest, Angus then asks, "Friends from back home?"

"Yes," I mumble, in his direction.

"No," returns Luke, at the same time.

Angus looks confused. My heart registers the danger and begins racing.

Attempting some inverted ventriloquism, I move my lips, but make sure the sound doesn't carry as I whisper into Luke's ear, "He means from New York."

"What?" asks Angus.

"Yes," I say, in Angus's direction, shaking my head affirmatively. "From New York."

"Yeah, we lived in the same building there," confirms Luke.

"That place on Riverside, where I visited you?" asks Deirdre.

"Right. Blimey, Rebecca, glad we're not living in New York now, eh?" he asks, referring, of course, to 9/11.

Luke then looks back and forth between me and Deirdre and shouts over the cable car's noisy grinding, "Did you two never meet, then?"

"No, don't think so," she says.

I shake my head in silent concurrence.

"Where are you living now?" asks Luke.

My heart maintains a steady gallop. "Uh, Broadway," I mutter.

He takes in Angus's tender age. "Where do *you* two know each other from?" he inquires.

"The hostel," returns Angus.

"Hostel?"

"Yeah, living at a hos-tel," I toss off.

Luke observes me astutely. "You sound like you've picked up an accent?"

"Really? No," I say, as Americanly as is possible.

"Oh, she does that," confirms Angus.

Angus assumes Luke is referring to the last intonation, to what Angus believes to be the mock-American he and I impersonate for fun.

Luke eyes around to see where we are. "Rebecca's always been bonkers," he adds.

"Anyway," I deflect, with some relief, "so for how long are you in town, Deirdre?"

"Just about a week now."

"Like it?" I follow up.

No matter what the circumstance, keeping the focus closely on the other person's thoughts and opinions always seems to end up being the best strategy.

"I do," she says. "It kind of reminds me of Brighton."

"I know, I agree. Where are you off to now?"

"Actually, just here, it looks like. We're going shopping," Luke says.

He touches Deirdre's shoulder and they start moving toward the exit.

"Nice to meet you," she says.

"Rebecca, give me a ring. Let's get together!" calls Luke, from the step.

"I will do! Cheers!" I shout back.

Luke does an awkward double take. And as I watch Luke and his cousin disappear into the shuffle of Union Square, two distinct memories of him vie for space in my mind: one of how his shirt collar got soaked with tears when we watched *The Color Purple* together on TV in New York and the other of how I had to hold my breath and squint my eyes, in order to avoid seeing or breathing in the dildos strewn all over the place every time I entered his San Francisco kitchen.

"That wasn't the bloke you stayed with when you first moved out here, was it?" asks Angus.

"Good memory. That's exactly who it was."

"So, he's a pornographer?"

"Afraid so," I return.

"How bizarre. You'd never know it."

"No, I know. He's a lovely guy, isn't he?"

"Seems like. Seems so straightforward."

"Well, just because someone does something a little dodgy, I guess it doesn't mean they themselves are dodgy, through and through, right?" I ask, attempting to rationalize my own deviousness a little.

"How about a killer?"

"Well, that's beyond dodgy, though, isn't it? But, even that. What if it was in self-defense?"

"We should meet up with him before you go. He *is* fit. Gay?"

"Don't think so."

"You don't fancy him yourself?"

"Well I did. I guess I still do a little, in a way."

"Why not totally? Because of the pornography?"

"I don't know. I mean, I don't rate pornography, but I do rate Luke. And somehow the two don't cancel each other out. But, then again, I guess, I don't know. In the end, yeah, maybe because of the por-nog-raphy. Though I real-ly hate to judge."

The Chosen Representative

As I hurry along Columbus to my afternoon job, anxiety continues to rise. How unlikely that Angus and I should bump into Luke like that! What would be the odds? I mean, I would expect an unpleasant coincidence or two occurring every now and then, but I just can't quite get my mind around how many near collisions there are every day. It's a virtual minefield.

Standing on the sidewalk outside the inn, I am unable to decide whether I'm just extremely unlucky to keep getting into these near accidents, or extremely lucky, to keep safely escaping them.

After another minute or two, feeling as if I've just finished a day's work, I head inside to start my shift. Before sitting down, I decide to treat myself, for once, to a proper tea, complete with a fresh pot of Darjeeling, two scones, and a monkey-dish each of gooseberry jam and clotted cream. A reward for surviving yet another close call.

Then, settling onto the soft pink sofa, I gaze out the window and find I am, as hoped, soon soothed. Leisurely sips of tea, together with the sight of Taco, the neighborhood Jack Russell, doing his daily back flips in the park do the trick.

In the same way it always feels good to return home to the hostel after a shift at the inn, each time I get back to the inn after a day at the hostel, it also feels good. In contrast to the scratched pans and general lawlessness at the hostel, somehow the matching china and tranquility of the living room at the inn offer a different, but equally reassuring, form of escape.

Just then Liverlable bursts in through the front door under armfuls of tatty folders.

"Rebecca!" he exclaims. "Am I glad to see you!"

"Oh, thank you. Likewise," I say.

"I've been on a train for two hours and I've been so crazed!"

"Why? What *hap-pened?*"

He holds up a paperback book. "Well, there I was, reading this English novel and I didn't know, I *don't* know – what does *weeds* mean? It's a British word!"

"Oh. Right. I'm not too sure myself," I return. "Perhaps I need to hear it in context."

"It's right here," he says, turning to the page. "She wore her weeds with quiet distinction."

"Weeds?"

"Yes, weeds."

"Hmm, might be an old word," I try.

"It must be. I guess I can look it up in a minute. But, it really was maddening!"

"Yes, I can well imagine."

"Here's one for you, then," he continues. "What's a cubbyhole?"

"You mean like a little built-in cubbyhole in a wall?"

"Nope."

I glance up at Liverlable's expectant face.

"Well?" he asks. "What do you think it is?"

"Well, actually, perhaps it's an older word, too, because it doesn't really ring a bell for me," I confess.

"It is!" he exclaims, visibly pleased to have stumped me in my own language. "Thirty percent of our guests are English, and I can't tell you how few of them get that one! It's another word for *glove compartment!*"

"Oh, I see."

"Anyway, never mind that. I've got some jolly good news, my dear."

"What's that, then?"

"I was just playing with the answering machine yesterday and I think I've figured it out."

"Sor-ry?"

"How to record," he announces.

"Oh. Good."

His eyes widen.

"Yes. And I've decided I'd like your voice to be on the hotel's outgoing message," he says.

"What do you mean?"

"You know, 'nobody is here to take your call' and all that," he explains.

"Oh, really?"

"Yes, absolutely."

"But, your outgoing message already sounds so lovely," I try.

"No, you've got a fabulous voice," he insists. "It's really sensational."

"Oh, I don't know. Truth be told, I'm real-ly rather shy," I demur.

"Don't be silly," chimes in an eavesdropping guest, peeking out over a copy of *The New York Times*. "You do have a great voice. I was listening to you take reservations the other day and I was thinking the same thing. You must be some kind of national treasure back home."

"See?" says Liverlable.

I think about biding for more time, but fear further protest might raise suspicion.

"Real-ly?" I dither.

"Yes!"

"Well, okay, then," I relent.

"Excellent," Liverlable says. He motions to me to follow him into the closet where the answering machine is kept.

Once inside, Liverlable fidgets with the machine, while I stand there by his side, in the dark cabinet beneath the steps, taking a series of furtive deep breaths.

"Now!" he exclaims.

"Hel-lo," I begin. "You've reached the Fil-bert Street Inn…"

He lifts his finger off the record button and plays back the new outgoing message. Inwardly I am imagining the look on Liverlable's face should my ruse ever be discovered.

"Perfect!" he exclaims. "It's perfect, isn't it?"

"It's awful," I return. I'm stunned. To my own ear the voice on the recording is every bit as false as the Rococo armchairs gracing the lobby. I've sprinkled the long, broad A throughout the message like chocolate shots.

"*Nobody* likes the sound of their own voice, my dear."

"You must let me try again," I entreat.

"No, it's just perfect the way it is," Liverlable refuses, as he guides me away from the machine and back into the lobby.

I grapple with the unpleasant notion of having just laid down a permanent sample of my scheming.

"You really do have a lovely voice," calls the guest, putting aside his newspaper. "Though I've always been partial toward British accents."

"Well, thank you. That's ve-ry kind of you to say."

"Whereabouts are you from?" he asks.

Liverlable, in the background, beams like the mother of an honor roll student.

"Arundel," I answer.

"I've been there," announces the guest.

"Oh, real-ly?" I exclaim, with the likely zeal.

"Yup, in '89."

"Ah, so it's been a while, then?"

"But I remember it very well," he assures me. "The Arundel River. We took a walk one afternoon on some beautiful grounds. You know where I mean? Just by the castle."

"Oh, yes, of course. It's funny. It's such a tiny place," I prattle. "Nobody I meet has even heard of it, let alone been there."

"Is that right?" he asks, with an air of satisfaction.

"Including people from England," I offer, obsequiously. I hope to flatter him toward a less specific exchange.

"The Duke of Norfolk," he says, instead, angling for even more precise pinpointing.

"How ve-ry impressive!" I exclaim.

For a moment I'm eased by being able to grasp the reference, thanks to the lucky coincidence of my former college being situated in the Duke of Norfolk's old summer house.

But he won't let up.

"Yes, and the split church," he continues.

"Yes."

"Right?" he queries. "That is in Arundel, isn't it?

"Oh, yes," I assure him, having no idea. "Very impressive, indeed."

"Yes, it's a church that's half Anglican and half Catholic, isn't that right?"

I do some quick multiplication. Saying "I don't know" could make me sound clueless. But, then, "no" could reveal me as an assured phony.

I opt for the emphatic bluff.

"'Tis indeed!"

At the same time I am gaining an intimate understanding of the notion that a person who lies hates the person they have to lie to.

"What I wonder," he starts.

Tripping over him to block his question, I cut him off with my stock deflection. "And what do you do?"

Startled by the suddenness of the shift, he hesitates. Not one to be so easily brushed off.

"For a career?" I elaborate, as if his hesitation was based on some kind of misunderstanding.

But he isn't sure he's prepared to yield the field. "Uh."

"Or, what *did* you do?" I practically demand, determined to steer myself toward safety.

"History professor," he gives in. "I'm a history professor."

"And have you got a specialty?" I press, as I try blinding him with my best glittery game-show-host smile.

"Yes. British history."

"Oh, right. That cer-tain-ly explains it!" I say. More fear builds inside me.

"Well," interjects Liverlable, as if on cue, "I guess I'd better get going. I have to go home and be nice to the dog. Or, *pretend* to be nice to the dog."

"Oh!" I return, seizing the opportunity to draw on the new subject. "That little toy poodle?"

"Yes, that's the one. The great thing about poodles, my dear, is they don't shed."

"Yes, that's quite the selling point, isn't it?" I ask.

"Oh, it makes all the difference. Did I tell you I have a cat, too?" he continues, in inadvertent cooperation.

"No, real-ly? What's he called, then?"

"Checkers."

"That's a sweet name," I say.

"Well, he's black and white."

"Ah."

"Checkers was a feral cat that I tamed," he says, proudly.

"How excellent of you."

Guest gathers up his glasses and pen. "The floors are beautiful, by the way," he points out.

"Oh, thank you," replies Liverlable.

"What are they, cherry?"

"No, actually, they're cumaru."

"Cumaru?"

"It's a sort of hybrid of woods, you know, passing itself off as mahogany," Liverlable explains.

"Well, could've fooled me," says the guest.

And, off they go, talking about how well kept the nightly polished floors are and speculating on whether the door cut into the floor originally went to a wine cellar.

Meanwhile, I muse over ideas of what's genuine and what's not. Over what gets celebrated and what doesn't. And why. And I wonder whether, despite being a reasonably competent counterfeit, I'm getting away with it all because others have a longing for things to be authentic; a yearning for the truth, however false.

I wonder whether the cumaru floors are not unlike the world's most iconic blondes, who, from Madonna to Monroe, have been brunettes. Maybe I, too, am like a British national treasure, as the guest referred to me, *because* I'm American. Perhaps, after all, it's the very perspective of being a foreigner, an outsider, which allows for one's study and understanding to become total.

Truth or Dare

I spend the whole next day trying not to think about how tonight is the night I'm going over Zoella's for dinner. So, when I get back to the hostel at half past four, even though Zoella is due any minute, the sight of Angus doing a striptease on the pool table provides one last very welcome distraction.

"Any particular reason why Angus is doing a striptease on the pool table?" I ask Sharon, when I get over to our booth.

"We're playing Black Jack Truth or Dare," she replies. "Want to play?"

Joining Sharon, plus a new girl, I pull up a chair. "But of course."

"Vic," says the new girl, in a familiar and natural manner.

"Becks," I reply, as I sit down.

I'm amazed by the way a few newcomers just seem to start out as hosteller-natives, without ever seeming to have to pass through the hosteller-tourist phase.

"Drink?" Vic offers, gesturing to her bottle of Irish cream.

"Oh, no, I'm all right. Cheers, though," I say, as I slide the two cards Sharon deals me off the table.

Seeing this, Angus jumps down from the pool table and rushes back over in order to receive his next hand.

Vic looks at her cards. "I'll stay put," she says.

"Same," I say.

"Hit me!" Angus demands, recklessly.

We all turn over our cards. Angus, again, has gone the furthest over twenty-one.

Sharon observes his initial nine of clubs and Jack of hearts.

"You're losing on purpose," she remarks.

"Balls!" denies Angus.

"Well, I'll come up with something that'll put him to the test," I threaten.

Angus glares in my direction. "I *dare* you to dare me, Becky!"

"After all," I observe, menacingly, "there's no real fun in daring an ex-hib-i-tion-ist to do a striptease, is there? So, let us open this dare up for collaboration. What, if anything, is considered taboo around here?" I ask.

"Not a thing," returns Sharon. "That's the problem."

"How about standing up and singing in front of everyone?" suggests Vic.

"Totally *un*embarrassing," vetoes Sharon.

"I've got it!" I exclaim.

"Go on, then."

"Fags."

"How so?" Sharon asks.

"Fags and mooching. Together they're almost taboo, right?"

"This is true."

"Okay, so, we dare you, Angus… You have to walk around the rec room holding an already lit cigarette, okay? And you have to bum one fag off five different people. *But*, as you collect them, the bummed fags must remain in plain view. And, of course, it goes without saying, there's no tel-ling them you're on a dare *or* smiling as if it's a joke."

A look of deathly composure mixed with great anticipation comes over Angus's face.

"You're wicked!" he exclaims, as he sets off on his challenge.

Just then Zoella appears.

"*There* you are!" she calls, reproachfully, tearing me away from the entertainment. "Are you not ready to go, then?"

"Oh, no, sorry, two more minutes. You've got to see this," I say. I bring her up to speed on the dare in progress.

We four then sit back and watch as Angus makes his rounds, earnestly approaching distraught-looking travelers who, observing his handful of cigarettes, begrudgingly part with their own most valued possessions, defying logic and their own feelings, as a safeguard against the only bigger taboo: appearing uptight.

Meanwhile, Harrison, who is now standing at the far end of the rec room, motioning for us to come out the side door, yells, "Zoella! Let's move it!"

As Zoella and I get up, Angus returns to the table and deposits his plunder at its center.

"Well done!" says Sharon.

"Here," offers Vic. She is still laughing as she pours him a glass of her Irish cream. "You deserve a drink for that."

Angus scrutinizes the glass of liquor a moment. Then he picks it up, downs it in one go, and lets tear one rampant, rip-roaring fart.

"Laaaaactose Intolllllerant!" he screams to the crowd.

"Let's move, Rebecca. Harrison is waiting," Zoella then urges.

"Oh, sure," I say.

"Not a moment too soon, eh?" she asks, referring to Angus's boorishness, as we disappear from the table.

"Right," I concur, allowing her to think she's rescuing me, as she guides me, like a lamb to slaughter, away from the relative safety of my make-believe family.

Cooking up a Storm

Out on the street, Zoella ushers me into Harrison's car. "After you, love."

I slip across the duct-taped leather seat to reach Harrison's side. "Cheers."

Zoella falls in after me, pulling the old Mercedes' substantial door to a heavy close and sealing us in.

"Nice wheels."

"Doesn't have to pass smog checks. Diesel," she explains.

"What the hell took you so long? I've been out here waiting for you two for twenty minutes," barks Harrison.

"Sorry, Harrison, we were playing some Black Jack Truth or Dare. I just had to see Angus go around the rec room with a lit cigarette trying to bum more."

"Well, in that case."

"Thanks," I say. "Because you're meant to be an easygoing hippy from the sixties and I'd hate to think you turned uptight."

He makes an illegal U-turn back down Montgomery. "Hippy? Not me. You got the wrong guy," he chortles.

"I thought we could do a sort of Thai pumpkin-prawn soup?" Zoella starts.

"Umm."

"Yeah, it's Nigella Lawson's recipe. You know her, right?" she asks.

I attempt to make up for in enthusiasm what I'm obliged to dodge in detail. "Oooh, that sounds *to-tally* gorgeous!" I exclaim.

"Or, maybe she's not on American tele yet," observes Zoella, supplying the supplemental clue.

"If she is, I've never seen her," I safely disclose. "Love Thai soups though."

She squeezes my hand in the same manner my aunt used to and presses the play button on their ancient tape deck.

"Smells like rain, maybe even thunder," she says.

We coast along at an easy speed, listening only to the crooning of Van Morrison together with the car's partially broken windshield wiper squeaking against the window. Harrison's worn flannel shirt feels soft against my bare forearm, and as we pass one country vegetable stand after another, I notice how comfy I feel. But I also think about how much cozier this outing would be if only it weren't laced with the dreaded fear of being busted.

After making a series of rights down little dirt roads, we come to a complete stop, before a little wood cabin, in the middle of nowhere.

"We're here," Zoella announces.

We each grab a bag of groceries and step out into the Eucalyptus infused air. A few steps and we enter the tiny cabin, which turns out to be even smaller than it looks from the outside. Complete with low ceilings and tiny built-in shelves everywhere, the scale reminds me of Gotthard's parent's houseboat.

Inside, the place smells like coffee grounds and wood smoke. A giant plastic garbage pail sits unashamedly in the middle of the kitchen floor, and I can't help envying its frankness. Even the fridge and the gas stove, which are antiquated and beaten up, are authentically distressed.

Zoella then brings me through a lopsided little passageway that leads to the back door. We step outside and take in the view. Acres of desert with a flaming pink sunset bleeding out over the horizon.

"Wow!" I exclaim.

"It's nice here, eh?"

"Yeah! And you have a *hot* tub!?" I ask, spotting the bubbling pool.

"Yeah, fancy one before we start cooking?"

"Sure!"

She unzips her nylon windbreaker. "Great! Let's take a quick dip. Should still be hot enough. Isaac and his housemates were just over using it."

Squatting behind the tub to undress, I glance cagily toward the house, lest Harrison catch a glimpse of me naked.

In contrast, Zoella strips everything off freely. Then she stands upright in the warm wind, revealing a body in perfect proportion.

Stepping in, she slowly submerges herself beneath the bubbly water. "It's hot enough, isn't it?" she asks.

"Yes, it's perfect. It feels great," I return, flopping in over the edge.

"Ahhh," she sighs, settling in.

Closing my eyes, I allow myself to connect with the essence of my own body. "Umm."

"Yup, we'll just need to clear all that brush away and put in some palms," she rambles, splashing me as she points to the side of the house.

I hear her words without listening to them. The heat of the water relaxes me and releases the feelings locked inside my muscles.

"Uh huh."

"California the business, or what?" she asks.

"Is," I reply, with deliberate brevity. The unlocking of feelings gives way to a peculiar sense of awareness, a sort of emotional presence that makes the idea of shaping an accent seem even more ludicrous a farce than usual.

"Beats October in ol' Blighty, eh?"

I stare up at the sky. Amidst the grandeur of spirit and nature, I take into account how relatively petty my own crime really is.

"I'd say so. So, you like California, then?" I ask.

"Love it, lovey."

"Me too."

"I mean, you never have to open a can here. Never!"

"Is Harrison from here?"

"Nope. Vermont."

"How long have you been together anyway?"

She floats up to take in the view. "About fifteen years. On and off, though. At least on the physical plane, that is."

"Why on and off?"

"Oh, it's been complicated. I always have to leave the country to renew my visa. And, he's always been a bit of a free spirit."

She extends her leg out of the water in a desultory manner.

"I think we're at a point now where we're sort of settling into some kind of mutual something, though," she says.

Observing the sharp arch of her foot, I say, "It seems like you two really know each other."

"Yeah, we do. We do that. He's my fella. How about you? What ever happened with your bloke, the one who came through on his way to Hawaii a while back? Griswold, or something, wasn't it?"

"Oh, Gotthard? We never spoke again."

"Really?" she asks, pushing some sweat beads from her forehead into her hair.

"Yeah."

"Sounds dramatic, eh?"

"Yeah, it was pretty strange. We'd been together for over four years. There was no... closure."

"What happened?"

I lift my feet out of the water, cross my calves, and place them on the edge of the hot tub, near Zoella's shoulder. I'm struck by how natural it feels to be hanging out with her.

"He just blew me out, actually."

"Why?"

"Well, in the end there were a bunch of reasons, but the original one, which I think was the catalyst for everything else was, well, in the beginning I told him I'd only slept with four people before him."

"He believed that?"

"He did," I reply, leaning forward to pick off some dead skin from around my toenails.

"And then what?"

"Once I fell in love with him, I wanted to be honest about everything. So I fessed up. But, it was like he never got over it," I say.

As I explain, I'm reminded of the principle that, ultimately, in this case, as in Gotthard's, the only really deadly thing is to lie halfheartedly, to lie and then backtrack.

"Yeah, never discuss numbers with blokes. You have to refuse to discuss it from the start. Absolute law."

I entertain the never-before-considered possibility that I could've just declined answering Gotthard in the first place, sparing myself the shame of lying and him the pain of betrayal.

"To-tally," I return. "I suppose I just did the whole trying-to-get-loved thing at school and in college. That racked up a few," I confess.

It's weird. I notice I'm offering more intimate details about myself than I ever would normally, almost as if out of some kind of twisted compensation for the main lie.

"Who didn't?" she replies. "You were just expressing a little Aphrodite, love. You have to be careful not to let the wrong goddess types, like Hera and Demeter, define you," she explains.

"Well, he didn't think it was too cool," I say. "Said it was something he could just never sit down with."

"That's a bit strong, isn't it?"

He'd only slept with two others before me, though," I disclose. "That's why I said four. I guess that may have had something to do with it."

"Two people?"

"I know."

"Maybe he had his own complex he was trying to put in your space."

I stretch to comprehend her lingo. "What do you mean by *in my space?*"

"If someone's not in a free space himself, watch out. They'll want to judge you. That's just human nature."

"Maybe. I don't know. The annoying thing was that he did manage to give me a com-plex over one of the things I didn't have a hang-up about. Made me feel like a right slag."

"Hang-ups are a great, big waste of time. Life's too short," she affirms. "A flash in the pan and we'll all be dead and buried, won't we?"

Wondering whether it's her own chaste circumstances that are affording her such freedom of thought, I ask, "How about you? How many people have you slept with?"

"Not too many, really."

"Oh."

"Maybe forty or fifty," she adds.

"Fifty?"

"Give or take."

"Fifty?"

"Yeah, not too many," she returns, seemingly unscathed by notions of social taboo.

"Not many?"

"Well not so many by Australian standards. On Phillip Island, anyway, sex is more like surfing – holy and free. Context counts."

"You think?"

"Sure. But, I mean, it's not surprising you bought into all that. Look what you've been up against." She looks at me empathetically. "You were raised in sexually repressed Britain, right?"

"Uh, uh huh."

"Then you came to Puritan America?"

"Right."

"And then you fell into the arms of Calvinist Holland, right?"

"Right."

"That's a lot. It's not that there's no value to any of it. Just that social strictures probably require some tempering, right?"

The more she works to understand me, the worse I feel. There's something grotesque about soliciting sympathy from somebody while simultaneously deceiving them. At the same time, I can't seem to locate the brake pedal.

"I guess when you put it that way."

"Oh, for sure, mate."

"I think I'm just trying to see myself ob-ject-ive-ly again," I continue. "Gotthard always saw me as, I don't know, as some kind of a sinner or something. Sinner is such a weird word."

"You?" she laughs.

I zoom in on her. Forcing a lighthearted inflection, I ask, "What's *your* definition of a sinner, anyway?"

"Sin? That's easy. It's actually an old archery term. All it means is you missed the mark. There's no moral ruling attached to it, like people think there is. All it means is, usually out of some kind of fear, you went and missed the mark."

Once again, I toy with the idea of just coming out with everything, telling the truth, here and now. Explaining to her, right this second, how *I* missed the mark.

I glance up at her face. She appears to almost be shimmering with integrity.

"What gets me though," she adds, sternly, "is when people miss the mark on purpose."

Once again, I beat a speedy retreat.

"But, if you ask me," she continues, "I say you dodged a bullet with that bloke."

"You mean like, *Rejection is God's protection?*"

"No, like he sounds like he was a bit joyless."

"Well, not always," I defend. "I guess, in the end, though, I did start to feel like I was trapped in a Strindberg play or something."

"Don't know how you fell for someone like that," she marvels. "You're so uncomplicated."

"Don't know about that. But maybe a Moliere play might've been a better fit for me," I say, considering *Tartuffe*.

"What about that Aussie bloke at the hostel?"

"You mean Stacy?"

"Yeah, now he's a bit of spunk, isn't he?"

"Umm."

"Yeah, well how about him?" she asks, splashing me playfully with some water. "What about him, for you?"

"Stacy is beautiful. Doesn't fancy me though."

"How do you know?"

"Well, for starters, every time I talk to him, he either treats me like a mate or ends up walking away."

"Oh, right, never a great sign, is it?"

"Nope."

"At any rate," she continues, "just to finish the point, though, you know, love, that being a virgin is about a lot more than *no sex*, right?"

"Oh, that doesn't mat-ter."

She reaches over the side of the hot tub and grabs the cooler.

"It's more about having... a virgin spirit. Anybody worth their salt gets that," she says.

"Right."

"Like someone who doesn't prostitute their heart or ideas or values. That's what virginity means, in the eyes of the gods anyway."

"You reckon?"

"Yep, I do. Someone with virgin ideas, for instance, is just someone whose ideas are still free. Like you," she says, opening the cooler and handing me a ginger hibiscus iced tea. "And as far as I can see, you're about as pure as they come."

"Don't be so sure," I suggest.

"No, *you* don't be so sure. And stop being so bloody hard on yourself, chook, would you?"

****

Back inside, Harrison, wrapped in a light yellow beach towel, pauses to observe the array of ingredients Zoella and I are setting up along the counter top.

"Looks interesting," he says, before dropping his towel to the floor and wandering, naked, down the narrow passageway toward the back door.

"Can you believe him?" Zoella asks.

I begin crushing the flavor out of the lemongrass stalks with the side of a knife. "Nice beer belly on him."

"Really!" she agrees. "He likes to shock."

She cuts the top off a giant pumpkin. "Can you believe how massive it is?"

"Oh, c'mon, it's not that big," Harrison calls behind himself.

"Where'd you get it?" I ask.

"Pumpkin patch down the road. Got her on sale, too."

"Uh huh."

"Guy Fawkes being nearly here," she adds.

Guy Fawkes?

"Or *Halloween,* as the Yanks call it," she muses, as she begins scooping out the pumpkin's seeds with her hand and shaking them into a blue ceramic bowl.

Then she hands me a bag of shrimp and a bunch of cilantro.

"Let's start with the coriander and the prawns," she suggests.

I wonder to myself what distinguishes prawns from shrimp, as well as what the difference is between coriander and cilantro.

"Shall I take the tails off?" I ask.

"What do you think? Nah, let's leave 'em on."

As I bathe the little creatures under lukewarm water, the pitter-patter of summer rain starts coming down on the sky light overhead. I have the distinct feeling of being out at sea in another century. And in the spaces between minutes, I feel anchored and calm.

"Well, they had a good life. I'm sure they were in the moment, right up until the end," Zoella says.

"Sure." My reply is perfunctory. I'm too busy stewing in my disappointment over the fact that now that I've finally come to find an atmosphere wherein I feel this at home, ultimately I'll have to break with it and them.

"That's where your mind was, huh? I know you," she says.

"Actually, I was just thinking about how nice this is, here, today," I say.

"Cooking is healing, eh? We should've done this sooner. But there'll be other times. You're coming back here after India, right?"

"Absolutely," I say.

Inwardly, of course, I am affirming the opposite. Once I'm gone, out of a little of respect for everyone, I know I'll never be able to pass this way again.

"Excellent!" exclaims Harrison, taking his first bite, as we all settle in around their candlelit kitchen table.

Zoella's eyes glisten in the shadows of the flames. "It came out pretty good, didn't it?" she asks.

Glancing past the pieces of pottery and photos of hostel family lining the windowsill, a birdfeeder hanging outside the window catches my eye.

"I love hummingbirds," I say.

"Yeah, just sugar and water. We see them all the time," she replies.

"According to science, they're not supposed to be able to fly," I say.

"Really?" they ask.

I correct myself. "No, sor-ry, that's the bumble bee."

Suddenly, I feel low. The disparity between how at home I feel in my heart and how estranged I know I really am makes me melancholy.

"How do you like our soup?" Zoella asks me.

"Oh, it's good. Real-ly good," I say.

"So, you don't like it, then?" she concludes, misinterpreting my depleted tone as some other kind of indirectness.

"No, I do," I assure. "I guess I just don't have so much of an appetite."

"You're kidding? You said you hadn't eaten anything since brekkie."

"No, I know. I think I'm just feeling a bit sad, actually. About leaving, that is," I offer, attempting a half admission.

"Well, you're always welcome. You can always come back," Harrison offers.

With his long, white braids and sober countenance, he looks like an American Indian chief. And the kindness in his voice makes me feel even lonelier.

I smile as I lean away from the table. "Sorry, suddenly I'm afraid I'm really feeling rather Moby," I say.

"Moby?"

"Moby Dick. Sick," Zoella interprets.

"Umm," I consent. "I feel a bit funny."

"Take a nap in our bed. I'll give you a nice hottie to curl up with," Zoella offers, treating me as a member of the family.

I glance toward their bedroom just off the kitchen, which, with its high sleeping loft piled with worn flannel sheets and down comforters, is like a beckoning hideaway.

I fantasize about how great it would be if I really did belong here and could legitimately fall in under all those comforters with a hot water bottle and just listen to their distant chatter intertwining with the sound of falling rain, without having to speak or think or worry.

"Seriously, please, feel free," she insists.

Unable to resist being seduced by the illusion of our closeness, I savor the option of respite. But just for a moment. Quickly, I remind myself of the nebulous nature of my status here. I can't forget that if they knew the truth I'd, just like that, become as unwelcome as I am welcome now.

It's a funny, familiar sort of double bind. It's as if there's some feeling, some belief, that I can be loved and unknown or known and unloved. I've experienced this bind before. Before this whole accent fiasco began, I mean. I've known this feeling.

"No, thanks, that's okay. Maybe I just need a little smoke," I finally reply, picking up a dark wood pipe off the window ledge. "Do you mind?"

"Go ahead," says Harrison. "The guy who fixed the drainage last week left it behind."

"What are you like?" Zoella laughs, delighting over a quirkiness

I suppose she supposes stems from caprice.

But as I light the stranger's pipe and inhale what's left of the tobacco, the act of doing anything seems to lend some semblance of order.

"What are you like?" Zoella asks again.

"What?" I challenge. "Women in the seventeenth and eighteenth centuries smoked pipes all the time."

"What kind of tobacco?" she asks.

"In this one? Tastes like a fine do-mes-tic cher-ry blend. No, I'm only kidding. I have no idea."

"You look better, love," she observes.

"Yeah, I'm fine. Just a wave of nausea. That was all."

Harrison stares at me, now resembling a sea lion with the shrimp tail sticking out of his mouth.

"So, give us the gossip. What's going on at the hostel?" he asks.

"Oh, I don't know. What do you mean?"

He chokes down the rest of the crustacean. "You know very well what I mean," he says. "Who's fucking who?"

"Oh, right. Well believe it or not, I don't real-ly know. In a funny way I think we're more like siblings there."

"We don't see the world as it is, we see it as we are," he dismisses. "You're just too innocent."

I like the thought of someone seeing me as innocent, in any context.

"But you must have some gossip," he continues.

"Okay, well, let's see what I can scrape up, then," I start.

Our communication begins to remind me of a Long Island Iced Tea, with all lethal dangers masked by the effervescence and deceptive sweetness of the soda.

"Tell me about Ike. Isaac getting any action?"

"I don't think so. At least I've never seen him chatting anyone up. Or vise versa."

Harrison roars with laughter, making me feel like a real ham. And I feel enveloped even deeper in the very brand of belonging to which I can never seem to get close enough.

"No?" he asks, egging me on. "How about Alan?"

"Also not. Not getting any action a'tall, I would say."

He lets out another bellow. His expression is warm and wide open. My craving to confess becomes almost tangible.

"You look so otherworldly, Rebecca," Zoella observes.

I am busy contemplating how a sudden confession might fare.

"Really?"

"Are you feeling Moby again?" she asks.

"No, I feel fine," I say. "It's on and off."

I determine, once and for all, that the confession would be chilling, not touching. It would result only in my being stuck here, in the middle of nowhere, at the mercy of two people who would no longer feel as if they even knew me. I can't lose sight of the facts.

"Well, it's not surprising, living at the hostel. Using that kitchen. Germs must be everywhere," she offers.

"Totally, same sponge since I arrived, I think," I joke, gloomily.

Back Home Again

As soon as Zoella drops me off, I race back inside the hostel and restore myself to the refuge that is the rec room. Falling into one of the dilapidated chairs surrounding the pool table, I am immediately calmed by the thought of lowered stakes and not having to be, comparatively, so *on* any longer.

Just as I begin to acclimate, a girl sitting next to me, who looks like she might be named Sage or Amethyst, leans toward me.

"Splif?" she asks.

"No, thanks, I'm all right," I say. Getting away from the Zoella danger is more than enough of a high for me.

She smiles alluringly.

"Actually, sure," I add.

She hands me the joint. "Humboldt's finest," she says.

With little frame of experience for marijuana, I appraise the joint appreciatively and give her a knowing wink. "Nice," I add, just before I take a long drag and launch into a violent fit of coughing.

She passes me her cup of tea while I give thank-you nods in between trying to catch my breath.

"Thanks. Sorry," I finally manage.

"You don't get off until you cough," she assures me.

Just then Stacy plunks into the empty seat on my other side.

"Becky, old gal?"

"Stacy."

He has a chipper look in his eye as he shucks the ear of corn he's holding and sinks his teeth into it.

"You can eat corn *uncooked?*" I marvel.

"Oh, for sure, mate, it's the best way," he says, handing me the cob.

I take the corn out of Stacy's hand and try a bite. "Hmm, that is pretty good. So, what've you been up to?"

"Hot off the phone with the oldies."

"Nice?"

"Yeah, my Nanna, she lives in a kind of guest house behind my parents' house."

"Uh huh," I say, picking some corn out from in between my teeth.

"Anyway, she has dementia. Yesterday my parents had a dinner party up at the house. Everyone was seated at this big table. And then Nanna came along, up the hill. She was dressed to the nines, with all her best jewelry and shoes and her handbag."

"That's sweet."

"And nothing else."

"What do you mean?"

"She was completely starkers."

"You're joking? She was naked?"

"Yeah, seriously. Mum had to jump up and go turn her around."

"Aww."

"But Nanna wouldn't have it. She began wrestling Mum in order to get to the party."

"Oh, no."

"Yeah, seriously. But in the end Mum won and got her to go put some clothes on."

"That's pret-ty funny," I say.

He shakes his head. "Love that mob."

"Homesick?"

"Never," he says, as he gets up and removes the cue from his opponent's hand.

Leaning back, I observe Stacy. I watch the way he interacts and think about how conduct around the pool table really typifies the standard for hostel behavior in general. You don't ignore people, but you don't kiss ass. Friendliness, of course, is valued, but only if it's natural. It can't be that fear-based variety. Seasoned travelers, natives, always seem to smell the difference. In short, everything here begins and ends with being true to yourself, something glaringly plain for some, extraordinarily complex for others.

I study the game with added interest for the next ten minutes, until Stacy's defeated opponent collapses in the seat to my left.

"Looking pretty stoned there," he remarks.

Attempting to sum up my thoughts, I say, "Pool is more than a standard of hostel etiquette. It's a met-a-phor for life."

He has a cockeyed frown across his brow. "What do you mean by that?"

"Pool is about having a vision. Once you can see the ball going into a hole, you can send it there. But, you have to be able to see it, feel it, know it first."

"I don't know. I just try to get the ball into the pocket myself."

"Oh, and that's where you lowball yourself," I explain. "Pun intended."

"Sure," he allows, with dull indifference.

"It's all about quieting the static of self-judgment and expectations," I continue. "Just be present with the task and with your own vision. Both in the game and in life. And when you do, that's when you don't have to *make* anything hap-pen anymore. It's effortless. You're in the flow. In the zone. Concentration and consciousness, without thought. Get it?"

"You think too much."

"Maybe so," I say.

Privately, I consider my words in relation to my own masquerade. Indeed, having to remain so focused on tone, timbre and vocabulary is what's liberated me from the self-consciousness that normally undermines me, not only with pool, but with the world, too.

It's as if playing someone else has given me my first taste of what freedom from my ego, and the resulting static, feels like. As if, for the first time ever, I've gotten into the zone. By default.

"Nice and easy," mutters the kid beside me.

"And you know where it's going," Stacy says to his opponent, as he releases an impossibly light touch which sends his four ball directly where he wants it to go.

Twisting toward the guy next to me, I resume, "See that? In pool, as in life, a light touch has the same effect as a slam, and is often more efficient."

"Profound."

"In other words," I conclude, "take the stress-free path. It leads to the same satisfaction."

"You want a game of foosball?"

"No, I've got to go pack."

"Where ya off to?"

"India," I toss off.

"Yuck, skipped India altogether. Not my cup of chai at all."

"Well, namaste," I say, as I get up and head off through the rec room's gold doors.

Then it hits me. Gold doors. Golden doors. *All* the doors here are *gold!* And I wonder why the significance of this has never registered before...

Instead of going to my room to pack, I detour and tear up three flights of stairs to the roof. Kneeling down on the blacktop still warm from the day's sun, I rifle through my pockets for my room key. Into the tarmac I etch:

Give me your tired, your poor,
Your huddled masses yearning to breathe free,
The wretched refuse of your teeming shore.
Send these, the homeless, tempest-tossed to me,
I lift my lamp beside the GOLDEN door!

What a workout! Breathing as if I've just finished climbing the steps to the top of Miss Liberty's lamp, I lean back against an air duct and I admire my handiwork. Although my mouth is dry from the marijuana and I'm desperate for some water, I stay put and contemplate the words I can't believe I still remember from seventh grade.

Didn't the hostel take me in when I was destitute, tired, poor, and yearning to breathe free? Wasn't I, too, tossed, homeless, to this place, where a lamp was lifted beside the golden door? It can't be a coincidence! No!

The Purple Parakeet has been my gateway to freedom, my Statue of Liberty! What the Statue of Liberty and the United States of America symbolized to the European immigrant, the hostel symbolizes to me. And just like the immigrants who sought freedom, I've found freedom, the freedom to be myself. Only the price I've had to pay has been to become British. It all makes such sense.

Then I lie back under the stars, which I know are up there, even if they're all obscured by the city lights. And I smile, from the inside, never before having felt so at home as I do here tonight, in exile.

A Shandy for the Road

The next day I am sitting on the steps alongside the hostel. I'm thinking about what I was thinking about last night on the roof. At some core level, it's true: I've never felt so at home as I do here, in exile. What's also true, however, is that I've never felt so guilty. Or so worn out.

How tired I am of avoiding topics, anticipating the thoughts of others, getting in there first with explanations before their questions can come up. It's hard to imagine that by midnight tonight all the hyper-vigilance will be over. Twelve more hours of lying and I'll be free. No mess. No repercussions. No casualties.

"Party outside the hostel!" Angus shouts, spotting me from the street.

As he begins striding up the steps with a pack of American Spirit cigarettes and a Snapple lemonade tucked under his arm, I rush to round up my stray thoughts and reinhabit my British self.

"Hiya, pet," I call, resuming the role I both adore and abhor.

When he gets to where I am, he plants himself behind me and begins massaging my neck and shoulders. I bask under the familiar energy coming off his hands.

"Oh my God, that feels gorgeous," I say. "You have no idea what I've been through last night. I fell asleep on the roof."

"Pretty soon you won't feel your shoulders at all. You'll be carrying your rucksack around all day," he reminds me.

"I know. Maybe not, though."

"How do you mean?"

"I read in the book that you can hire people for peanuts to carry almost anything. There was a picture of a bloke carrying a refrigerator on top of his head."

"Colonialist cow!"

"Does seem a bit grot-ty, doesn't it?"

"Can't believe you're off and away tonight," he reflects.

"You won't even notice I'm gone."

"Look at you, angling for appreciation," he says. "You're right, though, with the amount of talent I checked in last night, I'm not going to have much time to miss anybody. Plus, I'm off myself in two weeks."

"You won't miss me just a lit-tle bit?" I press.

He scrubs my scalp as if he's washing my hair. "Maybe a wee bit," he says.

"Don't tangle my hair, pray."

"Why? You'd look great in dreadlocks. Bet it wouldn't take much either."

Just then Zoella steps out the side door and dangles a bottle of beer with a lime squeezed into its neck before me. "One last beer for the road, lovey?" she asks.

"Umm. Cheers," I say, taking the beer from her hand and inching into the sun.

"What about me?" asks Angus.

"Go get one, if you want. They're right in the fridge," she says.

Angus removes the beer from my hand and takes the first swig.

"No, that's okay. I'll just share Becky's."

Squeamishly, I eye his hickey-covered neck. "Eww, I don't know about that," I say.

"What are you on about?" he asks.

I look at him knowingly.

"Uh, the love bites you're making no effort to conceal."

"Oh, I know. I like showing them off. I wouldn't worry about that, though. You need to start building your immunity up. Dusty said when he was in India half the time the restaurants washed their dishes in the bathroom anyway. Have a nice trip."

"How about let's mix the beer in with the lemonade? It'll be like a shandy," I propose, never feeling quite so authentically limey as in moments such as these.

Angus downs half of the lemonade to make room for beer.

"Good idea."

"Actually, I was on the Lonely Planet website today," starts Zoella.

"Uh huh?"

"Not to freak you out but there were some new warnings about traveling to India right now."

"Real-ly?" I ask.

"It looks like tension between India and Pakistan is really coming to a head."

"They're always fighting," Angus says.

He then squeezes me to let me know my massage has come to an end. "Do me?"

Getting up, I swap places with Angus and begin working his slight shoulders.

"I would just say, after 9/11, even though they'd never know it, I would be a little careful about admitting to being any part American, if I were you," returns Zoella.

"Well, I'm hardly going to deny a part of my national-ity!" I exclaim, with honor, as if denying something I am is somehow different from faking something I'm not.

"You have both passports, right?" she confirms.

"Harder! Harder!" Angus screams.

"You have a UK and a U.S. passport, right?" she repeats.

I loathe such closed questioning, confining me to *yes's* and *no's*. The questioning that forces me to lie by commission, rather than by omission. "Yes," I say.

"Well, at least, then, bring your British passport, rather."

"Hmm."

"For sure, at least do that," she insists.

I knead into Angus's shoulders with more force. "Yeah, I will. Thanks for the idea," I say.

"That's more like it," he says. "I like it really hard."

"I'm going to need a thumb massage after this," I note.

"You two are a real pair," Zoella observes. She disappears back into the rec room.

I start to get up. "Actually, I have to get going to work, too," I say.

"You're working today?" Angus asks.

"Yeah. That reminds me, will you pick up my last check and deposit it for me after I'm gone?"

"I don't know. That's a lot to ask," he says, following me into the kitchen. "What's it worth?"

"Oh, I don't know," I say, rummaging through my cubbyhole. "How about a nearly full box of Taylors of Harrogate and, here, an unopened bottle of – ooh la la – premium olive oil?"

"Not good enough. What can you splash out on for me today?"

"How about a new lighter?"

"So tight! How about a Dim Sum lunch at least? It'll be like your going-away present to me."

"Fine," I say, handing him everything from my cubby. "You know this is yours anyway."

Shrewdly, he removes the premium tea from its box and immediately stuffs it into a decoy Safeway tea box to better protect it from pilfering.

"Cheers, dear," he says.

"Pleasure. What's yours to me?"

"I already have it. I'll give it to you when you get back from work."

"Oh, really, a pre-arranged going-away prezzy? I'm touched."

"I'll walk you to work," he offers.

"And walk me to work too? So doting today."

"No, I just don't want Alan to find me. I'm going to skip my shift. I'm going to pretend I didn't get the schedule. And we can get my Dim Sum on the way."

****

Angus and I amble down Columbus in silence. It's a silence I've experienced with him many times before. A silence that says everything and manages to convince me, despite all I've done, that there's a certain sanctity to our friendship.

"So, how often do you visit your mum in Arundel?" he asks, ruining the moment.

"Oh, almost never," I reply.

Angus sticks an arm in the open window of a Chinese restaurant we're passing and removes a bottle of soy sauce from the table.

"Well," he says, doctoring up his to-go platter of Dim Sum before returning the bottle through the window, "we should all have a reunion next time you're back. I'm going to move to London after I get back anyway."

I picture this reunion taking place at my mother's nonexistent thatch-roofed cottage along the Arundel River. "Okay."

"You should just move back to the UK, really. Ten years is long enough to be away from home," he says. Then he places the rest of his plate beside an old homeless man passed out on the sidewalk and links his arm under mine.

The Show Must Go On

"I have been on hold for ten minutes. I just need to confirm my flight," I say.

"Flight number?"

This, of course, is when the other line at the inn rings.

"Oh, no. I'm sorry," I tell the airline representative. "Would you hold on for just one moment?"

"Hello dear," starts Liverlable, the second I pick up Line Two.

"Oh, hel-lo, sir, it's you! Can I put you on hold for a moment? Am just finishing up a reservation," I lie.

I click back over to a disconnected Line One.

"Hello? Hel-lo?" I return, frantically.

"Hi, I'm back," I then say to Liverlable.

"Very good, dear, you're making reservations up until the last minute," he praises.

"Yes," I say, as I buzz a rich, bohemian-type guest through the front door.

"Well, was just calling to say thanks a billion for all your help. We're sorry to see you go," he says.

"No, thank *you*. It's been a pleasure working here," I say, returning the passing guest's wave.

"Great, when you get back from your trip, if you want a job, we'll always try to accommodate you here," he says.

"Oh, that's ve-ry kind. Thank you ve-ry much," I return.

I place the phone down and redial the airline.

Following another five minutes of listening uneasily to easy-listening music, a person finally answers.

"Hello, I'd like to confirm my flight and make sure it's on schedule, please."

Just then, emerging from the staircase that leads to the kitchen, Reggie, the inn's houseman, interrupts me. "Rebecca, Rebecca!"

I hunt for my flight number. "Not now Reggie," I whisper.

"But, Rebecca!" he insists. "There's a man in the kitchen."

"What are you *talking* about?" I snap.

"A man in the kitchen! He has a *knife!*"

Picturing a wandering guest merely fixing a sandwich in the kitchen, I cry, "What *man?*"

"This man," announces the intruder who, as if on cue, makes a surprise entrance through the same door Reggie has just shut.

"Oh!" I exclaim. It's the rich bohemian man I just buzzed in. But up close I can see he is no rich bohemian type, but more a shabby criminal type. And as his detached-looking eyes brazenly dart around my desk area, a fetid body odor begins to emanate from beneath his armpit-stained T-shirt. Not a guest at all.

He smiles mordantly. Very slowly he extends his hand.

"Hel-lo," I stall, cautiously.

I don't want to join with him by shaking his hand. At the same time I'm scared to risk provoking him with the slight of rejecting it.

"Mark Halpern," he says, pushing his chapped hand even closer to mine.

I distance myself from his offering, albeit in a less provoking manner than I believe would have been possible without the assistance of my accent.

"Yes, how can I help you?" I ask.

He holds up a check and stares at me.

"Can I help you?" I repeat.

"I want to cash this check," he says.

"And you're a guest here?" I ask.

"Yes. Mark Halpern," he says. He grabs a few of our crackers out of his coat pocket and scatters some crumbs across the floor as he brings them to his mouth.

Reggie shudders at this new mess, which will be his to sweep.

"Well, we don't cash checks, I'm afraid, even for guests, sir," I try, attempting to dignify him into complacency. His nostrils flare.

"Perhaps you might try Bank of America just down the street, Mr. Halpern. I know they're open until five o'clock," I offer.

"No, no. You gonna do it," he blurts out. Suddenly I wonder if the deferential tone of my inflection might be a liability, rather than an asset.

"I beg your pardon," I say.

I sense the best strategy is to continue treating him like a guest in the hope that it will influence his interest in behaving like one.

"You is gonna cash this check for me," he repeats.

"I'm afraid we don't have cash here anyway," I say.

His eyes scan the desk area until he locates the cash box. "Oh, you got the cash," he affirms, knowingly.

"I'm afraid we don't. We only take credit cards here," I say, undermining my authority with further explanation.

"Don't be fuckin' with me," he warns.

The doorbell rings, and I look at him aghast, as if to suggest I can't imagine any *guest* would be capable of such impropriety. Then, I buzz Mr. Rogers, our eighty-eight-year-old guest, in through the front door.

Mark Halpern, taking Reggie hostage, leaps into an adjacent closet.

"Well, what a day!" exclaims Rogers.

I note a crouched Halpern-in-hiding. His expression seems to be saying, "One word and I'll kill you both."

"Did you have a nice walk, Mr. Rogers?" I ask.

"Just to San Jose and back," quips the old man.

I smile at Mr. Rogers. I realize he is not the person to scribble and slip an S.O.S. note to anyway.

"Did I tell you my son is getting married?" Rogers starts.

"No, I don't think so," I return, grateful to his faulty memory for biding us some time.

"My son is getting married," he says.

"Oh?"

"He's forty-seven and lives with two cats. She's forty-three. Neither of them have ever been married. And he's not queer!"

"That's amazing," I acknowledge.

"Yar. What time is check-out?" he continues.

"Noon."

"Can I have a wakeup call at 11:59?"

"Certainly," I say, distractedly. I'm wondering if Halpern has a gun as well as a knife.

"Thirty-five people at forty-six dollars a plate, plus thirty-nine dollars per bottle of wine," he continues.

"Pardon?"

"That's what I'm paying for all this."

"Oh, yes, that's not cheap, is it?" I answer.

"Thirty-five people at forty-six dollars a plate, plus thirty-nine dollars per bottle of wine," he repeats. "And who knows how much they're going to drink."

Mustering a look of commiseration, I reply, "Indeed, I suppose it could get rather expensive."

"I know, and I'm the one who picks up the tab. But, then I guess he is forty-seven and living with the two cats."

"Yes."

"Now," he says, looking around the lobby. "This used to be a whore house, right?"

"No, actually," I contradict, gently. "I believe it used to be a pharmacy."

"Yes, I remember that, too. But before that it was a whorehouse. I was only six then."

"Oh, okay. I didn't know."

"What's your name?"

"Rebecca."

"My name is Tom. That's Tom with one 'o.' Tom Rogers. Did I tell you I was a third officer, then captain, in the Army?"

"I don't think so."

"Well, one thing about getting older, Rebecca, is that you don't have to give a damn!"

He takes an oatmeal cookie off the silver tray. "Cookie's pretty good," he says, taking a bite.

"I'm glad you like them," I say.

Absentmindedly, he puts it back on the tray. Meanwhile, Mark Halpern's impatience becomes audible.

"Well," Mr. Rogers explains, "I do everything. I even make buttermilk pancakes. And, now I'm going to sit down and have a pear. Or at least a part of one."

I recognize an opportunity to retreat to the kitchen in order to call the police. "Yes, can I get you a knife?" I ask, eagerly.

"No, thank you. I'm going to go upstairs and lie down. What do I do if I have to call down for something?"

"Just press zero, Mr. Rogers."

"Yowser!" he exclaims.

He heads toward the stairs to tackle two steep flights.

"I'm sorry we didn't have anything available on the elevator side," I call behind him.

"You did. I requested room nineteen. You know why I took it? I took it because it was cheapest," he explains, resolutely. Then he disappears up the steps to the safety of his chamber.

"Yeah, that's right. Beat it, old man," resumes Halpern, immediately emerging from the closet. "Now, you!" he says to me. "Move it."

"Yes, indeed. If you'll just excuse me a moment," I say. I am filled with adrenaline as I carefully inch past him. "I'll just go and get you your cash, then."

To my amazement, Halpern doesn't object. He lets me slip right by him. Bounding out the front door, I leave a terrified-looking Reggie behind, trapped in the desk area. But, at least I'm safe. I'm alive.

Breathing in the fresh air, I make a run for it. I rush into Donatello's, the neighboring restaurant, past people who all seem to be dining without a care in the world, and make a beeline for the hostess.

"Call the po-lice! Call the po-lice!" I instruct, my voice now quivering with a trace of hysteria.

"Hello," she says, calmly. "Can I help you?"

"The Filbert Street Inn! It's being... *ransacked!*"

She hesitates, as if assessing my mental state. Nearby rubberneckers take in the sideshow.

"Please, just call the police," I insist. "I work next door. A man has got-ten in and has been ransacking the kitchen and is get-ting ready to rob us and God knows what else."

She digests the information and begins dialing.

"Thank you ve-ry much," I say. I realize I've never used the word *ransack* before.

Then I hurry back to the hotel in order to keep Halpern in place until the cops arrive. The minutes go by like hours as I pace back and forth in front of the inn. Finally, with flashing lights and a silent siren, they appear.

A young pink-cheeked policeman with a heart shaped face and pale blue button eyes steps out of the cruiser.

"Hi. I'm Officer Murray. What's the problem?" he asks.

"A man has got-ten into the inn. He was telling me I had to cash a check for him and he was eating crackers," I prattle.

He turns back to the second police car and signals to them that they don't need to stick around.

"Okay, and has he threatened you?"

"Reggie, our houseman, said he had a knife in the kitchen."

"Right, okay. He still inside?"

"Yes, that's him, right there," I say, pointing at Halpern through the big window.

Spotting me, Halpern then rushes to the door. "You get it?" he asks, urgently, before seeing the policeman.

"No," I mutter.

As Murray steps into plain view, Halpern stares at me disbelievingly. "You got the *cops?*"

I look away awkwardly.

"Said you was going to get the cash," he accuses.

Shaking his head cynically, Halpern almost manages to make me feel as if I were the criminal; as if I betrayed him.

"Let's see some ID," Murray says to Halpern.

Halpern offers Murray the same edgy handshake he offered me inside. "How you doin'?" he starts.

"Okay, funny boy, you have ID or not?" Murray snaps.

Halpern sways noncommittally, gazing at Murray through his heavily-lidded brown eyes, as if trying to hypnotize him.

"Cuff him," Murray commands his partner, who grabs Halpern's arms, cuffs him, and locates his wallet.

"Okay, looks like his real name's Webster," he reveals.

Knowledge of Halpern's own duplicity toward me absolves me of mine toward him. I shoot him a disappointed frown.

"Was just tryin' to cash a check," reasons Webster.

"Not true!" I protest, vehemently, in a burst of courage.

He glares at me.

"You were ransacking the kitchen," I continue. "You had a knife, and you were trying to make me cash your check with our pet-ty cash!"

"Okay, take him in," Murray tells his partner. "I'll stay for questioning."

****

"Well, thank you for coming so quickly, Officer," I start, as Murray and I make our way into the hotel lobby.

"That's my job, ma'am."

"Can I offer you some coffee or some cookies?" I ask.

I almost make a joke about being sorry not to be able to offer him a doughnut, but decide a Brit might not have that degree of cultural literacy.

"A cup of coffee would be great," he replies. "Thanks."

Murray points to a trail of crumbs. "He do this?"

"Yes, he was eating everything," I say, as I hand him a porcelain cup full of coffee.

"How'd he get in?"

"He was buzzed in," I say, attempting to avoid ownership of the oversight.

"By you?"

I settle onto the plush pink sofa, reunited with the dignity and comfort of being on the right side of society.

"Yes. I mistook him for a guest. How long will he stay in jail for?" I ask.

"Depends. Usually about four hours."

"*Four* hours!?" I exclaim. I am jolted by the thought of Halpern returning to settle the score with me before I even get off my shift.

"Yes, at the most."

"But, that's ridiculous. You can't keep him any longer? He broke in here and ransacked the kitchen!"

"Not the way it works, unfortunately."

"Isn't there anything I can do?"

"Well, even that's only if you're willing to file a citizen's arrest."

"And what's that?" I inquire, righteously.

"Well, are you a legal resident here?" he checks.

"Yes," I say, reminded of my own criminal status.

He winces as he downs a sip of the diesel North Beach brew.

"Where'd you get the accent?" he asks.

"Well, I grew up in England," I fumble, wearily.

"Whereabouts?"

Uggghhhh.

Although not being allowed to be honest in this particular instance feels almost sickening, I slog on. "Arundel."

"But, you're legal here?" he verifies.

It's now time to churn out my most worn-out line, the one that no longer seems to leave me feeling at least half honest. "Yes, my dad's American."

"Then, yeah, you could go ahead and file one. Your mother English?" he pries.

"Right," I confirm, with ever more nerve than shame.

"I'm the same," Murray says. "Surprised?"

"Sure."

"Had an Irish mother and an American father."

"Fancy that?"

"Yup, my mother's family's from Cork, originally," he says. "But, I didn't get the accent. Got here too early for that."

For some unknown reason, I feel sorry for *him* for believing me.

"Right."

"Anyway, but if you want to go ahead and file a citizen's arrest," he continues.

"Hmm, and how long would he stay in jail for then?" I ask.

"Four hours."

"I don't get it."

"Four hours, but he'd get a summons to appear in court."

"But, how long would he be on the loose in between the four hours and the court?"

"Anywhere from thirty to forty days. We only have one DA to review about forty misdemeanor cases a day."

"Misdemeanor cases?"

"Well, actually this is more of what we call a wobbler. It's not a felony. Your colleague said he was brandishing a knife. But he didn't threaten him with it."

"Oh."

"We have a lot of cases, ma'am. And if I can be perfectly honest with you, this particular case would probably get dismissed before it even got to court because the chances of prosecution would be so slim."

"I see."

"As a citizen, you do have a right to go after him civilly though," he says.

"That's okay. I don't think that'll be nec-ess-ry," I reply.

****

After work I pack up my Tetley's and Hob Nobs and, for the very last time, stagger away from the little inn. Feeling disheveled and out of control, I then hurry home, braking before each corner, my eyes peeled for Halpern-Webster along the way.

As I zigzag through the raucous street noise and drunken tourists crowding the North Beach side streets, I keep checking behind myself, to make sure I'm not being followed. I don't feel anything like myself.

Then it hits me. The danger and the fear are finally congruent. What's going on for me on the outside is finally matching how I feel on the inside. There's even a perverse sense of balance. Alas, a tangible outer threat is attacking my inner well-being to the same extent that my fear-infested psyche has been threatening my outer reality.

Before getting to the hostel, I duck inside the corner deli. I throw a cheap bottle of Pinot Grigio and a pack of gum up on the counter, behind which the usual manager is stationed. He greets me with a familiar smile as he rings me up, no longer offering me tips on how to distinguish denominations of U.S. currency. I offer back a perfunctory nod and grab a straw. I have one agenda and one agenda only right now. That is to get away from this insanity as quickly as possible. To get it all back down a few notches. Because it's gone too far. Even for me. It just has. At this point, I don't feel like I could handle *one more thing*.

For She's a Jolly Good Fellow

As I draw nearer the Parakeet, my nerves calm. Until I enter the hostel, that is.

Inside, handmade posters line the entire staircase. And on the posters there are drawings of a wavy-haired girl riding a magic carpet, under which it's written:

"Becky's Going Away Party: 8:00 p.m. til 2:00 a.m.!"

"Boo-hoo! Bye-Bye, Queen Becky!"

"Becks Forever!"

My heart begins racing.

As I ascend the stairs, I find myself struggling between feeling honored by the tribute and wishing there was some way I could actually be worthy of it.

Approaching the stairs' summit uncertainly, I have deluded hopes of weaving myself into the fabric of the party, slowly, at my own pace. This notion is quickly dispelled when Angus, spotting me as soon as I spot him, announces, "She's here!"

"Surprised?" queries Zoella, as Angus leads some of the others in a guttural round of "For She's a Jolly Good Fellow."

"Yes! I *am* surprised!" I exclaim.

I am then mauled by knowing nudges and pats on the shoulder. One kick in the rear.

Alan looks at me suspiciously from behind the front desk.

"Angus didn't leak?" he asks.

"No, he didn't, actually. I'm completely surprised!" I declare, with satisfaction. My bar is set so low these days that being able to avow *any* form of truth, however unconnected, makes me feel just a little less the liar.

"Surprised he didn't leak, you mean?" Alan asks.

"That too."

"Aw, we're *so* going to miss you," starts Zoella.

My own reply is more reserved, "Same." Never do I overlook how tenuous the unmerited affection actually is.

But Zoella then springs a hearty hug on me. She rocks me tightly for a minute, managing, once again, to strengthen the illusion of my really belonging here after all. This causes my eyes to water up a little, for all the wrong reasons and, maybe, for some of the right reasons too.

She takes a step back and, with an outpouring of feeling in her face, looks me deeply in the eye. Though I seem to be responding with equal emotion, in fact, I am exhibiting a mere mannerism, a device necessary to obscure my own guilt. Yet, like a Russian doll, the guilt itself is still only another smokescreen, a cover-up masking, in truth, that which exists still more deeply: an authentic affection.

"Thanks, old gal," I manage.

My thoughts swim into one another, whirling to recover some semblance of harmony.

"So, what time are you off, then?" she asks.

"Soon, actual-ly," I start, taking advantage of the opening. "An hour and fifteen minutes, to be exact. Must go grab my gear, in fact. Should have it down here when the shut-tle comes."

"If you have a trademark," she starts, familiarly.

"Sor-ry?"

"Organized. You're very organized, eh?"

I attribute the said trademark, in part, to my real ancestry. I think, too, of my paternal grandmother, Leah Lamb.

I think about Leah's closet with its three hundred different pairs of shoes, and matching handbags, everything meticulously labeled and neatly arranged. All that order, all that illusion of control, perhaps just symptoms, outlets for unacknowledged fears. Has that trait been passed down to me? Or maybe I'm just your garden-variety obsessive. Either way, I don't tell any of it to Zoella. That's another identity.

Instead, feeling estranged, I force a terrible we-really-do-know-each-other-pretty-well-by-now sort of smile. Too much pre-meditated structuring has finally exhausted me. It has conquered my desire to connect. I long for natural dialogue and casual conversation. It's as if I am reaching the end of the line. And not a moment too soon.

****

After retrieving my backpack, I glide steadily down the stairs, until I am obstructed by a group of people, who appear to be in some kind of a meeting, on the second floor landing.

"There you are! I was afraid you'd *gone!*" exclaims Daniel, recognizing me before I see him.

"Oh, Daniel! What are *you* doing here?"

"Got back this afternoon," he says. "This is my crew."

He makes a brief round of introductions: cameraman, sound-man, and associate producer. All offer obligatory nods.

"This is Rebecca, men. She's the one who's gonna get us minted."

"Sorry?" I ask.

"My commissioning editor went for it."

I cock my head slightly, trying to take in what he's telling me.

"Did you not get my message or my e-mail, then?" he asks.

"No, I guess I didn't."

"Oh, that's crap. The bloke on the phone said he'd be sure to get the message to you. Should've given a second ring, as well, perhaps. Just had so much to do. Christ, I'm bloody glad you're still here, though."

My mind races. "Yeah, just, really."

"Sorry?"

"Just, I'm *just* still here," I explain. "I'm off in an hour."

"What?"

"I'm off. I'm leaving."

He looks at yet another "Bye, Bye, Queen Becky" poster hanging on the wall behind me. Then at my backpack.

"This is for *you?*"

"Afraid so."

"That's perfect!"

"Huh?"

"*Booze-free Brit is Belle of the Ball!*"

"Oh, yeah, I guess," I reply.

"Well we've got to move it then, don't we? There's no time to spare."

Somehow, managing to forget that this whole subplot was something I brought on myself, I feel martyred by Daniel's demands. I feel like some kind of worn-out circus performer who has been out there again and again, night after night, and who has finally had enough.

"I know this is bad timing, but the thing is I'm not sure I can do this tonight. Frankly, I'm really just not up to it," I manage.

"Not up to it? Are you joking? Do you know how much red tape I had to cut through to get this assignment off the ground? You're damn well not backing out now."

"It's just that I've had a real-ly long day. I'm knackered. I'm not up to per-for-ming. I can't tell you how *done* I am."

Daniel leans in so close that I can smell the coffee on his breath.

"Look, Rebecca," he whispers, "don't worry about it. We'll be completely unobtrusive. Just go about your business, *sober* of course, and you won't even know we're down there. Frankly, mate, you don't have a choice, okay?"

"I guess I'll just see you downstairs, then," I say.

****

Downstairs, with my wine and backpack in tow, I sneak through a back entrance off the kitchen and head for the supply closet sprinkler room, where nobody except Alan or I ever go.

Ducking through the pantry's low entryway, this is the first time I'm not in there to round up ingredients for a meal I'm cooking. I'm just looking for a place to collapse. Crashing onto a tub of peanut butter, I then lean back against a giant bag of poppy seed bagels and let out what feels like the first breath I've taken all day. A few minutes all alone and I'll be able to cope with the party.

Removing my bottle of wine from the back of my bag, I use all of my strength to push the cork of my Pinot Grigio into the bottle with a blunt knife, like Gotthard once taught me.

As I commence with a few cork-obstructed sips, the theme song from the night Angus and I were dancing on the tables begins playing.

Cries of "Where's Becky?" "Has anybody seen Becky?" carry into my little hideout.

Shit!

I drink purposefully, half in merriment and half in reckless desperation, as I gear up to rejoin the celebration. But, none of it works.

Suddenly, it's as if I'm split into two separate people – at once, both fantastically popular and horribly false. And I start to wonder at how two identities, so mutually exclusive, can possibly coexist.

I sit back down and take stock.

Stop it, Becky. You're losing it. This is not the time for these kinds of questions. You'll drive yourself balmy. Balmy!? You don't say "balmy." You're using British slang in your own head now? Stop this! Get a hold of yourself. You are leaving in an hour. You're almost there. Everything is okay. You are not a bad person. You love them, too! You have not deceived anyone, not in your heart.

Suddenly the door swings open. It's Frances! She eyes my bottle of wine.

"What in the world are you doing…"

"Oh, God, not you! Go away!" I exclaim, as I slip off my peanut butter chair.

"…in here?" she finishes.

I get up off the floor and push past her, making my way back out into the bright kitchen.

"I can't just stand by and watch this happen," she calls behind me. "I thought I could, but I can't."

"Leave me alone!" I demand.

But she closes in on me. "Please, Rebecca," she pleads. "Just take another meeting. Just come with me to *one* more meeting!"

"Frances, look, I know I said I was trying to stay sober, but the truth is what I told you in the beginning. I *don't* actually have a problem with alcohol."

"Rebecca, you were drinking in a *closet.*"

"It's because I wanted to be alone! And because I didn't want *you* to see me!"

"Do you think being afraid someone is going to see you drinking is *normal* drinking? Do you think it's normal *thinking?*"

"Yes! Because I'm not hiding it for the reasons you think I'm hiding it!"

"Just the fact that you use the word *hide* in relation to drinking. How much more closeted can you be?"

"So sorry, ladies," interrupts Stacy, squeezing past us to the refrigerator in order to execute a perennial beer rummage. "I seem to always be walking in here during your… lover's rows."

I shoot daggers at him which, for the first time, are not lost on him.

"You all right, Becky?" he asks, forebodingly.

"No, I'm not all right!" I snap.

"Easy, old girl," he says, locating his beer booty. "I knew you were no lipstick lesbian, but I didn't take you for a… never mind."

Although up until now I've managed to be the teapot steadily on the cusp of the whistling boil, this commentary, at this particular point in time, adds the fractional degree of heat that sounds the alarm.

"Shut up, Stacy!" I shout, losing control. "Stop *pretending* you think I'm gay, just because of that one night in the sauna! You know good and well who it is I like. Or make that *liked!*"

"Huh?" Frances returns.

"I do?" asks Stacy.

"Yes, and I'm not an alcoholic either!!!" I screech.

A small crowd, including Daniel and his crew, gather to observe the spectacle, their expressions echoing the surprise of both Stacy's and Frances's.

Daniel is whirling his arms and shaking his head. I can tell he's pleading with me not to blow the ruse of being an alcoholic-in-recovery.

"You tell 'em, girl," chimes in Angus.

Stacy is wearing a puzzled smirk. "I get the feeling we have to be very careful with how we proceed," he says to Frances. "Rebecca's in a bit of a mood today."

"For Christ's sake, you guys!" I holler, unwittingly reclaiming my very own voice, "I'm… I'm…"

"What?" prompts Angus, playfully.

"I'm an *American!*"

"Huh?"

"What are you on about?" challenges Stacy.

"See, I told you she'd give us a show," I hear Daniel whisper to his associate producer. "This is the *real* fake-out."

Then, to me, Daniel is mouthing the words, "Brilliant! Yes!"

"I can't lie anymore!" I exclaim.

"Good," interjects Frances. "We're only as sick as our secrets!"

I see Daniel nudge his camera man in the rib, signaling him to zoom in for the big moment.

I fall back into the pile of beach towels used for drying dishes.

"So, I'm just going to tell you the truth," I say, continuing in my real voice.

"Nice try, but not too convincing," scrutinizes Stacy, still determined to take the lie for granted and to doubt the truth. "Nothing more grating than an English girl doing an American accent!"

"No, Stacy, it's worse than that," starts Frances, wringing her hands. "She's hiding again. She uses an American voice when she's afraid. When she's uncomfortable being herself," she explains. "She's done it before, at an AA meeting."

"No, Frances," I correct. "That was my real voice that day."

I decide to pass the point of no return. "You see," I divulge, "the truth is… The *truth* is…"

I feel Angus's eyes zooming in on me even closer than the cameraman's telephoto lens.

"The truth is… I'm doing a linguistics study at Stanford University."

They look at me expectantly.

"Being here, this has been my field work," I continue. "I'm sorry to have had to deceive you all."

Stacy shakes his head, cracks a beer, and grabs his pool cue.

The rest of the crowd carelessly melts away, too.

Angus remains. His face looks uncharacteristically sober.

"Are you serious?" he asks.

"Yes. No. Yes about faking the accent. No about the degree. But, I can explain…"

He looks disoriented. And my biggest fear is realized: not that he'd be angry, but that he'd somehow be creeped out by me.

"See," I start, commencing with the big confession, as the soundman lowers the boom a few inches over my head, "I was substitute teaching and…"

Angus knocks the boom with his fist and looks fiercely at Daniel.

"Could you lot not fuck off for a minute? She's not sober, by the way? She's faking that too!"

Then he just looks at me as if he doesn't know who I am anymore. In return I start almost speed-talking, my words tumbling out wildly now, as if any indecision might make me want to take it all back.

"Look, I was dealing with the whole Gotthard fallout, which you already know all about," I point out.

. He takes a deep breath and begins searching my features accusingly. "Are you *okay?*" he asks.

My voice now starts to quiver. I feel ugly in a way that has nothing to do with looks.

"Just, please, give me a chance to explain better. I swear."

He waits in anticipation.

"So, my lease was up. I just needed a place to stay for two nights until the teaching interview I had," I continue, anxiously.

"From New York?" he asks.

"No, actually, I was living in Berkeley before here."

He shakes his head.

"But, everything else is true," I appeal. "And I did live in New York for ten years. And I *am* from Connecticut."

"And you were born in East Sussex then?"

"*West* Sussex," I correct.

"Were you born in *West* Sussex?"

"No."

"So, you never lived in Arundel?" he continues, with a look of increased distrust.

"I did."

"So, you *are* from Arundel?"

"No. I only lived there for a year."

"So, you're not half English?"

"No, not really."

"Not really?"

"No, then. I mean, I suppose... in spirit. No. Not. Not half English."

"Why are you making me drag this out of you!?" he demands, misinterpreting my nervousness as more withholding.

"I'm not. I'm willing to explain everything."

"Carry on, then," he prompts. "I haven't got all night."

"So, I called here. Alan said I couldn't stay because I was American – or a local, rather. And so I called back a minute later in the accent and then..."

"And then you just decided to live here this whole time while pretending to be someone else?"

"Something like that."

"I understand," he says, thinly.

"See, all the other hostels were booked. And, anyway, I really did want to stay here."

"And that was so important that it was worth it to lie to all of us about everything?"

For a moment, I am speechless. I don't know how to explain to him that it wasn't like that. When, of course, it was.

"How desperate can you be?" he asks.

My words, like a popcorn machine, now start exploding every which way. "Oh, I... I wanted to tell you from the beginning. I really did. It was complicated. But I wanted to. But I couldn't. And there was a new tenant moving in the next day. I felt too guilty. And then Mexico didn't work out. Well, I was going to tell you, but then..."

"But, then, *what?* *Why* didn't you just say?"

"Because one thing sort of led to another. It was too hard."

"Too hard to say, 'Hey, mate, I'm American. I lied.'"

"Yes, I'm afraid so."

"Well," he starts, with a look I don't recognize. "That's a bit too average for me."

"Look," I attempt, more authoritatively, "the truth is there was nothing involuntary about any of it. It was all deliberate. It was all choice. I admit to everything. All I can say is that, to me, the choice itself made more sense, in context."

But he just holds a repellant hand up to me. "Please!" he says. "No more. I feel like I'm about to be ill."

With that, Angus walks off. And Daniel storms over, exclaiming, "That was *brilliant!*"

"Hmm."

"I'm at a complete loss for words, Rebecca."

"Me too," I tell him.

"How ever did you come up with that whole story? Had you scripted it in advance?"

"Uh, Daniel."

He grabs my right shoulder and gives it an affectionate shake.

"No, you're a star. You're brill. To come up with that plot twist so you could actually transfer the American scam here. It was stellar."

"Please, no," I protest. "It's not what you think."

"Too right, it's better. *Never* would I have come up with it. It was genius. You're an *icon* of deceit. You really are going to mint us with this."

"No, I'm not."

"Stop being so bloody English, Rebecca! Just take the bloody compliment, would you?"

"I'm not being English."

"Too right you aren't being English. Just listen to you go. There isn't even anyone around. And listen to you. Method acting, I think they call it."

"Huh?"

"That's what the Yanks call it, I think."

"Look, it's crazy but…"

"No, it's not. Not at all. It's just one method. I think it started in New York. It's pretty mainstream now, actually. Meryl Streep, Nicole Kidman, they all use it."

"Would you just listen? Please."

"Go on, then."

"I have to tell you something that's going to sound crazy. But, it's the truth. The real truth. The thing is, I really *am* American, okay?"

"You're absolutely outrageous, you know that?"

"I'm serious."

He pauses a moment and then bursts into laughter. "You'll stop at nothing. Will you?"

"No, seriously, I'm American. I *am*. It's being British I've been faking. Except with you, Daniel. With you I've been *faking* being American on top of that."

Suddenly something in his eye shifts. It's like a switch flips and he does a double take. "Jesus, you're serious, aren't you?" he says.

"I am, I'm afraid."

"So, you mean, you actually *are* American?"

"Yes."

"And you actually tricked me into believing you were English, faking being American?"

"Yes."

"Whoa."

"Are you angry?"

"Angry? You're absolutely shameless!"

"I don't blame you for being angry."

"Angry? Do you want a job?"

"You *must* be kidding."

"I couldn't be more serious, Rebecca. Crikey, we could take this on the road to hostels all over the U.S. Make a bloody series out of it. I can see it now: *The Counterfeit Brit!* It's a scream! Do you not see how priceless this could be?"

But Daniel could not be more mistaken, and the price is what I know I'm just about to start paying.

****

Sure enough, moments later, I am alone, outcast, standing small in the middle of the big, empty kitchen. It doesn't even feel like the same kitchen anymore. It's not the same kitchen. Because I'm no longer Queen Becky.

Suddenly, like the mercury rising in a thermometer, I feel something awful rising up inside of myself. It feels like there's been some kind of toxic dump in the pit of my stomach and it's slowly seeping everywhere, flowing up through my chest and throat, and down through my arms to the tips of my fingers. At the same time it's as if I'm being smothered. I know I have to get away from these feelings. Because if I don't do something, anything, I feel like I'm going to *die*.

The problem is, as much as I know I have to do something, anything, at the same time, I feel completely frozen. As if my feet are cemented to the floor.

Mustering all my reserves, I will myself to lift a limb. It feels wholly unnatural at first. But, one at a time, I just put one leg in front of the other until I'm walking.

Once in motion, I make my way through the rec room to the front desk. I have to keep going. I have to take some other kind of action. I have to win Angus back. Get him to see I'm still me. Still her. That she and I are the same *we*.

I grab a pen and a piece of scrap paper and rack my brain for something to write. I try to think of some quote from *Thelma and Louise*, Angus's favorite movie, but nothing seems relevant, except for the part where they drive themselves off the cliff.

After another minute, it comes to me and I begin scribbling onto the paper what I can remember of a favorite Joan Crawford quote, after she was busted as a jewel thief in *The Last of Mrs. Cheyney*:

"You weren't so wrong about me. You thought I was a nice girl with the heart of an adventuress. Whereas, really, I'm an adventuress with the heart of a nice girl."

Then I look around for someone to summons.

Conveniently, Frances is planted neatly in one of the purple salon chairs beside the French doors.

My approach is slow, stealthy. I have total composure suddenly, like a madman on the verge.

"Frances?" I ask, gingerly. "Could you please give this note to Angus for me?"

She is, indeed, the one person to whom I suspect I can still afford to speak.

She looks up at me and pauses. "It's like I said the night of the last big party," she says.

"Sorry, I don't remember."

"When we act on our vices, even in small ways, it wears on our self-esteem, even unconsciously. Then we don't have the self-assurance we need to stand up for ourselves," she says. "This is the right context for that point, I think. Integrity and humility. You need both, Rebecca."

"Got it. I follow. I follow now. I do. Will you, though? Give this to Angus?"

"You're supposed to make your own amends, directly," she starts.

"Right, of course," I say.

She studies me a moment.

"I *shouldn't* enable," she continues. "But, you know what? I think just this once it would be okay. To perform the duty of a messenger is, after all, a form of service, too."

"Oh, thank you, Frances! Thank you."

"Not at all. Glad to be of service," she replies. Then she vanishes into the rec room.

From a safe distance, I watch as Frances presents my note to Angus. He reads it himself with a poker face and then passes it counter clockwise around the table. I begin sinking as, one after another, like the beads on a graduated pearl necklace, the disapproving head-shakes grow larger and larger.

Still, none of this surprises me. Despite this being an anything-goes kind of hostel, a place where you can rob the register, hightail it to Mexico for a few months, then return and manage to reclaim your desk job, somehow I've always suspected that what I've done is in a different realm. Premeditated deceit wouldn't be tolerated.

In another minute Angus gets up and heads over to where I'm standing.

I stare at him meaningfully as he approaches. He holds my gaze.

"I'm sorry," I utter. Unexpectedly, the weight of three months of resisting these words comes crashing in on me.

For a split second it almost looks as if the tiny muscles around his pupils are relaxing.

"Angus," I continue. But then I stop myself, judging it prudent to avoid testifying to any further emotions just yet.

He hands my note back to me. "Why don't you stick to using your own words, as well as your own voice?" he says.

"Okay. I will. I'm really sorry, Angus. I'm really sorry," I say again.

Listening to my own voice I notice there's something different about it. Aside from the obvious lack of accent, there's a tenor of humility, a kind of goodness I haven't heard in it for years and years.

"I," I continue. But he turns on his heel and disappears.

With that one action, the pendulum swings again to the other side. I feel neither humble nor good. To my surprise, I realize my worst fear isn't my worst fear: his disdain *is* as bad as his being creeped out by me.

I'm extremely thirsty suddenly. And I feel as if I'm about to throw up.

"Rebecca, your shuttle is here!" Alan then shouts into the rec room, with a customary harshness that makes it difficult for me to judge whether or not he's heard the news.

"I'll be there in a minute," I rally the courage to call back, before I head for the bathroom.

****

Locking myself in a stall, I fall, still in my jeans, onto the toilet seat. I hang my head between my knees and listen to my heart beat, never remembering feeling quite so leaden.

"Don't sweat it," says a voice from the next stall.

I look down at a pair of paint-covered construction boots.

"What?" I ask.

"No big deals, Rebecca," returns Isaac.

"How'd you know it was me?" I ask.

"Don't rely on what I see," he states, mystically.

"Oh. Or what you hear, I suppose?"

"Or what I hear."

I sit still a moment, wondering why Isaac never said anything about any of it before.

"You know," I confess, staring at the gimp bracelet Angus wove for me, "the whole thing just kind of happened."

"Yeah."

"I'm just afraid they think it was out of some kind of spite. It wasn't. It was more like serendipity. I know it sounds weak, but, in a funny way, the accent was almost... accidental."

"I believe you. It's okay. I believe you. Just, people don't like to get duped. That's all," explains Isaac.

"I know."

"They don't hate you, though. They hate that you've made them question their assessment of reality. There's a difference. It's like the *Uncanny Valley* thing or something."

"Uh huh."

"Rebecca?" he continues. His tone is philosophical sounding.

"Yes?"

"Can you pass me some toilet paper?"

I tear off a few squares with which to dry my sweaty palms before handing him the rest of the roll.

"Thanks."

Unhitching the door, I inhale the bathroom's signature bleach scent one last time.

"Guess I'll see ya around," I say.

"Oh," Isaac replies, with an audible smile. "I'll be around. And around."

****

As I exit the bathroom, I take a deep breath, perhaps the deepest one in months. Convinced the details of the drama will have by now spread throughout the hostel, I cross the lobby in what feels like slow motion. Again, it's like in the dream where you have to get away, but you can't move your legs. Sound is distorted too. I hear sound bites. Sharon's voice says, "It's freaky." But the scorn is more felt than heard. The verdict is in. Worst of all, I know it's fair.

Somehow I manage to make it through the thirty-foot lobby to the top of the torn turquoise steps. I feel both relieved to be escaping and awful to be leaving like this. To be fleeing the identity I escaped *to* in the first place seems backwards. Yet, as sure as the original lifeline doubled as an albatross, the original albatross, it now appears, is my lifeline.

"Not so fast!" a voice calls behind me.

Already almost halfway down the stairs, I consider just making a run for it.

"Wait!" the voice insists.

Swinging around at Stacy's entreaty, I look up at him and prepare to take whatever I have coming.

He comes down a few steps to meet me.

"I've got something to say," he starts, shaking his head disapprovingly.

"Uh huh?" I return.

But, it's also a relief. A relief to finally be escaping the court of my own conscience. And all the terror that implies.

"I just wanted to say," he continues, looking me square in the eye. "Look, I'm an idiot, okay?"

I stare down at my free-bin-salvaged sneakers, not trusting myself to look back at him without crying.

"You?"

"Yeah."

"You mean you aren't mad at *me?*"

"Because you're really a Seppo?"

"A Seppo?"

"Septic tank. Yank," he translates.

"Oh. Well, yeah," I say, softly.

"Nah, mate, it's a *corker* of a prank. Can hardly wait to tell my mates! Mad at myself, for being such an idiot."

Overwhelmed by the mercy, I rush to reassure. "*You* weren't being a fool! *I* was lying!"

"Not about that, ya goof."

"Oh. What then?"

He takes a deep breath, as if to summon courage.

"I feel like a drongo, okay? But the whole time I really did think you and that girl, the one with the green hair, were an item."

"Frances? You mean you weren't just winding me up with all that?" I ask.

"*Me?* No, Becks, I thought *you* were taking the piss."

"How do you mean?"

"I just kept feeling like something wasn't dinky-di from the beginning."

"Dinky-di?"

"Dinky-di. You know, the real thing, genuine."

"Oh."

"But I couldn't work out what it was. Figured it was that you were just flirting with me, for sport. You know, when really you were into women, into her. Shining me on, like."

"Why would anybody do that?"

"I don't know. I might be a little complicated. Just, I've been down a road like that once before," he adds. "Wasn't heaps of fun."

"Oh. Well, no. I wasn't. I mean, that wasn't what was dinky-di. Or what wasn't dinky-di. If that makes sense?"

"It does now, Becks," he says, softly. "Guess you could say we've sort of just been speaking different languages?"

"You can say that again," I whisper.

Stacy takes a baby step toward me then and presses a little piece of paper into my palm. Then he moves his head a bit closer to mine and stops. I lean in some, too, meeting him in the middle.

In reality, the kiss only lasts for a few seconds. But it's finally real. And, like a kid on a trampoline, relishing that split second between rising and falling before flopping back down again, I savor the moment.

Then, closing my hand around the little piece of paper, I nod goodbye to him and head off down the steps of the Purple Parakeet, for the very last time.

****

Out in the open air, the moment lingers, along with the feeling of Stacy's lips. Opening my hand, I look at the note he gave me. It reads:

Becky, let's keep in touch: I'mAtThePubInAmerica@hotmail.com – *Stacy*

I digest the possibility of actually getting to continue a friendship with Stacy, as my whole self, and suddenly it's as if there's an extra foot of space all around me.

Just as this feeling begins to soften me, though, something hard whacks me on the back.

I look down. A third of a baked potato is at my heel.

I look up. Angus, my sniper, is sitting carelessly on the inside of the windowsill.

"She's gone, Alan!" he shouts. "Now we can break out the *good* beer!"

The shuttle van blows its horn then. I pause. I dare to take one last look up at Angus, who is looking back at me with an earnestness that cannot be mistaken.

"See ya, ya Pom," he calls.

I pick up the potato and lob it back at him through the open window. And I know, in some way, everything is going to be okay.

****

"Every time I pick up from this hostel, it's the same thing," begins the shuttle driver.

"What?"

"Waiting ten to fifteen minutes while you say your goodbyes."

"Oh."

"You have to say your goodbyes *before* your shuttle pickup. You're not the only one I have to pick up, you know."

"Sorry."

He lunges across the dashboard for his clipboard. "So, what airline are you?" he asks, impatiently.

"Oh, um, I forget," I say. I shuffle through my bags for my itinerary.

"Well, that's another thing you could get in order *before* I get here."

I raise my papers up to the window, straining to make out the name of my airline beneath the blinking billboard signs of Broadway.

"C'mon," urges the driver. "You've got to *know* these things."

"You're right," I say, restoring my ticket to its envelope. "American. I'm American."

❧ACKNOWLEDGEMENTS ❧

I am grateful to Linda Case, my editor and aunt, whose generous commitment to this project wholly transformed it.

With particular thanks, too, to Henna Marie, for her infectious enthusiasm and for being a rule-breaking example. As well as to my many dear friends, for their thoughtful feedback and suggestions.

Most of all, I am obliged to the "Purple Parakeet" and all of its former inhabitants, not only for providing the alternate universe that inspired this story, and for never deporting me, but for being the first lighthouse on my long journey home.

Rachel Eisenwolf lives authentically ever after in Portland, Oregon, where her accent enjoys the drizzle.

Made in the USA
Lexington, KY
23 January 2013